HELL'S HALF ACRE

A gripping murder mystery full of twists

JACKIE ELLIOTT

Coffin Cove Mysteries Book 2

JOFFE BOOKS

Joffe Books, London
www.joffebooks.com

First published in Great Britain in 2021

Cover art by Nick Castle

ISBN: 978-1-78931-794-7

*In memory of Terry South and the stories
of the real Hell's Half Acre.*

CHAPTER ONE

"Shh, shut up, he'll hear you."

The oldest boy crouched down behind a tree and gestured at the other two to do the same.

They hunkered down as low as they could go and squinted into the sunlight reflecting off the retreating morning tide.

All three boys were breathing hard, anticipating the morning's hunt. They could see their breath billowing white in the chill of the spring morning as they waited.

The trio had gathered early as planned, slipping out of their respective homes and meeting on the boardwalk.

They had walked together, not speaking much and keeping their heads down. Nobody took any notice of them. It was quiet at the government dock and the marina. The herring boats had left hours before, and now only early morning dog walkers and the occasional wharf rat — ex-fishermen or oddballs who lived on their boats against all the Coffin Cove Marina rules — hung around, waiting for the coffee shop to open.

If anyone had paid them any attention, they might have wondered where the three boys were going. Their demeanour suggested a purpose. Their furtive glances indicated that purpose might not be entirely innocent.

The comrades passed by the boat ramp and took the stone steps down onto the pebbled beach below the cliff. The tide was still out, so they opted to jog along the hard sand until they reached the far end of the bay. A rocky outcrop where the cliff had crumbled marked the edge of the public beach. Beyond that point was a smaller secluded bay, surrounded by clusters of pine trees. Narrow trails disappeared into the woods, but the bay was only accessible from the beach when the tide was out. At the nearest end, driftwood piled up, flung by the winter storms and spring tides to the edge of the forest.

The boys had scrambled over the grey hunks of timber to find a lookout point.

They could see the length of the beach, and their prey had emerged from the cover of the trees, causing the youngest boy to squeal with excitement, earning him a glare and a reprimand from the oldest.

The three observed their prey in silence.

Silence. They knew all about hunting. The oldest boy had been on a hunt. He knew all about tracking an animal. He'd learned how to be quiet, to remain downwind and out of sight. He'd passed on this information with authority to the other two, who had listened in admiration. The oldest boy had automatically assumed the leader's role. He had planned the hunt and identified their prey. For several days, they had watched and learned.

Their prey was amusing himself on the beach, squatting down in rock pools, poking at the seaweed with a stick.

"Where is it? Give it here."

The smallest boy dug into his shorts pocket and pulled out a whistle.

The leader grabbed it. "Ready?"

The other two nodded, holding their breath.

He blew the whistle, shrill and piercing, three long blasts, and then collapsed, stifling giggles.

"Watch him, watch him, what's he doing?"

The prey looked up. He seemed to be waiting. He didn't move, still knelt down in the tidal pool.

"Blow it again!"

The leader did as urged, and the three were rewarded as the prey took off running, almost straight towards them.

"Heads down!"

The three hit the ground and waited until the prey's running feet had passed by.

"Quick, quick, follow him!"

The three, experienced in the art of hunting small animals and birds with pellet guns and slingshots, moved as silently as they could, pursuing their largest target ever into the dense trees that bordered the beach.

This was the furthest they had ever been into this part of the forest. All three had been warned.

"Stay off Whilley's land. He'll shoot first and ask questions later."

But the boys were even more fascinated by the overgrown property that jutted out on the rocky end of Coffin Cove beach and stretched right up to the gravel pit. And they had made it their business to casually bully the mysterious Whilley boy who appeared from time to time to pluck starfish from the pools or toss rocks aimlessly into the ocean.

They had called to him once to play on the beach, as they tried to spear fish with sticks they had sharpened themselves or attempted to knock "shit-hawks" out of the sky with well-aimed pebbles.

The boy always ignored them and dashed back into the bush.

Now he had become their plaything, a focus of cruel attention whenever they found him. And the whistle was genius, guaranteed to make him run.

Trying not to rustle the dry undergrowth, they followed their prey up the hill.

He was quick, knowing how to navigate around the rotting tree stumps and moss-covered rocks. It was hard for the boys to keep him in sight. They could see by his upright body and lack of hesitation that this was a route that the Whilley boy had run many times before. He didn't once look down to check his footing.

They nearly gave up. The three came to a halt at the foot of a steep incline. The Whilley boy was nowhere to be seen. The smallest boy put his hands on his knees and bent his head, taking deep breaths.

"We lost him!" the leader said. He was mad. "You slowed us down!" he shouted, pointing at the smallest boy, who flushed red. He didn't want to be left out.

"Shh!" The middle boy signalled them to be quiet. He pointed upwards, and they saw the Whilley boy running along the top of the ridge above them. He must have circled the incline and doubled back.

The hunters didn't have time for that.

The three scrambled up the bank, the quickest way to get back in the chase. At the top, the trail was flat and open, and the boys could see their prey in the distance. They took off again, eager not to lose him.

The trail curved to the right and met a gravel road, forming a fork. The boys slowed to a halt. The Whilley boy had disappeared again.

"Over there!"

The leader gestured wildly. About a hundred yards in front of them, obscured by tall cedar trees, was the roof of a building.

This must be where the Whilley boy lived.

The boys stood stock still. The plan had been to chase their prey. They hadn't thought what to do if they caught him or got near him. Now they were trespassing.

"Let's go back!" the smallest hunter whispered.

But the leader didn't want to lose face.

"Let's look," he commanded.

The three moved along the trail at a slower pace and hid in the undergrowth as much as possible. As they got nearer, they had to scramble over coils of rotting rope, rusty barrels and stacks of wooden pallets half swallowed by brambles.

The boys followed the trail as it made one last bend to the right, and then they were standing in front of a wooden gate. It had sagged and was half detached from disintegrating wooden posts. From either side of the gate, a badly maintained wooden fence enclosed an overgrown yard. Two old fishing boats sat on blocks, the paint peeling from the hulls, and rusty drums perched precariously on the bows.

A faded sign attached to the fence read "Whilley's Net and Twine".

"Ma? Ma!"

The boys, startled at the sound of their prey's voice, scrambled to get out of view. They could other hear voices. The oldest boy dared to put his head up.

"Holy shit," he whispered urgently to the other two, "look at this!"

A human mountain shuffled out of a run-down cabin behind the boat debris in the yard. The boards of the decayed deck creaked under the weight of this gigantic creature, with matted grey hair hanging over its face.

"Why are you here?" the Mountain wheezed.

One boy moved, and a branch creaked.

The prey looked round, but they were saved by the Mountain, who gestured with a surprisingly bony hand.

"Go inside."

The prey did as he was bid.

The Mountain shuffled further outside.

She was covered in a grubby, greying smock that flowed almost to the ground. As she shuffled alarmingly nearer to the boys' hiding place, they could see swollen ankles and dirty feet.

She edged nearer the fence.

Don't move! *The leader looked fiercely at the other two, who crouched as small as they could get in the undergrowth.*

The Mountain stopped just a yard or two away.

She let out a long rasping sigh, and the boys tensed, expecting to be hauled out of the bushes.

Instead, she bent down slowly and hitched up the grey smock high enough for the boys to glimpse matching grey hair matted to her crotch.

Horrified, they watched as she let out a stream of urine that splashed her feet and steamed off the grass.

This was too much.

Unable to stand it any longer, the smallest hunter let out a gurgle of revulsion and turned and ran. The other two followed him, not caring how much noise they made. They crashed through the bush, whooping and running until they rounded the corner on the trail and dived into the bush.

The oldest boy skidded to a halt. The other two bounced into each other and fell to the ground.

They laughed and rolled in the moss, heady with relief at not being caught.

"Did you see? She PISSED herself!"

"And she showed her dirty old 'C'."

Shocked into silence momentarily by the hint of that forbidden word, the three looked at each other and started laughing again.

The smallest hunter blurted, "Shh . . . stop . . . do you hear that?"

The oldest boy pulled a face. "I don't hear noth——" and then he stopped, frozen in fear.

An eerie cackle, high-pitched, got louder and louder.

The boys stood up and turned around, wildly looking to see where the noise was coming from.

"What's that?" the smallest one asked, near to tears. "Where are we?"

In their excitement, the three hunters hadn't noticed where they were. They were in a clearing. Tall fir trees rustled above them. The ground was spongy with moss, and they were surrounded with mounds of old stones, half-covered with brambles, circling them like forest monsters guarding their lair.

"Where are we?" the smallest boy repeated, his voice rising in panic. "I don't know this place."

The cackling stopped.

"There . . . it's nothing," the oldest boy said, taking charge again. "We just took a wrong turn. The beach must be down there." He pointed to a trail leading out of the clearing.

"Come on, don't be scared. She can't have followed us. She was too fat."

That made them all giggle, the tension broken.

Then they heard a different noise. Starting softly at first, then louder, a baby was crying.

Without another word, the three took off running down the trail and further away from the hunt.

CHAPTER TWO

Weak sunlight streamed in from the doorway. Walter propped the heavy wooden door open with an empty beer crate.

"Sunlight is the best disinfectant," he muttered out loud.

Even after decades of running the Fat Chicken pub, Walter had never got used to the morning-after yeasty stench of beer splashes on the floor and drips on every table. As the morning sun illuminated the inside, a wall of dust hanging in the stale air became visible, as well as the sticky rings and smudges on the bar top. The light refracted off the glass optics above the bar, making Walter squint as he walked back to his stool and attempted to focus on his laptop screen. He swore softly to himself, moving the screen back and forth. Not that he wanted to see the numbers.

He wanted a drink.

Putting off his bookkeeping for another day was a bad move. But the idea of pouring a couple of inches of amber liquid over a few ice cubes and allowing the pleasant buzz to push away any nagging thoughts of bills and debt — well, that was indeed an inviting idea.

He sighed, adjusted his seat again so the sunshine was no longer obstructing his view and continued to input the totals from the pile of stained paperwork he had pulled out from behind the cash register.

How long had it been since he last did this? Can't have been three months, surely?

But the invoices went back to April. Walter checked the date and saw it was 7 June. That would explain the increased number of calls to his cell phone from 1-800 numbers. Collection agencies. And the rent was due. *Past* due.

Walter sighed again.

Sales were down. Costs were up. Profits had been dwindling for the past five years — now they were non-existent. Walter had no savings left. He gazed around the pub. It hadn't changed in years. The walls and ceiling were still yellow, even though smoking was banned these days. The booth seats were faded and torn in places. There was no money in the budget for renovations, not even a flat-screen TV to attract a crowd for Sunday afternoon football or the Stanley Cup play-offs.

Walter had been attending the recent planning meetings. As much as he welcomed a new waterfront development and investments in tourist attractions, he wondered how the Fat Chicken would fare against a smart new bistro or wine bar. Cheryl was an excellent cook and their pub food was popular, but they'd had no competition except the tiny pizza place, and they still couldn't make it work. He'd voiced his concerns to Cheryl. Naturally optimistic, she'd pointed out that if there were more visitors to Coffin Cove, business was bound to improve.

"A rising tide lifts all ships," she'd said and kissed him.

"I hope we can last until then," Walter muttered under his breath as he added up the last of the receipts and stared down at the total. In the red again. As he wondered how he was going to break it to Cheryl, he heard her footsteps clicking down the hallway from the kitchen. Bruno, their dog, stirred from his sleep and struggled to his feet. He whined and wagged his tail as she bent down to scratch his ears.

"How's the bean-counting going?" she inquired. Cheryl always smiled. She had one of those upturned mouths that lent itself to smiling and a sunny disposition that usually lightened Walter's naturally dour manner.

"Oh, fine," he said, snapping the laptop shut. *I'll tell her later*, he promised himself, *when she's not busy*. Once again, he rationalized away the opportunity to confess to his wife that his dream, the business he had convinced her would make up for not having the family they had both wanted, was just about over.

"Just about," he muttered. "But not today."

"Remember that Nadine is coming with the dance troop this evening for a rehearsal." Cheryl hadn't heard his last remark, and she stood in front of him, hand on hip, looking amused at the pained expression on Walter's face. "Come on, how can it hurt? Maybe we'll get a few new customers, something different!"

Walter was certain that scantily dressed, middle-aged women wobbling their oversized midriffs around his regular crowd of truck drivers and fishermen would certainly be different, but not in the way Cheryl was expecting. And worse than that, it was Nadine. He knew one thing for certain: there was something in it for her. She did nothing out of the goodness of her heart. If she even had a heart.

"Belly dancing?" he said. "Really? How much is it costing us?"

"Not a penny." Cheryl started squirting bleach on the counter. "Nadine arranged it as the first event of the Heritage Festival. All we have to do is provide some Greek food."

The Heritage Festival was a summer-long event intended to boost tourism. It was the first one that the new Tourism and Economic Planning Committee had arranged.

"Well, food costs money!" Walter protested.

"Just get in some samosas or something — appetizers, nothing fancy."

"Samosas aren't Greek," Walter grumbled.

"Walter, please try to be enthusiastic, we need to increase sales, right? I'm not stupid. I see you avoiding picking up your phone and doing the accounts. How are the numbers anyway?"

"I have to go out." Walter avoided his wife's gaze and her question. He put the laptop back in its case, grabbed his cigarettes and headed towards the sunshine and distraction. Bruno followed him.

The Fat Chicken looked over the waterfront of Coffin Cove. The perfect location for a pub, for tourists and locals alike: fishing boats, commercial and sporties, were tied up at the docks, a two-minute walk from the pub, and a boardwalk stretched around the bay, with steps to the sandy part of the beach.

The Fat Chicken should have been rocking. But this was Coffin Cove, and even though the rest of Vancouver Island seemed to be thriving, it felt like this small town had been in a permanent recession for as long as Walter could remember.

Walter stopped and surveyed the building that had once held all his dreams for the future. At one time, he'd intended to knock out the back wall and install French doors leading to a shaded patio area. And upstairs, instead of the cramped apartment and storage rooms, he and Cheryl had planned a large conference facility. They would rent it out to smart young millennials and entrepreneurs, who would relocate to Coffin Cove, attracted by the cheap real estate and outdoor lifestyle.

Walter lit his cigarette and let the early sunshine warm his shoulders. The sun danced and sparkled off the ocean, but Walter could see only five fishing vessels moored there. There had been nine last year, and fifteen the year before that. Fishing was shitty, the forestry business was shitty and it had hit this little community hard. The two sawmills had cut back to one shift each, and the pulp mill had just shed another fifty employees.

Coffin Cove had relied on the resource industry for the entire 150 years of its existence, and there was nothing to replace it. So far, the millennials and entrepreneurs had avoided the tiny fishing town. And Walter didn't blame them. But maybe the Heritage Festival would kick-start a new beginning.

Walter stubbed out his cigarette, half-smoked.

Don't want cancer on top of everything else.

He walked down to the boardwalk, followed by Bruno. The dog settled himself under the little table at the front of Hephzibah's café.

There were upsides to living in the back of beyond, Walter thought, as he took a steaming mug of freshly brewed coffee from Hephzibah herself. She handed him a warm muffin, winking.

"On the house. Us business owners need to look after each other!"

The big branded coffee emporiums and fast-food outlets had not bothered with Coffin Cove. Instead of paying ten bucks for exotic flavours and frothy toppings, it was still possible to get a cup of morning joe for under two dollars.

And a great view, Walter thought, as he sipped his coffee and bit into a Morning Glory breakfast muffin — one of Hephzibah's specialities. On sunny mornings, sitting in a warm breeze and hearing the clang of the boats shifting in the swell of an incoming tide, Coffin Cove was idyllic, and Walter didn't want to be anywhere else.

As he sipped his coffee, he felt a little better. Maybe he was overreacting? He and Cheryl had weathered financial hardships before, and they could do it again.

Walter looked around. There did seem to be more people than usual on the boardwalk. And wasn't someone telling him just the other day, a new business was renovating one of the empty stores in the old strip mall? Maybe the new young mayor was living up to her promises after all.

The election last fall had been a surprise. Dennis Havers had been on the city council as mayor for as long as Walter could remember. Dennis was also his landlord. Thinking of him made Walter wince a little, as he remembered his unpaid rent. Still, Dennis hadn't called in yet. There was a time when Dennis would stand at his door with his hand out, first thing in the morning on rent day. But Dennis was living through worse times than Walter. Last year his son Ricky had gone missing, and in the fall, to everyone's amazement, Dennis lost the mayoral election.

Coffin Cove had their very first female mayor, Jade Thompson.

Walter and many of the regulars in the pub had laughed when Jade announced her candidacy. Men had always run Coffin Cove. It was a West Coast resource town, founded on mining and then forestry and fishing. Sure, they employed women at the fish plant back in the day and they worked in the grocery stores and whatnot, and some of them even ran little businesses selling trinkets, but mayor? The plaid-shirted men snorted in derision. "And she'll never win by posting her face all over the internet. Nobody in Coffin Cove bothers with social media. *She'll never win.*"

Walter remembered how Cheryl's face had darkened when she slammed the men's beer bottles in front of them and started furiously polishing glasses with her back to the bar.

"C'mon, honey, they don't mean anything by it. You've got to admit, it's unlikely she'll win. But good for her, giving it a try, eh?"

That had made Cheryl angrier. She hadn't spoken to him for the rest of the evening, leaving him to close up the bar on his own. The next day, she left early and was out for most of the morning. Walter had been relieved to see her walk back in the bar, her face lit up with her customary smile. His relief faded when Cheryl announced she was helping Jade Thompson with her campaign.

"There's lots of us," she'd said defiantly. "We've set up the campaign headquarters at Hephzibah's."

When Jade won, Walter wasn't surprised. Her campaign committee, led by his hard-working wife, had knocked on doors, shaken hands and kissed babies. They'd tweeted, posted videos and put up posters. They talked to weary business owners and promised change. They campaigned on turning the fortunes of this small defeated community around. They promised to dismantle the old boys' club — a swipe at Dennis Havers' shady business dealings — and they revealed their vision for building a new commercial and residential development on the waterfront, by tearing down the derelict fish plant.

"It's about time women ran this town," Cheryl had declared. "You men had your chance."

Walter privately agreed with her, though he laughed and rolled his eyes with the guys at the bar. But even they were coming around to Jade Thompson's proposals.

That last campaign promise alone had caught the town's attention. The fish plant and the pier were crumbling into the ocean. Worse than that, it had been the scene of a murder the year before. Walter hadn't been near the dump since they'd removed the crime tape, but Peggy Wilson, the motel owner, was constantly complaining that the gruesome evidence of a killing still remained. Nobody had been back to clean up the blood. Rats scurried in and out, while rust and oil contaminated the bay where the pier stood. It was a reminder of a tragic time in Coffin Cove.

Walter shivered at the memory.

A shadow fell over him.

"Mornin', Walter."

Walter looked up to see the tall bulk of his old friend, Harry Brown, blocking the sun. Beside him was a young woman who smiled and thanked Harry and disappeared into the café.

Harry was one of the last commercial fishermen who tied up at Coffin Cove. He'd been forced to retire early when the fishing boom ended but had made enough money to pay off the money owing on his boat and buy a cottage in town. Harry, towering above Walter, was a solid wall of a man, wearing the customary fisherman's uniform — canvas bib overalls and a wool sweater. He was also a solitary man, with a resting expression that was neither welcoming nor forbidding. His penetrating blue eyes were the only clue to his Norwegian heritage, though his year-round dark tan hinted at his native blood. The *Pipe Dream*, his old aluminium purse-seiner, used to be his livelihood but was now home to just himself and the occasional visit from his grown-up daughter, and he rented his cottage to his sister, Hephzibah.

Harry bent down to pat Bruno.

His young companion emerged from the café and handed Harry a mug of coffee.

"Thanks again, Harry, I appreciate it. Dad said you'd be the man for the job." And with a big smile and a nod at Walter, the woman walked down the boardwalk.

Harry sat down at the table with Walter.

"So?" Walter asked, noting Harry's smug expression. "What was all that about? And who is she?"

"That was Katie Dagg, Lee and Nadine's girl."

"Little Katie?" Walter could hardly believe it. "How old is she now? I thought she was still at school."

"Just finished university. And back here as the new Coffin Cove Museum curator." Harry acknowledged Walter's surprise with a grin. "Yeah, I know. I remember when she was born."

"God, I feel ancient," Walter said, then frowned. "The old museum is opening?"

Harry nodded. "Yep, in the old building at first, then in the new development. They hired Katie last month. She seems to know her local history, that's for sure."

"And what did she want with you?" Walter asked. "Some of your fishing stories?" He chuckled.

"Kind of." Harry ignored his friend's teasing. "She's hired me to do trips along the coast, pointing out where the rum runners and smugglers operated. For tourists. I've got my first booking in a couple of weeks."

Walter was astonished. "She's paying you?"

Harry nodded and smiled. "Not bad pay, as it happens."

"What do you know about smuggling?" Walter asked. "Family connections, maybe?"

Harry laughed. "I wouldn't put it past Ed to have done some smuggling at some point."

Ed was Harry's father, and Walter knew him well. Ed had dabbled in all sorts of nefarious activities in his life, so it was a fair comment, and Harry took it as a gentle joke. When Ed was younger, he'd had a vicious temper, especially when he was drunk — which was often — and Harry's mother, Greta, had left when he was still young. She'd taken his baby sister, Hephzibah, with her and it was only when the two siblings were adults that they'd finally begun a relationship. Greta had since died, but the siblings were still close. Harry had even helped Hephzibah set up the café.

"Actually, it was Clara Bell who got me interested in the old smuggling stories," Harry said. "They used the old mining tunnels. There's a whole network of them, and the smugglers extended them as far as they could to the coastline, so they could move barrels of hooch right out to the beach. Then they got picked up by a boat in the middle of the night and whisked down to Seattle or the Oregon coast. Back in Prohibition times."

"Clara Bell, who used to run the museum? Is she still alive?" Walter said, surprised again.

"Yes, and yes. She's very much alive and kicking. She lives up near Ed. I used to visit her when I was a kid. You know how she used to have the museum filled with boxes?"

Walter nodded. "You could hardly move in there."

"Right. Her place is worse. Always has been. Jam-packed to the rafters. She must be one of those hoarders, I suppose. But she knows her local history, and she dug out an old map of the mining tunnels from years ago. And then I did some of my own research. I've even been in some of those tunnels. They're quite dangerous now, though."

"Well, my friend, I didn't know you had all this knowledge, but it's paying off now," Walter grinned. "Must be easier than fishing."

"You're right about that. And now I can share my wisdom with the rest of the world, thanks to Katie Dagg." Harry smiled back and drained his coffee mug.

Walter shook his head. Cheryl was right. It *was* time the women ran things around here. He couldn't help poking fun at his friend a little more. "You'll be famous," he said. "Maybe your friend Andi will interview you for the *Gazette*."

Andi Silvers was the reporter for the local paper. She had investigated the murder at the fish plant and managed to uncover all kinds of secrets previously buried in the murky history of Coffin Cove. It had been fascinating, and for a while, the Fat Chicken had seen an uptick in business as Coffin Cove experienced its first influx of "murder tourists". Harry had helped Andi with the investigation somehow. He'd been tight-lipped about it, but Walter knew Harry well enough. He was quite taken with Andi Silvers.

Harry didn't bite. "I'll be a legend," he said comfortably. "Anyway, I've got to get on." Harry got up and picked up his empty coffee cup to take inside to Hephzibah. "And I nearly forgot, when's that belly dancing night at your place?"

Walter's head shot up, looking to see if Harry was teasing him back, but the man looked serious. "Friday night. Why? You thinking of coming?"

Harry shrugged. "Sure, why not? Somethin' different. Anyway, see ya later."

Walter watched as he handed his mug to Hephzibah and left the café. He laughed to himself. His old friend wasn't fooling anyone. Harry knew Andi would be there. And Walter was sure there would soon be an article about Harry's smuggling tours in the *Coffin Cove Gazette*.

Wonders would never cease. Harry hadn't been romantically involved with anyone for years. Walter thought he and Andi would make a good couple. Sure, Harry was older than Andi, but that didn't matter these days. Both of them needed to settle down, he thought. It was time Andi moved out of the apartment and got herself a permanent place . . . Ah! Walter slapped the table. Rent! Andi hadn't paid her rent yet. Well, that would cover a couple of bills.

Bruno barked, interrupting his thoughts, and Walter stood up too. Time to get back to the Fat Chicken. Maybe he should be more enthusiastic about this Heritage Festival. Maybe a half-naked Nadine Dagg would turn the business around. He laughed to himself and felt optimistic. And if things were really looking up in Coffin Cove, maybe he would pull out those old plans for a patio and . . . Walter bumped into a man coming out of the café. He was several inches taller, and Walter had barrelled into his chest, preoccupied with his thoughts. Walter stood back, embarrassed, and apologized. He saw the man was dressed in an expensive sports jacket and crease-free chinos. His fashionable haircut was greying at the temples. He looked like a businessman from the mainland, Walter thought, and wondered if he was the type of person the new mayor was hoping to attract to Coffin Cove. This guy looked like he had money. The man was looking Walter up and down, with a curious expression on his face. Walter was aware of his unshaven appearance and beer-stained T-shirt he'd grabbed off the floor this morning.

"No worries," the man said eventually, moving around Walter and leaving the café. A waft of expensive aftershave lingered.

Walter saw Hephzibah staring after the man.

"See something you like?" he asked, winking.

"Oh, no, it's not that," Hephzibah smiled. "Although he looked a little more . . . well, *businesslike*, than my usual customers," she said diplomatically. "No, it's just that I'm sure I know him from somewhere. But I can't think where."

Walter looked out the door at the man's tall figure striding down the boardwalk. There *was* something familiar about him.

An old memory surfaced briefly in Walter's mind but was gone before he could grasp it.

"Sorry, Hep," he said, "can't help you. Anyway, got to get back to the grind."

Walter hurried back, hoping to catch Andi and collect her rent payment before she left for work.

CHAPTER THREE

Andi Silvers woke with a start.

In her dream, she was hanging on with all her might to a narrow ledge. Her fingertips were sore. Her arms ached and she was screaming for help. But because it was a dream, no sound was coming out of her mouth, and her only option was to cling on until her muscles were too tired to hold on any longer and she let go.

Nausea overcame Andi as she clawed her way back into consciousness, just as she had been about to plunge into the murky fathoms of her dream hell. She had to lie still until the feeling subsided and her mind cleared from the fog. Her arms and hands throbbed. She clenched and unclenched her fingers. The dream had seemed real enough for her to grip her pillow in fear. Her bedsheets were damp with sweat.

"This is normal," she whispered to herself. The counsellor had warned her. The dreams were a mechanism the brain used to clear and reset the unconscious mind. Eventually they would pass into nothing, but occasionally a nightmare might be triggered by something in her subconscious, and she would be tormented again.

It had all sounded like bullshit to Andi. But she had to admit, the bad dreams did come less often these days. But she wished they would go away for good.

Jim, her boss, had recommended the counsellor. Not so much recommended, Andi remembered, as insisted. He'd made it part of the conditions of her return to work as a journalist and assistant editor at the *Coffin Cove Gazette*.

Andi had argued, of course.

"If you don't like it," Jim had said, "complain to HR. Oh wait . . . that's me." He had beamed at Andi and pointed to the door. "Don't come through that door again until you are completely healed. Body and mind."

Andi had been to the counsellor once a week for three months to appease her boss and then found excuses not to go. Working was the answer, she told Jim. *I'll just get back on the horse, and I'll be fine.*

Reluctantly, Jim had agreed.

Andi rubbed at the scar on her thigh. A little over a year ago, a very dangerous man had shot her. She had been pursuing a story. It was her job, and she was bloody good at it, she knew that. But she was also impulsive (*undisciplined*, Jim called it) and inclined to cut corners. These bad habits, combined with terrible judgment when it came to men, had contributed to the loss of a glittering career at a national news outlet the year before. Andi had taken the job at the *Coffin Cove Gazette* — the only opportunity offered to her — and expected to be filing dull reports about city council meetings and garage sales for the struggling local paper. Coffin Cove was an isolated fishing town with a dwindling population on the east side of Vancouver Island and barely attracted enough tourists to keep the only motel booked through summer. The rest of the island, though, was a Mecca for surfers, fishermen and outdoor enthusiasts.

The run-down town sullenly refused to go bankrupt and be swallowed up into the suburbs of Nanaimo, the nearest big city. Every year, the pulp mill located at one end of the Cove, combined with a handful of just-viable businesses and a crumbling residential infrastructure, scraped together enough tax dollars for another year.

When Andi first arrived, she couldn't understand why Coffin Cove wasn't overrun by developers, with all the cheap real estate available in the coastal town. But there was only one road in and out. There were few amenities, and frankly, the locals weren't that friendly. They had regarded Andi with suspicion and sometimes downright hostility. She could attribute some of that reaction to her chosen career. People these days didn't trust the media. But it was more than that. In some ways, Coffin Cove had closed itself off from the world. The inhabitants complained about the lack of stores, cell phone coverage, not enough work, and decreasing numbers of children keeping the elementary school open. But should an outsider point out deficiencies, the locals would bridle with indignation and mutter about the "good ol' days" and "damn blow-ins".

People reluctantly began to accept Andi after she had helped uncover the truth behind the death of a local teenager. Years ago, the drowned body of Sarah McIntosh, the daughter of a local businessman, had washed up on the beach. Andi had made it her business to solve the mystery, even going against the advice of her boss.

Andi's story had started out as a clash between local fishermen and environmentalists and had ended up as a murder investigation. She had rediscovered her old tenacity as a journalist after being fired, and her relentless digging uncovered a link between this murder and a twenty-five-year-old missing persons mystery. Andi's persistence had been rewarded by getting shot by the prime suspect.

"Your own goddam fault!" Jim had shouted at her, while she was lying in the hospital. "All this haywire bullshit got you fired once, and this time you nearly died!"

He had calmed down, and Andi knew that this man who had given her a chance and was now her friend was shaken by the events.

But his words hit home, and for months her confidence had been in pieces. Jim had only allowed her to cover local events when she first started back at work, and now she was beginning to think her old instinct for a good story might never return. As the nightmares lessened, worries about her future surfaced, and she often lay awake obsessing over the same questions. Was she still a good journalist? Had she ever been? And what was next? Just growing old and lonely in a tiny rented apartment writing fluff pieces?

Andi touched her scar again, remembering how difficult the last months had been.

"ANDI!" Someone thumped at the door.

She jumped and winced.

"Andi? Are you in there? Your rent is late again!"

Andi lay still with her eyes closed, hoping that Walter would go away. As she listened for his retreating footsteps, her cell phone trilled from somewhere under the heap of clothes. She dug around, forgetting her hangover for a moment.

Work.

"Shit." Andi turned off the cell phone and slumped back on the bed.

"Andi, I know you're in there."

"Walter, I'm really sorry, I'm sick," Andi called out. Well, she felt like crap, so it wasn't a lie. "I promise I'll bring you the rent later today."

Silence.

She heard Walter's steps echoing away.

Andi heaved herself into an upright position. She needed money, she needed to get out of this apartment, and the only way to do either of those things was to get back to work. *Real work.* And in the last few weeks, she'd finally got the whiff of a story. Well, it might develop into a story, Andi wasn't sure yet, but it looked intriguing. She'd made a promise to help someone. Ricky Havers, the mayor's forty-two-year-old son, had gone missing. The mystery had fuelled the Coffin Cove gossip factory, not least because Ricky owned the town's first and only weed emporium, but so far there were no clues at all. Andi was investigating every angle possible, but the fact was, one day Ricky was at work and the next he was gone. There was no sign of a struggle and nothing missing from the store, not even cash. The local RCMP had conducted a few half-hearted searches, not willing to invest resources because Ricky was a grown man and free to vanish if he wanted to.

It wasn't until Dennis and Sandra Havers, his parents, exerted some family influence over a senior member of the RCMP, that they dispatched Andi's old friend, Inspector Andrew Vega, to Coffin Cove to "oversee" a thorough investigation. He too found nothing. Ricky Havers was gone, and the only thing to do was wait until he turned up.

Dead or alive.

Andi was now convinced of two things. First, Ricky's plight involved foul play. Second, the new mayor, Jade Thompson, who'd unseated Dennis Havers a few months after his son's disappearance, knew more about Ricky than she was letting on.

Andi had no proof of this. She was relying on a few small clues and her gut instinct. Andrew Vega and Jim Peters had been quick to point this out. Usually that wouldn't have stopped her. But the problem was, she was worried her gut instinct was not reliable. Not at the moment, anyway.

There was one person who thought Andi could solve the mystery, though, and that was Sandra Havers, Ricky's distraught mother. Andi had given her word she'd continue investigating Ricky's disappearance, especially when Sandra handed her some intriguing information. So now, despite her horrible night, Andi had made a promise and now she needed to get out of bed and get on with her job.

* * *

The *Coffin Cove Gazette* had moved from a tiny run-down office on the outskirts of town to a "suite of spacious modern work spaces overlooking the ocean". At least, that's how the landlord had advertised it, and although Jim Peters had discovered that the roof leaked when it rained hard, and only one wall heater worked properly, at least he had his own space now. And the new office, updated computer equipment and stylish office furniture signified an upturn in business.

Jim Peters had inherited the *Gazette* from his father. An anomaly in Coffin Cove back in the seventies, he'd always had wanted to be in the newspaper business. Instead of heading to the mill or a fishing boat when he left school, he went to university and got a degree in journalism. He came back to Coffin Cove to work with his father, but his new wife disliked Coffin Cove and left Jim alone to raise their young son. Paul went off the rails when he was a teenager, and when he left home, Jim left too. For a couple of decades he worked for national and international media organizations, reporting the news from around the globe. He returned to Coffin Cove when it was apparent that both the *Gazette* and his father were in ailing health.

Jim, a small, slender man, leaned back in his office chair, clasping and unclasping his fingers, as he always did when he was thinking.

The *Gazette* had undoubtedly profited from last summer's tragedy. The murder of a prominent activist, the uncovering of a decades-old murder of a local young woman, all against the backdrop of a conflict between the working men of Coffin Cove's traditional resource industry and environmental protestors . . . Well, if that wasn't a great story, Jim didn't know what was.

Andi had investigated and written a series of captivating articles that put the independent *Gazette* on the map and earned both Jim and the paper a good payday. Since then, Jim had shaken off numerous offers to buy the business from regional media organizations. He had launched an online version of the paper and even had a social media strategy.

All was good from that point of view, but great stories came at a cost — and in this case, two people were dead. The inhabitants of Coffin Cove had been shaken by the events, and Jim knew that Andi had suffered over the last year. He had to push her to turn in an article a week.

He sighed. Andi was talented. But she'd become obsessed by the disappearance of a local man a few months before.

Jim trusted Andi's nose for a story when she was functioning at full capacity. But he was worried about her recent investigations. Jim hadn't intended to snoop — at least that's what he told himself when he was picking the lock on Andi's desk drawer. Careful not to disturb the contents, he flicked through the hanging files until he came to one marked "Havers" and another labelled "Thompson". He pulled them both out and found Andi's usual thorough work. The Havers file contained archived articles, yearbook photographs and scribbled notes about the Havers family and Dennis's tenure as mayor. All as Jim expected. Andi wrote several articles about Dennis during his recent re-election bid, and he expected her to do her homework. The Thompson file was considerably thinner. Andi was right about one thing, Jim thought: Jade Thompson was a bit of an enigma.

Jim leaned back in the chair again.

There was nothing here to link Ricky Havers with Jade Thompson. They'd attended the same school in Coffin Cove, but Ricky was a few years older than Jade. She'd been a serious-looking, plain little thing with big round glasses. In his day, Jim thought, they'd have called her a swot. After graduation, she'd left Coffin Cove and gone to university on the mainland. After that, she'd worked her way up the corporate ladder in a big property development company. Ricky, on the other hand, was a jock. He'd played football and excelled at baseball. There was even one article about a national team scout inviting Ricky to a summer baseball camp for rising stars. It hadn't come to anything. Ricky never left Coffin Cove, and to all accounts, he'd only left his parents' basement a few months before he disappeared. Ricky hadn't held down a job since he'd left school. Dennis Havers had been exasperated by his only son and didn't make a secret of it, Jim recalled. Ricky was lazy, entitled and did little except smoke dope all day long. The contrast between smart, hard-working Jade Thompson and Ricky Havers couldn't have been starker.

So why was Andi so convinced?

When Ricky went missing, he was the proprietor of the Smoke Room, the first and only legal marijuana store in Coffin Cove. Dennis had bankrolled the whole venture, realizing maybe the only chance he had of ejecting his adult son from the basement was to hand him ready-made financial independence. And what better business for Ricky Havers than a store selling his beloved marijuana?

Dennis's decision attracted controversy. The Smoke Room was located in the run-down, deserted strip mall near the Coffin Cove trailer park. Dennis owned the strip mall, and while everyone agreed the property was an eyesore and badly in need of upgrading, there were rumblings of dissent in the community when Dennis proposed opening a legal weed store.

Dennis pushed it through the planning committee, despite a lengthy petition from disgruntled nearby residents. One name that caught Jim's eye in Andi's notes was Summer Thompson. Andi had underlined it, and in the margins, written a date. Jim thumbed through the file. He saw the date referenced and an interview between Andi, Summer and Jade Thompson.

Jim vaguely remembered Andi wanting to interview Summer. He checked the date again. It was a few days before Ricky went missing. He shrugged. Probably Andi wanted to get a few comments on record about the Smoke Room. Summer Thompson was the organizer of the petition opposing the store. The trailer park tenants were worried the store would attract customers looking for more than weed. Drug dealers on the island had switched to opioids almost immediately after recreational marijuana became legal.

Jim smiled ruefully. The petitioners were probably right. It was likely Ricky Havers would dabble in a more lucrative, illegal inventory, along with the government-sanctioned weed, oil and edibles. When Ricky went missing, the most popular theory was that he'd encroached on someone's territory. Someone who didn't resolve their business differences around a conference table.

Andi hadn't found a shred of evidence to connect Jade Thompson with Ricky Havers, let alone his disappearance. Jim read through her interview notes. All she had were a series of coincidences. Jade had apparently reacted "in fear" when she heard Ricky's name. She had been evasive when Andi questioned her about Ricky and the Smoke Room. Summer Thompson clearly disliked Dennis Havers, and not just because of the Smoke Room. She had hinted at Dennis's nefarious past. All Andi had was her intuition, but was it sheer coincidence that Ricky disappeared a few days after Jade appeared in town?

Jim wondered if Andi was still traumatized. A gut feeling for a story was one thing, but Andi was imagining bogeymen and conspiracies. It wasn't like her. One sentence in her notes stood out to Jim: "*Summer Thompson is not what she seems.*" Andi sounded like one of those crazy bloggers, not a serious investigative journalist.

The thing was, Coffin Cove did have a questionable history. It was an isolated town, accessible only by one potholed road or by boat. The location was perfect for anyone wanting to drop off the grid. From the coal mining days to the boom years of fishing, Coffin Cove had always attracted the shadiest characters. Nobody asked questions, and they got paid in cash. Draft-dodgers assimilated into the population in the sixties, and as far back as Prohibition, Coffin Cove had been a favourite with smugglers and drug dealers.

Newcomers were viewed with suspicion. Despite having a very healthy gossip network, residents clammed up around people they didn't know. There was a mistrust of any kind of authority — police, the Canada Revenue Agency, the Department of Fisheries and Oceans.

Jim could see how Andi had got caught up in Coffin Cove's outlaw mythology. Andi was getting carried away with the thought of criminal masterminds around every corner. The reality was that most people in Coffin Cove were trying to scrape a living and were working for cash under the table. The worst crimes committed here were undeclared income and unpaid payroll tax, Jim thought.

That was why the new mayor was making so many waves. Her plans to revitalize Coffin Cove's economy were not being met with enthusiasm from everyone. With new businesses, provincial grants and municipal improvements came increased regulations, property taxes and closer scrutiny of those operating in the grey area of legality.

Jade Thompson was a disrupter. And disruption, in this small community, was not popular.

Jim gathered up all Andi's paperwork and replaced the files in her desk drawer. As he ran his fingers over the file hangers in Andi's drawers, he noticed an oversized manila envelope jammed at the back. He pulled it out. It had been hand-delivered to Andi and had her apartment address at the Fat Chicken scrawled on the front. Jim frowned. That was strange. Andi usually had her mail delivered to the office. Knowing he was now really invading Andi's privacy, Jim shook out the papers from the envelope. Then he wished he hadn't.

"Damn it, Andi," he said out loud. Sometimes Andi operated in the grey area too. This was one of those times. The papers were from the British Columbia Business and Incorporation Registry. It took Jim less than a few seconds to see Andi had got a search from the Transparency Registry of Private Companies.

The provincial government required private companies to register, among other things, the names of individuals who had significant interest in their businesses. Someone had sent Andi the results of a search on Dennis Havers.

Jim groaned. There was no way Andi had obtained this legally. Only authorized representatives of certain agencies could get this information.

He stuffed the documents back in the envelope, resisting his journalistic curiosity to examine them. He couldn't help noticing one company name because Andi had marked it with a bold question mark. Abandoning his misgivings, Jim had a quick peek. He didn't recognize the business, "Knights Development Ltd", but the listed shareholders were familiar.

Apart from Dennis Havers, there were three names: Daniel Ellis, Wayne Dagg and Art Whilley. Jim had never heard of Daniel Ellis, although there was an Ellis family in Coffin Cove. Wayne Dagg was Lee's older brother. Lee Dagg was a local electrician, but Wayne had left Coffin Cove long ago. Jim stared at the last name. He should know it, he thought. Was it an old story his father had worked on? He couldn't think. He shoved the envelope back into the desk and locked it.

Jim could see no connection with the Ricky Havers case. But Andi was digging deep and taking risks.

Jim was angry. Andi knew better than to break the law for a story. She'd pushed boundaries before, and it had cost her dearly, but she hadn't crossed the line at the *Gazette* until now.

His first impulse was to confront her and demand an explanation. Fortunately, his anger dissipated as quickly as it had come. He cared about Andi and admired her talent. He was also touched that she had turned down other opportunities to stay with the *Gazette* after her articles garnered so much attention. He knew Andi was struggling, but maybe he hadn't realized how bad it was. Andi's confidence had taken a beating before she came to Coffin Cove. She'd pushed herself to get to the truth of an old murder, and in the process had been shot. Now she was trying to deal with the aftermath by throwing herself into another investigation — even if there was nothing to uncover.

Andi's preoccupation with Ricky Havers and the Thompsons wasn't healthy, Jim concluded. It needed to stop for her own benefit.

Andi was very loyal to Jim. And he intended to support her. But Jim also knew Andi was unlikely to let her investigation go until she could see for herself there was no story. Just a sad mystery about a man who made some bad life choices.

Jim had an idea. He picked up his phone and put it down again. He frowned, picked it up and tapped in the number before he had time to change his mind again.

"Andi, it's Jim here. You're late. I've got an assignment for you. Call me back — or better still, meet me in the office." He ended the call.

He took a deep breath. Andi had convinced him it was better for her to get back in the saddle. He hoped she was right.

CHAPTER FOUR

Katie Dagg unlocked the door to the Coffin Cove Museum. The outside of the wooden-framed, one-storey building was freshly painted. The contractors had finished the day before and a new sign was due to be installed at the end of the week. Katie was pleased with the progress.

She stepped inside and smiled. The interior was unrecognizable from the cluttered, dusty space she'd inherited from the previous curator.

Katie and her father, Lee, had invested hours of sweat equity to transform the dark musty interior into a spacious, open-plan layout, with the appropriate lighting to accentuate the exhibits.

Along the two main walls of the museum were the permanent glass cases with artefacts and photos which all told the history of Coffin Cove. The centre of the main hall would house the revolving themed exhibition.

This was temporary accommodation for the museum. A brand-new home, complete with art galleries and a separate theatre room, was planned for the new waterfront development. Until then, Katie had to make the best of this space on a limited budget. But she was delighted with the results so far and confident she could make the museum a success, even in this old building.

Katie called her father from her office, to tell him Harry Brown was on board, quite literally, with her plans.

"I knew Harry would help," Lee Dagg said. "He knows quite a few old stories about the smuggling racket at Coffin Cove. He'll keep your clients entertained."

Katie was looking forward to welcoming visitors to the Coffin Cove Museum, but she was sad the renovation phase was coming to a close. It had been fun working with her dad.

Katie smiled again when she ended the call. Lee sounded so happy for her. It had been a while since she'd heard him so upbeat. She knew it was because she'd moved back home and taken her first job after university in her hometown. She could tell her father was ecstatic although he'd argued about it. "Why not get a job in Vancouver?" he'd implored. "Get off the island, see the world. You're wasted in this backwater!"

But Katie had always loved Coffin Cove. She was a homegirl at heart, and the chance to start her career telling the stories of this isolated, overlooked town was more than she could ever have hoped for. Katie didn't see dilapidated houses and the deserted fish plant. She could almost hear the noise of a busy fishing port, the fishermen cussing and women laughing as they gutted and cleaned the catch. In her mind's eye, children were playing in the yard until the bell pealed out from the old, one-room schoolhouse. She knew the town was famous for the boom days of coal and once attracted workers from all over Canada to work in forestry and fishing. Coffin Cove was also infamous for smuggling, the rum runners using the disused mining shafts as escape tunnels to move illegal moonshine across the border to Prohibition America. Katie also wanted to tell stories from before the European settlers found the resource-rich paradise. She intended to include the little-told history of the indigenous people who called the island home. Katie had reached out to descendants of the first people who had lived in the cove and pieced together the island's stories from their perspective. She had comprehensive plans, and she knew Mayor Thompson would support her.

Katie had enthusiastically described her ideas to Mayor Jade Thompson at her interview.

"History should be alive," she'd explained. "How exciting to imagine the stories of Coffin Cove as you stand on the very spot where history was made! Much more interesting than glancing at a few old exhibits in a glass case."

Mayor Thompson had agreed with her, especially when she'd laid out her business plan. She'd hired her immediately. For the first year, Katie would clean up the old museum, which was currently housed in a boarded-up converted cottage, and when the new development took place on the waterfront, Mayor Thompson promised her a new state-of-the-art facility.

This was Katie's dream job. She didn't care about the tiny salary, though the mayor had also promised to double it if Katie could make the museum profitable in one year.

Katie had already heard from her father about the new mayor. He'd said things were changing in Coffin Cove, and Katie could see this quiet woman had a determined air. She thought they'd work well together.

Katie also had personal reasons for wanting to return. She was worried about her dad. Katie couldn't remember a time when the Dagg family were happy together. She had memories of summer camps, days at the beach and rare wonderful occasions when he would beckon her to jump in the truck and go to work with him on a Saturday morning. But even when she was a small child, she'd sensed tension between her parents. Katie had little in common with her mother, Nadine. This hurt her when she was very young, but Lee had made up for Nadine's indifference. Katie had always been a daddy's girl.

Katie wasn't sure if Nadine would welcome her back when she took the curator's job and moved back permanently to Coffin Cove. She wished they could find some common ground. But Nadine had always seemed to resent her. She talked about 'missing out on her best years' and was obsessed with appearing youthful. Katie knew her mother had spent a fortune on plastic surgery and dental work in recent years. It was money Lee and Nadine could ill afford. Although Nadine earned a decent wage working for the city, she'd always spent every penny, leaving it to her husband to pay the household bills. Nadine also hated living in a rented house.

The Dagg family home belonged to her father's brother. Katie had never met Uncle Wayne, but she surmised he was successful because Nadine would often throw the same vicious comment at her father when they were arguing: "I married the wrong brother — I should never have settled for you!"

Katie was certain Lee needed her. During her last year at university, she'd heard the strain in his voice every time they spoke on the phone. She rarely talked to Nadine. Katie knew the business was struggling. Lee was under constant pressure from Nadine's spending.

Nadine had said little when Katie moved back. "You must pay your way," was her only comment. "Your father barely provides for us now."

"Of course," Katie had said, giving her mother the expected kiss on the cheek. "Until I get my own place." *And I'll take Dad with me*, she thought to herself.

She was sad about her relationship with Nadine but had long since come to terms with it. Luckily, she'd had a lot of positive female influence in her life, so she hadn't felt the lack of maternal love too badly.

When Nadine was working or just couldn't be bothered to watch over her, Katie spent most of her time with their neighbour, Terri South. She and her husband Doug didn't have children of their own, and Terri loved to fuss over Katie.

It had been Terri who first sparked Katie's love of history. On rainy Saturday afternoons, Terri would pull out all her old photographs of Coffin Cove and tell Katie stories of when she had been young. Katie was fascinated with the past. She'd visited the old museum when the curator was Clara Bell, an elderly, grim-looking woman who did little more than scold children visitors and smack their hands if they touched the dusty glass display cases. Old Clara also had boxes piled up everywhere, so the tiny museum was cluttered and dirty, and only two or three people could visit at a time.

Katie was daydreaming about Terri now. She couldn't wait to show her friend around the new Coffin Cove Museum. Terri had hugged Katie tight when she'd arrived home. "I've missed you so much, honey," she had whispered to Katie. "And I know your dad has too."

How different life would have been, Katie thought, if Dad and Terri had got together. It had been a childhood dream. She knew Terri loved her husband Doug, although Katie had always been slightly afraid of him . . . Her phone dinged and interrupted her thoughts.

She glanced down. She'd set an alarm to remind her of her schedule today. Katie had a meeting with the Historical Society at noon. The Heritage Festival was starting soon and she was planning a series of tours. Harry Brown was now on her list, and she'd been enthralled by his stories of Coffin Cove as an infamous haven for smugglers.

This afternoon's meeting was a little different, although the historical site in question was in her own backyard. Katie was excited. She'd discovered an old Coffin Cove legend by chance.

When she'd arrived at the museum two days previously, she'd found a man trying the door and peering in through the window.

"Can I help you?" Katie had asked.

The man was tall and well-dressed, in a sports jacket and smart trousers. He was clean-shaven, and Katie caught a whiff of aftershave as she walked up the steps to unlock the door. He smiled at her.

"Just wondering if the museum was open," he said, still smiling. "Do you work here?"

"I'm the curator." Katie enjoyed saying that, and she smiled back. She explained about the renovations and invited him in to look around.

"Wow, this is amazing," the man said. "You've done wonders with this place."

"Oh, have you been here before?" Katie asked. "I don't think I know you. But then, I've been at university for the last few years," she added, feeling silly. Of course there were new people in town.

"I was here years ago," the man said. "I'm back because of business. I'm a real estate developer. Always been interested in this little place. I visited the museum once before, but it was cluttered and a fierce old lady told me off for touching the glass." He laughed.

Katie smiled. "Clara Bell. She is quite the character."

She gave the man a quick tour, explaining how and where the exhibits would be presented. Remembering her sales pitch, she said, "The Heritage Festival starts soon. We'll be ready for that, and I'm arranging a series of historical tours around the town, if you're interested?"

"Sounds fascinating. If I'm here, I'll certainly make time. Actually . . ." The man looked at her and then murmured, almost to himself, "No, probably just an old legend," and shrugged.

"What is?" Katie asked, instantly curious.

"Well, I heard an old story once about how Coffin Cove got its name and I always wondered if there was any truth in it. It was about a priest who built a chapel in the woods."

"A chapel? I don't know of any chapel . . . There's an old church in the valley. Could it be that one?" Katie asked.

"No, it was built of stone, but if it still exists, it will be derelict now, I'm sure. It's supposed to be haunted by the ghost of a child. Apparently, the priest insisted on carrying out burials beside the chapel, even though he was warned that the area was too wet. He dug a grave for a small child who died, but before they could fill the grave, there was a tremendous storm. The coffin was dislodged by massive

35

waves and washed out to sea. The child still haunts the chapel because he or she didn't get a proper burial, or so the legend goes. And hence the name of the town . . . Coffin Cove, see?" The man laughed again. "Don't mind me. It's only an old story I heard once."

Katie shook her head. "I've never heard that one. Where is the chapel supposed to be?"

He thought for a minute. "I think it's somewhere in the wooded area by the gravel pit. There are some trails down to the beach. Do you know where I mean?"

"I do," Katie said, surprised. "I live right by the gravel pit."

"Oh, so you would know those woods?"

"Well, I was never allowed to play on the trails. There are so many old mineshafts around there my dad was always worried I would fall in one. So apart from one main path to the beach, I've never explored much."

"Well, as I say, probably just an old tale." The man cocked his head to one side and looked at her. "If the chapel exists, it would be a fun addition to your tour, don't you think?"

Katie beamed. "What a good idea! Maybe I'll take a hike out there."

She could hear her dad coming through the back entrance of the museum.

"That's my dad, I'll ask him about it," she said.

"You do that." The man held out his hand. "Here's my card, Miss Dagg. Good luck with the new venture. I look forward to those tours."

And he was gone.

Katie shoved the card in her pocket.

She asked Lee about the chapel, but he looked at her blankly.

"Sounds like an old wives' tale to me," he said. "Ask someone in the Historical Society. But be careful if you go hiking out there. Those old mineshafts are overgrown and bloody dangerous."

He and Nadine had been in the midst of another row. He'd been drawn and preoccupied, so Katie left it at that.

Mr Gomich, Katie's old history teacher and president of the Coffin Cove Historical Society, had chuckled when Katie called.

"I haven't heard that old story for years," he said.

"So there's really a chapel?" Katie asked, amazed.

"Supposedly. But I don't think it dates back that far. I think the Whilley family built it. They used to own the property your house is on, and that stretch of land down to the beach was in their family for years."

Katie said, "Mr Gomich, do you think the society members would be up for a field trip?"

CHAPTER FIVE

Nadine admired her newly constructed breasts in the mirror. Cautiously, she lifted each one and checked underneath. The scar lines had faded. That was a relief. On Friday, for the first time, her new breasts would be on public view. Well, not uncovered, of course, but the belly dancing outfits were quite revealing, and she expected that her enhanced chest would get quite a lot of attention. Nadine liked attention. She turned from side to side to admire her profile, focusing on her upturned nipples and ignoring the rolls of belly fat that obscured her nude crotch.

Nadine had "invested" a considerable amount of her husband's money in the renovation of her chest and the removal of all body hair.

Hair, when it wasn't growing on a head, revolted her. So did fat, and that was the focus of her next expenditure.

As she advanced through middle age, Nadine was making her body a project, with four main objectives — remove wrinkles, fat, body hair and "cankles".

She couldn't stop time, but she would defeat the gravitational pull and effects of aging on her body, she had decided, using her husband's bank account as her main weapon.

What next, she thought? *Liposuction?*

As she mused in front of the mirror, the bedroom door swung open.

Lee Dagg marched in, pulling off a grubby sweater. He looked at his naked wife. "Are you getting dressed? You'll be late for work. I can't get your car to start. I'll get Doug South to look at it. Take mine. I'm using the van today."

"Come here and look," Nadine demanded, ignoring her husband's words altogether. "What do you think?" She stood, posed with her hands on her hips, her head on one side, thrusting her chest towards him.

"Expensive, that's what I think."

Undeterred, Nadine gyrated her hips, and she sashayed towards him. "Come on, I bet you want a feel, don't you?"

"For fuck's sake, Nadine."

To Nadine's annoyance, Lee appeared unimpressed.

"Pathetic," she hissed.

"Get dressed. You'll be late."

Lee disappeared into the bathroom, and seconds later, Nadine heard the shower running.

She spent a few moments more examining herself in the mirror and then dressed for work. Short skirt, tight blouse — also expensive and paid for by Lee, even though he seemed determined to ignore her efforts. Dennis had been appreciative, but he wasn't at the office to admire her anymore. She sighed.

She told herself her husband's rejection didn't bother her. She had unfettered access to his bank account (she didn't make much from her city clerk position) and she desired nothing more from Lee. Just his money. The problem was, the cash was running out. The electrical business was barely able to sustain itself, let alone provide the quality of life she deserved. Now Katie was home, and all Lee could do was run around after her. All the hours he was spending at that dusty old museum and he wasn't even getting paid. It didn't matter what she did, Lee acted as if she didn't exist.

Nadine felt her anger rise.

What did Lee expect? Of course she'd gone looking for attention elsewhere. Well, it was time. She was going to make a decision, once and for all. It had been OK, carrying on with Dennis at the office. It had been fun. Made her feel warm inside, the way it had been when she was young, even before Lee. Before she'd settled for second best. But it wasn't enough now. Dennis wouldn't mess her about anymore. *After all these years*, she thought, *I deserve better.*

* * *

Lee stared at himself in the mirror without smiling as he picked up his razor blade.

Just one swipe, he thought. It would all be over. He visualized lying down on the tiled floor and just letting the life seep out of him.

He shook his head to get rid of the thought.

He couldn't do that to Katie. His little girl needed him, and he would be there for her, no matter what. The only love left in his life, he reckoned, was for and from that girl.

The only reason he stayed with Nadine was . . . well, where else would he go? And Nadine would make sure she took every penny to start over with a new man. He knew that. His wife, shaking her flabby stomach and oversized breasts, disgusted him. He knew that her new hobby, belly dancing, was just an excuse to spend evenings rubbing herself up against as many men as possible. She probably had her next partner lined up already.

He had stopped being jealous years ago.

"Just the occasional expensive grope is all I get from her," Lee muttered as he shaved.

Ouch, shit!

He had nicked himself. As he watched the blood drip from his chin, he gripped the washbasin with both hands, as if to stop himself falling.

He felt a dark weight on his shoulders, and the ground seemed to shift underneath him, as though to signify an upheaval to come.

He steadied himself, dabbed a tissue on his cut and finished his shave.

Get a grip, Lee.

It had all been different in the beginning. Nadine was charming and fun. He knew she liked money, and back then, before they were married, he'd had lots of cash. Business was good in those days. Lee had competed with many suitors. Nadine was pretty — round face with dimples, baby-blue eyes and a hint of mischief in her eyes. He wasn't the first love of Nadine's life. Well, money was her first love, he knew that now, but he wasn't the first man either. He didn't care. Nadine was a prize.

Even during the first euphoria of love — or was it lust? — he'd felt a few nagging worries. Nadine was overly concerned with image. He'd bought a brand-new pickup truck, even though he'd just started the business and couldn't really justify the extra outflow of cash. Nadine expected expensive gifts and nights out — even over to the mainland. When she said "yes" to his marriage proposal, it had cost him a small fortune to get the perfect ring. But all this made Nadine happy, and that was all he cared about.

At first they had rented a small basement suite, but Nadine wanted something bigger. Lee had no money to buy a house, even though real estate was cheap in Coffin Cove. But with some help from his friends in the construction industry, he could build his own house. And he had one option: the overgrown piece of property belonging to his brother, Wayne.

Wayne had been wild. Coffin Cove wasn't big enough for him, he used to say. When he and Lee were little, they were close. They went fishing and hunting together. But when they were teenagers, Wayne drifted away. He preferred to spend his time at the old gravel pit and hung out with a biker gang. At first, the bikers were harmless. Just a bunch of guys who loved their bikes and riding together. Lee spent time at the gravel pit occasionally, but he soon felt uneasy around Wayne's new friends.

Wayne had also befriended Art Whilley. "The Whilley boy", as most people called him, was seriously weird. His old man used to mend nets and splice rope for commercial fishermen. Fred Whilley was a quiet man, by all accounts, and well-liked. But his wife was a monster. Even Lee, as a child, had heard the rumours of neglect, abuse and even violence towards Art Whilley. He was a small boy for his age. Lee remembered Wayne and his friends bullying him. Art spent all his time in the schoolhouse, never playing with the other kids, just reading and reading. When the bell went for end of school, Art Whilley would scramble for the door, yank it open and run as fast as he could, with Wayne and his friends in pursuit. They thought it was a game. Lee thought it was cruel.

Lee never made sense of how Wayne and Art came to be friends. Art Whilley eventually lived on his own by the gravel pit. His mother died, followed by his father, and all Art had left was the small dirty cabin he lived in, and the old net shed full of his father's tools and rusty marine parts.

Soon the biker gang were partying at Art Whilley's house after racing up and down the quarter-mile strip of tarmac behind the gravel pit. The parties were wild and noisy. There were complaints, but the police seemed unable to do anything about it. The biker gang grew in popularity, and Lee remembered how they would leave Art's place en masse and drive recklessly through town, throwing beer bottles when they were bored and drunk. Soon the rumble of engines on a Saturday evening was a signal for residents to go inside and lock their doors.

After months of being terrorized by the Knights, as the biker gang now called itself, the residents started referring to Art Whilley's place as Hell's Half Acre.

Lee remembered confronting his brother.

"C'mon man, people are tired of this shit. Can't you get them all to calm it down a bit? Talk to Art, get him to stop the parties."

Wayne laughed. "Not up to Art anymore, bro. I own Hell's Half Acre now."

"How come?" Lee asked, suspicious. He was sure Wayne hadn't bought it legitimately, although his brother was always throwing around wads of cash. Lee had long suspected Wayne was dealing harder drugs than just the odd joint.

Wayne laughed. "Won it in a poker game, man. Lighten up a bit. Come to a party, you'll have fun. There's more than beer, if you know what I mean." He winked at Lee.

Lee knew what he meant. He meant weed and drugs and girls. Even Nadine. She was up there often, partying and doing God knows what. Wayne must have read his mind because he punched his brother in the shoulder.

"Still sad about Nadine? Tell you what, I'll get her back for you."

Lee wanted her back. He couldn't help it. So when she knocked at his door a week later and fixed him with those blue eyes, he'd welcomed her back. Nadine was his girl. Lee wiped from his mind any thoughts of who she'd been with and what she'd done, and even why she was back. It was a fresh start.

Shortly after that, a fire broke out at Hell's Half Acre. The cabin burned to the ground. Art's body was never recovered, but many of the subdued partygoers testified he'd been inside. Lee discovered Wayne hadn't been joking. He was the registered owner of the property. Coffin Cove City, sensing an opportunity to rid the community of the biker gang, the drug problem and a nuisance property all in one go, sued Wayne Dagg.

But Wayne was gone. He'd left Coffin Cove without paying the city a penny. He didn't say goodbye to Lee, just moved on. The biker gang dispersed too, and the community heaved a collective sigh of relief.

Brambles and weeds soon consumed the scorched earth at Hell's Half Acre.

Lee had to pay some outstanding property taxes when he applied for a building permit for Hell's Half Acre. The disinterested clerk who handed him the paperwork didn't seem to care the property belonged to Wayne.

Over the next six months, Lee worked early in the morning and late at night to clear the land and build a small two-bedroom house. It wasn't elaborate, but it was new, and Lee had saved enough money to buy some new furniture. The net shed was the only reminder of the past and Lee intended to replace it with a brand-new workshop for his electrical business.

One evening, Lee persuaded Nadine to go for a drive. They left Coffin Cove and drove up towards the highway. When Lee took the left turn towards the gravel pit, Nadine stared at him.

"Why are we going this way?" she demanded. "I want to go back."

It hadn't been the celebration Lee was hoping for.

"Are you insane?" Nadine screamed at him when Lee explained what he'd done. "You want me to live at Hell's Half Acre?"

She'd sobbed, and Lee, bewildered, tried to calm her down.

"It won't be Hell," he'd whispered, hugging her tight. "We'll make it Heaven." The words sounded corny, even to him.

Finally, Nadine agreed to move in. But things went downhill from there. The economy collapsed in Coffin Cove, and even though Lee would drive anywhere on the island for a booking, many other electricians were looking for the same work.

Nadine managed to get an administrative job at City Hall but fell pregnant with Katie. She didn't want a baby. She screamed and blamed Lee for their financial predicament and threatened to have an abortion. Lee begged her not to, and to this day, he didn't know why she didn't.

Gradually things got back on an even keel. Lee picked up a few contracts from the city. He suspected Dennis Havers pushed the work his way to please Nadine. He'd seen the way Dennis leered at his wife. But they needed the money.

Now, Nadine seemed focused on spending everything he earned. She had a good wage from her job, but Lee knew she squirrelled that money away. In the last year, Nadine had run up his credit card bills and emptied the savings account. She'd spent money on her breasts, her belly dancing outfits and trips to Seattle with her dance troop, and even put a deposit on a brand-new car.

It was getting too much to bear. Maybe Nadine had been right. It was insane to live at Hell's Half Acre. Lee wasn't superstitious, but it felt like his life was cursed.

He looked at himself in the mirror. Where had that energetic young man gone? What was left for him now? Katie, he reminded himself. How could he think his life was cursed when he had Katie? He was so happy to have his daughter back, and he was proud of her new job but worried she had returned just for him.

Thinking of Katie always made him smile. He loved working at the museum with her. She was full of creative ideas for the old building, and already he was looking forward to the grand opening. It would do Katie good to be in the spotlight for once.

The sound of a car leaving the driveway reminded him that Nadine wouldn't enjoy any attention being showered on Katie. She'd never had time for her daughter. Now Katie was home and all grown up, he'd noticed Nadine staring at her daughter with a weird expression on her face. Was she jealous? What kind of mother is jealous of their own kid?

He dried off his face with a towel and went into the bedroom. Nadine had left clothes strewn on the floor and the bed unmade. Lee tidied around and pulled the bedclothes straight before hunting around for a clean shirt. Nadine was making a point of not doing any housework since he'd fired the expensive housekeeper in an effort to keep his bank account in the black.

Giving up his search, he pulled on the least grubby T-shirt he could find and gathered up all the dirty clothes to fill the washing machine. He'd have to talk to Katie. Maybe she could help out. He knew she wouldn't mind.

For a second, he had a vision of himself and his daughter in their own place.

"What the hell?" he said out loud. What was wrong with him? Katie deserved her own life. Shaking his head at his own selfishness, Lee grabbed up more dirty laundry for the washer and left the bedroom.

Lee turned on the machine and listened to the gushing water. He didn't feel like working today. He had things left to do at the museum, and he wondered for a second if, afterwards, he and Katie could take the afternoon off and go on a road trip somewhere, like they did when she was a kid. He used to take her with him when he had work in different parts of the island. He wanted her to see a world outside of Coffin Cove. He wanted her to escape someday. Like he dreamed of doing.

His mind wandered back to those days. He had never wanted to be an electrician like his dad. He wanted to get off the island and go to Alberta. Work in the oilfields, maybe. Leave like Wayne had. Why hadn't he done that? There had been a chance, but then there was Nadine smiling at him, wanting a pretty wedding dress and a diamond ring, taking his breath away.

He sighed. How things had changed.

Lee turned to leave the laundry room. He caught sight of a sparkly ribbon caught in the closet door. It looked like a Christmas decoration. Lee pulled the door open to get a closer look.

"Damn you, Nadine," he shouted.

Hanging in the closet was Nadine's brand new belly dancing outfit. She hadn't bothered to remove the price tag.

Just about a month's income. The dress glittered at him and Lee felt like ripping it to shreds with a knife. Didn't Nadine care about anyone except herself?

Lee knew the answer to that. He couldn't go on like this. It had to end.

CHAPTER SIX

Jade Thompson looked out of her office window, the only one in the building facing the ocean. She felt her spirits lift. Warmer, brighter weather was on its way. The sun felt warm through the office window, and Jade stood there for a moment, enjoying the peace of the early morning.

Jade allowed herself some optimism. It might be a new beginning for Coffin Cove. At last. So far, legal struggles and tough financial negotiations had overshadowed her tenure as the new mayor of Coffin Cove. But it had been worth it.

Coffin Cove had been in an economic mess for as long as Jade could remember. The heady days of the fishing and forestry booms were long over. Coffin Cove had squandered every penny, it seemed, with nothing left for a rainy day, and no means of raising any more cash from the struggling residents and business owners — those few who remained, anyway.

Jade wondered, not for the first time, what on earth she had been thinking when she announced her candidacy for mayor.

It had been a difficult few months.

Fired up with determination, Jade had worked hard at her campaign. She knocked on every door in Coffin Cove, handed out leaflets, pledged to do her very best and smiled winningly at sceptical voters. She promised she would reinvent the town, attracting tourists and developers, and most importantly, jobs. She reassured the community there would be an end to the shady backhanders and dodgy deals rumoured to be the "business model" of the incumbent mayor and his inner circle. People at least listened, and at the end of the campaign Jade was hopeful of the outcome and certain she could not have done any more. But despite her hard work, she was as astounded as both her opponents and supporters when the results of the mayoral race were announced and Dennis Havers' reign as mayor of Coffin Cove was finally over.

Jade Thompson was both the youngest and the first female mayor to serve Coffin Cove.

After election day and the celebration at Hephzibah's café, the headquarters of the Thompson campaign, Jade was officially sworn in. But then it rained. As the euphoria of winning wore off and the enormity of the task ahead of her became apparent, the dark grey days reminded Jade of all the reasons she'd left Coffin Cove years ago.

Not that Jade doubted her ability as mayor. She was smart — not just academically, but street-smart too. She'd learned how to be cunning, how to be patient, how to gently talk people into doing things her way, even if they didn't want to. No, Jade was a natural politician. It was abandoning her privacy that Jade feared most. Her ability to fade into the background. It had been an effective survival technique, and without it, Jade felt exposed.

On her first day, Jade made a brief speech to the staff at City Hall. The small crowd dutifully clapped, but Jade saw suspicion and scepticism on some faces, mostly from the staff who'd been employed there for years. She saw the raised eyebrows and exchanged glances as she laid out the way she would run the show from now on.

"The past is the past," she'd said. "Nobody will be blamed or judged for what went on before. From this day—"

she looked meaningfully at the silent staff — "we will have one mission only: to serve the people of Coffin Cove. They pay us. We work for them. Every project, every decision, every dollar spent will be in pursuit of that mission. Everyone who understands that and works towards that mission will continue to have a job. If there are people who have a different agenda — well, at some point, they'll be looking for alternative employment."

Jade saw the odd smirk. She knew it would be an uphill battle. But she smiled and told herself they would soon see she was serious and capable. Jade was used to being underestimated. People glanced at her forgettable face, obscured by large glasses, and mentally categorized her as a coffee girl or filing clerk, if they didn't know better. Jade didn't mind. She liked the look of shock on the faces of self-important corporate types when she arranged her files, her notebook and her tablet at the head of the table and called meetings to order. She laughed inwardly when men in suits shifted in their chairs and attempted to keep up with her rapid absorption of facts and figures and her quick-fire questions. She liked that she could be unobtrusive. She heard things. People told her things, things they shouldn't, not realizing she internally filed every scrap of information. Jade had an amazing memory and a meticulous attention to detail.

Jade's focus was born out of a disability she kept hidden. She was dyslexic.

She had hated school when she was little. She was plain, needed braces and wore large glasses. The kids mostly ignored her unless she was called upon to read out loud in class. Jade couldn't understand why the words and letters seemed to swim around in front of her, swirling into a jumbled mess when she tried to read. The mean kids laughed at her. Time after time, she'd sink down into her chair, flushed with shame and humiliation. It was years before Jade was diagnosed. Until then, she'd trained herself to memorize pages and pages of textbooks and assignments, so she could stand and recite whole passages, keeping her eyes trained on the pages, so nobody knew she wasn't reading. She learned to study in-depth, paying attention to detail. Jade was always prepared, her tasks well-researched, so when she looked around at her new staff, she already had a good idea of who would stay and who would look for a new job.

The run for mayor, uncharacteristically for Jade, was conceived in a flash of anger. More than just anger, Jade acknowledged. It was rage — rage at injustice, which had accumulated over decades.

Summer Thompson, Jade's mother, moved to Coffin Cove in the eighties, a refugee from the freewheeling chaotic days of the previous heady decade.

She was a "blow-in", as the locals called the drifters, artists and get-rich-quick schemers who materialized when Coffin Cove's economy boomed. Summer was a talented artist, pretty and engaging, and Jade grew up surrounded by bohemian people who talked art, politics and philosophy late into the night. They mostly took no notice of the plain little girl with her nose in a book.

Although Jade didn't know her father, she never wanted for love or fun. Summer took her on camping trips to the beach, where they'd collect driftwood and shells for art projects, and roast hotdogs over a fire. Jade had her best memories of Coffin Cove from those times, the sun slipping down behind the cliffs, Summer and Jade huddled under a blanket until it was pitch dark. For a while, the two of them had lived on Hope Island, a tiny community of women who created a commune of sorts.

Jade liked to think of them as a duo battling against the world. She'd arrange Summer's finished pieces in the yard to attract sales from the trickle of tourists in the summer and make sure her mother ate when she was especially engrossed in her art. Summer encouraged Jade's academic progress. "My little professor," Summer used to say fondly to her daughter. And, "You're smart. You can do anything, go anywhere. Get away from Coffin Cove and make something of your life." She'd saved as much cash as possible for Jade to go to college.

Jade loved college. The last years at school in Coffin Cove, she'd suffered from panic attacks. She wasn't popular. The popular girls were the pretty ones who gathered together at lunch breaks and giggled about boys. The boys they liked were the ones who had trucks. Trucks with gun racks, boys with beer who liked to race their trucks in the gravel pit while the pretty girls watched. Or the sports jocks who strutted and preened and expected adulation.

They never invited Jade to join the crowd and giggle about boys. The girls were not openly mean, they just huddled and whispered when Jade was near, and sometimes they laughed.

Jade didn't care that she wasn't popular. Until that one day. She preferred not to think of that day.

When Jade was at college, she discovered her weapon: her intellect. She had always been smart, with good grades, but in college she excelled. Her professors had wanted her to study law, but she rejected that option. She studied business and economics because she knew that money, not law, equalled power. When she graduated, she was snapped up by a large property developer who soon discovered Jade's ability to negotiate contracts with steely resolve.

"She cut their head off before they even knew they were bleeding," she overheard one partner say in awe after she saved the company millions, by refusing to back down or even move an inch during particularly sensitive transactions.

Jade took that as a compliment. She also took the bonus with a curt "thank you", refusing the invitation to the celebratory dinner. She still wasn't popular.

Jade knew some of her decisions as mayor would not be received well. Some of the residents still disliked blow-ins. They preferred to think of themselves as outlaws in a renegade town, keeping business to themselves. But business hadn't been good for decades. Not since the days when lumber and fish fed the town's economic boom. But those days were gone now, and Coffin Cove needed a financial lifeline, one that benefited the whole community, not just opportunists in elected office.

After Jade took over, she worked on uncovering the damage Dennis Havers had done. She opened files, worked through budgets, studied reports. While the rain pounded outside, Jade made it her business to know all the financial secrets of Coffin Cove. Dennis Havers had never considered the possibility of losing, she thought, because he had made little attempt to cover his tracks. There weren't actual records of backhanders, but the inflated tenders for city contracts — sometimes with no evidence of work having ever started, let alone been completed — showed that Dennis was skimming. The same names came up repeatedly.

The atmosphere at City Hall for that month was hushed and apprehensive, as Jade worked long hours with her door closed.

But she made headway. She was true to her promise. She never fired anyone or used the word "fraud", but a quiet word in a clerk's ear, pointing out accounting discrepancies, was usually enough to prompt a quick note of resignation.

When the new fiscal year rolled around, the budgets were balanced. Jade had acquired provincial grants and long-term loans to invest in the town. Applications for business licences were up and the planning department reported an increase in applications for new building work. Jade had big dreams for the town, and today, for the first time, she believed they would come true.

She turned around and sat at her desk. She had some letters to sign, and after that she promised herself a walk to Hephzibah's to get a large mug of milky coffee. Her latest project, the Heritage Festival, kicked off next week, and Hephzibah would let her know if there was a buzz of enthusiasm in the town about the festivities. Jade hoped so. An early start to the tourism season was what everyone needed.

Still work to be done, she admonished herself. *Can't celebrate just yet.* And she focused on the pile of paperwork on her desk.

Jade had her head down, working through her pile, when she heard a slight cough.

"Excuse me."

She heard a man's voice and looked up.

A tall man was standing in the doorway, smiling.

"Sorry to interrupt," he said. "You are Jade Thompson, oh . . . my apologies, Mayor Jade Thompson?" He was still smiling, but Jade couldn't sense a mocking tone. She didn't stand on formalities, but she didn't tolerate disrespectful comments either. But there was no hint of either, and the man didn't move to walk into the office.

"Yes, I'm Jade Thompson. Come in."

The man was well-groomed, and Jade thought he'd be in his late fifties or early sixties. Carrying a manila envelope, he walked to Jade's desk and stretched out his hand. She shook it. Jade noticed his handshake was firm, but his hand was soft and his nails were trimmed.

He held out the file, and as his sleeve moved up his arm, Jade caught sight of a tattoo.

He saw her looking.

"Sign of a misspent youth, Mayor," he said, and his smile widened. "Don't judge me."

Jade could not help but smile back. She associated tattoos with the bikers of the bad old days of Coffin Cove. But she knew it wasn't fair. Many people had tattoos now. It didn't mean they were in a gang.

"I'm a property developer," the man said, with no preamble. "I'm interested in developing the old fish plant site." He nodded at the envelope. "The details and my offer are in there."

Jade took the envelope and frowned. She had uncovered Dennis Havers' plans for the now derelict fish plant. The site was one of the few pieces of real estate still owned by the city. Once, it had been the centre of Coffin Cove's thriving seafood industry. Fishing vessels lined up to unload their daily catch at the pier, and the plant hummed with the sound of conveyor belts moving mechanical rivers of shiny fish to be cut and processed. The fish plant was one of the major employers in the town. For decades it had stood silent and empty, save for the odd vagrant who camped there and the gulls that lined up on the rusting rails of the pier, as if paying homage to the days when they were sure of easy meals of fish guts.

"Thank you," Jade said, "but I haven't put that project out to tender yet."

The man chuckled. "Word of your regeneration of Coffin Cove has reached far and wide," he said. "I've been looking at the potential of the town, and that waterfront site . . . well, let's say it could be a goldmine. For everyone."

Jade was secretly pleased. This was what she wanted: for people to see beyond the decaying infrastructure of Coffin Cove and instead picture what the town could be. She needed people with vision. Maybe this man was one of them.

Still, she kept her cool. "Thank you," she said. "I'll be happy to look it over."

"Please do. I'll be in town for a while. But I won't take up your time, you look busy." He gestured to her desk.

"Well, thanks again," Jade said awkwardly, as the man had made no move to leave.

"I hope you don't mind me asking," he blurted, "but . . . Thompson? Are you any relation to Summer Thompson?"

"Yes," Jade said, feeling uncomfortable. Who was this man? "She's my mother."

"Thought so," he said. "You look like her."

"You know my mother, Mr . . . ?" Jade was getting a little suspicious now. Was this man a friend of Dennis Havers', fishing for information, perhaps?

"Oh, a long time ago," the man said, ignoring the obvious hint for his name. "Back when I was proud of my tattoos," he laughed.

Don't be silly and paranoid, Jade told herself, as the man excused himself and left the office.

She sat back down at her desk and opened the envelope. She slid out a sheaf of papers and recognized the legal format. She scanned them, looking for a name, but the cover letter was signed by a lawyer's firm she knew from her days working in Vancouver. They referred to their client as "Knights Development Ltd".

She'd never heard of them.

Sighing, she pushed the papers back in the envelope. That development was a long time in the future, and right this minute, she had work to do.

On second thoughts, she stood up.

It was such a lovely morning, maybe she'd run out now for coffee and enjoy the morning air. She deserved a few minutes out of the office.

"You want some coffee?"

For the second time that morning, Jade wished the door was closed.

"No, thank you, Nadine." Jade forced herself to smile. "How are you this morning?"

Before Jade could tell her office manager to close the door, Nadine Dagg interpreted the polite words as an invitation to sit down and actually tell Jade exactly how she was.

Jade was forced to listen to Nadine's never-ending list of complaints about her office colleagues. Nadine was one of Dennis Havers' most valuable employees — at least in her own opinion. Jade wasn't oblivious to the rumour that Nadine had been far more than an employee to Dennis.

Jade looked at her, not listening to her voice, and wondered what on earth Dennis was thinking, if the rumour was true. Sandra Havers may have been older than Nadine, but she had kept herself in shape and was a stylish, well-groomed woman.

Nadine Dagg was nearing her mid-fifties, Jade guessed. This morning, she was squeezed into a tight black leather skirt and a red shirt that strained over her chest and midriff. She wore her faded blonde hair long, with one streak of purple, and was heavily made-up, with pencilled-in eyebrows and bright lipstick.

Jade imagined that Nadine would fit in perfectly on the back of a Harley, clinging onto a pot-bellied, bearded biker. In the city office, she looked as if she should be paying a fine for loitering outside the Fat Chicken all night, rather than managing the office.

Nadine was oblivious to the inappropriateness of her dress. In fact, it was obvious that she thought she looked sexy. Many a male employee had smiled politely at Nadine and then been subjected to a full-frontal "seductive" move. Nadine reminded Jade of a coiled snake, waiting to strike and consume her prey.

Jade disliked Nadine but had to admit she was passably efficient at her job.

"Oh honey, you look so tired and stressed, what's wrong?"

Jade bit her lip. She hated being called "honey" or "dear", but she let it go, just hoping to get rid of Nadine as soon as possible.

"Absolutely nothing, Nadine, I'm fine. What's on the agenda for today?" Jade was brisk. Nadine's syrupy tone, she knew, was designed to elicit some small morsel of information that she could file away and use to her benefit, or even just for her entertainment. Jade had long since discovered Nadine's love of gossip.

The accounts department had already lost a couple of junior clerks who'd made the mistake of confiding in Nadine, only to find they were the subject of wildly false rumours that spread throughout the city offices. As with a dangerous swaying snake, it was best to show no fear and no signs of weakness.

If Nadine was offended at Jade's abrupt tone, she didn't show it. She moved smoothly into business mode and the next few minutes were at least productive.

Then Nadine got up to go.

"Nadine, did you see a man in a sports jacket leave the building this morning?" It occurred to Jade that Nadine, who never missed a thing, might know the man. She told Nadine about the unscheduled meeting.

Nadine pursed her bright red lips. "No, I don't know who that could be," she said. "I'll ask around. What company did he work for?"

"Oh, I have it here."

Jade pulled the envelope out of her drawer.

"Here it is. Knights Developments Limited. Are they local?" She looked at Nadine, who shrugged.

"Never heard of them," she said.

As Nadine left the office, one of the junior clerks barged in. "Sorry to interrupt, Mayor Thompson," she said.

"Yes?" Jade was getting short-tempered now.

"Jim Peters phoned from the *Gazette*, Mayor, and said to remind you about the interview at ten."

Jade sighed. She'd forgotten. She thought for a second about cancelling but then nodded at the clerk. "Thanks, I'll make sure I'm free." She might as well get it over with. She'd agreed to the interview, and she liked Jim Peters. The *Gazette* had been neutral throughout the campaign and refused to print anything negative or mean-spirited about either candidate. Since she'd been in office, Jim had printed positive articles about her progress, urging the community to give their new mayor their wholehearted support. So she owed him an interview, at least, she thought.

"And close the door, would you?" Jade called out at the retreating clerk, hoping, finally, for some peace and quiet.

CHAPTER SEVEN

When Katie arrived at the gravel pit, she saw a small red truck already parked. Mr Gomich was waiting for Katie. As she drove closer, she could see he had a companion. She had hoped he would bring other members of the historical society, but her heart sank when she saw the other person was Clara Bell.

Clara had retired as museum curator just as Katie returned to Coffin Cove, but the couple of times they had met, Katie had felt the elderly lady's hostility. Maybe she was upset because she'd had no support from the city, Katie had wondered aloud to her father. "And now I have a budget and the promise of brand-new facilities? I'd be annoyed too," she'd said.

"More like she's a grumpy old bag," Lee had replied.

Maybe Clara knew something about the mysterious chapel, Katie thought as she waved and smiled. Harry Brown had told her earlier that Clara helped him with locating all the old mining tunnels.

Clara Bell was one of Coffin Cove's "characters". She lived out of town on the original homestead her family had claimed back in 1846, just as the Treaty of Washington divided off United States territory, allowing the British control of Vancouver Island. She lived off the grid still, with electricity from a diesel generator and water from a well.

Clara was a forbidding figure. She'd been old when Katie was little. She looked no different now, except her wild mane of hair was white. Her face was smooth, with few wrinkles giving away her age, and her dark eyes were sharp and piercing. And at the moment, Clara was glowering at Katie.

Katie tried to stay positive. This was a learning experience, she thought.

Mr Gomich greeted her enthusiastically.

"Hello there, Katie! I'm excited about our adventure this morning. I've brought Clara with me. She'll be a huge help — there's very little she doesn't know about our local history."

"That's wonderful." Katie smiled at both of them, ignoring the sullen expression on Clara's face.

"Is that a map?" she asked Clara. The old lady was holding a roll of yellowing paper.

Wordlessly, Clara marched over to the truck and pulled down the tailgate. She spread out the paper. Katie was surprised to see it was a hand-drawn map. She could see the gravel pit marked, a few trails and some other symbols which meant nothing to her. Katie didn't know much about map-making, but it looked to scale.

"Did you do this?" she asked Clara. "It's amazing."

"I mapped all the area," the woman said, in a friendlier tone. "See that there?" She pointed at the map. "That's your house, Hell's Half Acre."

Katie smiled. Her mother hated it when the elders in the town called their home that old name. Katie had heard the stories about gangs and parties but had never taken much notice. She thought her mother was being oversensitive.

"You ever walked much in the bush?" Clara asked her. Her voice was gravelly, as if she were a heavy smoker, and she was abrupt.

"No. Just that trail. From our house to the beach. Dad always told us there were abandoned mineshafts and it was too dangerous."

"He was right," Clara said. "The shafts are here and here. The chapel is between them, in a clearing right here." She was gesturing at her map, but Katie was looking at her, amazed.

"So there really is a chapel?" she asked.

"'Course there is. Why else are we here? Some damn goose chase?" Clara snorted, as though Katie was the most ignorant person she had ever met.

"It's just I'd never heard about it until the other day. And the story about the priest and the coffin."

Clara looked at Katie as if she were mad and then threw back her head and laughed.

Katie was getting annoyed now, but at least her lack of knowledge had broken the ice with the irritable old woman. When Clara stopped laughing, she took Katie's arm.

"Come on, I'll show you, dear, and tell you the true story. This way," she called over her shoulder to Mr Gomich.

"That's just an old wives' tale," Clara explained to Katie. "There was no priest, and no coffin bobbing out to sea. Coffin Cove got its name from the shape of the bay. It's a recent name. The natives who lived here long before we arrived had their own name."

"And the chapel? Who built it?" Katie asked.

"Noah Whilley. The great-grandfather of the most recent Whilley. Poor little Art Whilley lived on your property before your uncle conned him out of his inheritance and all the hell-raisin' started." Clara looked sharply at her. "Your mother knew all about that. But maybe you're not like her, eh?"

This was news to Katie. Lee had always been vague about her uncle's story, and Nadine never spoke about her past. What did Clara know?

But before she could ask more, Clara was striding through the bush, with Katie and Mr Gomich struggling to keep up. Clara was wearing a long dark skirt, just as Katie remembered from the old days in the museum. But Katie caught a flash of sturdy hiking boots under the folds of material. Clara was fitter than she looked and moved nimbly over the gnarled roots and loose gravel on the narrow trail.

Why hadn't she ever noticed this trail before? It was more than an animal trail, and it seemed to be clear, as if it were walked regularly. Maybe it wasn't just Clara who knew her way around the bush. She made a mental note to ask Terri.

Although they were walking in the shadows of the undergrowth, Katie caught glimpses of sun lighting up the path.

"Not far now!" Clara called out, sounding confident.

There was a sharp descent, and then all three of them were standing in brilliant sunshine. The trees had parted above them, and they were standing in a clearing.

"Here," Clara said triumphantly.

Katie looked around. She didn't see anything at first, except tall fireweed and yellow yarrow.

"I don't . . ." she started to say, but Clara pointed out a mound at one side of the clearing. When Katie got nearer, she could see it was a pile of stones, covered with wild grass. When she looked closer, she could see the vague rectangular remains of a structure.

"I see!" Katie said. "This is amazing!"

She visualized telling the story to small tours of visitors.

"How old are the ruins, Clara?" Katie asked.

Clara shrugged. "Maybe a hundred years," she said. "I've never found much on the chapel. Probably all the old paperwork burned when Art did."

"Was it just a family chapel?"

Clara nodded. "Back in those days, people in Coffin Cove were either one way or another. They were drunkards or churchgoers. The drunkards were serious about their drinkin' and the churchgoers were serious about the Lord. There was no meetin' in the middle. Noah Whilley was serious about the Lord, and so he built his own chapel. Probably because he thought it was easier than pushing through all the drunk folk in town to get to the Lord. I dunno what he'd have thought 'bout his place bein' Hell's Half Acre. Probably turn in his grave."

Katie was alarmed. "Are we walking on family graves?"

Clara's answer was drowned out by a sudden screeching sound that made Katie grab Mr Gomich's arm.

"What on earth?"

Clara chuckled. "Maybe it's old Noah, telling us to get off his holy ground."

Katie stared at her, not knowing what to think, but realizing Clara was enjoying her discomfort.

"You never heard ravens before, girl? You've been too long on the mainland."

Katie smiled, relieved. She'd forgotten about the ravens. The "tricksters" of the forest, Lee had told her. They can make all kinds of noises — sometimes it sounds like a person laughing or a baby crying.

"Oh, that fits with the old story," she said. "People weren't hearing the ghost of a child, they were hearing ravens."

"Exactly," Mr Gomich said. "Wonder how that old story came about?"

"Probably to stop young 'uns falling down mineshafts," Clara said. "No point telling 'em it's dangerous, makes 'em want to explore all the more. But frightening them with ghosts and bogeymen — well, that'll keep most kids away."

"And the graves?" Katie asked.

"Not likely. None of the Whilleys, that's for sure," Clara said. "I've checked, they're all in the cemetery in town. Except Art. There was nothin' left of him."

Katie wanted to know more about Art Whilley and his demise, but Clara had found a stick and was poking around at the edge of the clearing.

"There used to be a corner of the chapel still standin'," she said, "somewhere around here, I think."

Katie took some pictures with her phone.

"What do you think, Mr Gomich? Would this make a good tour for visitors?"

She and Mr Gomich chatted about making the trail wider or seeing if there was easier access from the beach. But Katie broke off her conversation when she heard Clara exclaim, "Oh my Lord!"

Katie hurried over. Clara was bent over and peering into a part of the ruin which must have once been the corner of the chapel. It was obscured by brambles, but Clara had found two stone walls joined at an angle.

The old lady was on her knees as if she were praying. She was motionless, and for a second, Katie thought she might be having a heart attack.

"Clara, are you OK?" Katie rested her hand on the woman's shoulder.

"There," was all she said. Clara had freed a brownish round object that at first glance seemed to be attached to the stone wall. Katie leaned closer, confused. Moss and brambles obscured Katie's view, so she reached out her hand to pull the undergrowth away.

Clara grabbed her wrist. "Don't do that, girl."

Annoyed, Katie pulled away from the old lady's grasp, and got on her knees to have a better look.

Then she realized she was looking directly into the empty hollow sockets of a human skull. She covered her mouth to stop her scream and stumbled backwards away from the sightless gaze.

CHAPTER EIGHT

"This is your assignment." Jim handed Andi a sheet of paper.

"The Heritage Festival?"

"That's what you get for being late. Go and interview the mayor and then write something nice about the celebrations here in town. We need copy by Thursday afternoon. I promised the mayor a mention before the launch party at the Fat Chicken."

"How is belly dancing part of Coffin Cove's history?" Andi asked, casting her eye down the festival schedule.

"No idea. It can be your first question," Jim said cheerfully.

Andi shoved the paper in her purse and eyed Jim with suspicion. She got up to leave, saying, "I thought you were interviewing the mayor."

"Sit down, Andi."

Jim's tone was serious, so Andi did as she was told, but didn't look happy about it.

Jim looked at her for a moment.

"You look like shit," he said, always direct. "How are you doing?"

Andi sighed. "I'm fine. I just slept badly," she admitted. "A nightmare." She shrugged and then sat silently.

He softened. "Look," Jim said gently, "you went through a terrible time last year. The occasional nightmare is to be expected, isn't that what the counsellor said? I know you're bored with this stuff—" he gestured at the paper in Andi's hand — "but it keeps your mind busy. Routine is good for you. Cover this festival, and then, if you're sure you're feeling up to something more . . ." He took a deep breath. "Look, I don't think you have any evidence at all to link the Thompsons with Ricky Havers' disappearance. But I will help you. We'll start from the beginning and see if we can re-interview everyone connected with Ricky and go where the story takes us."

Jim got a smile, a spark of the old Andi.

"Sure, sounds good."

She got up to go and then stopped.

"Jim, there's something I haven't told you."

Here it comes, Jim thought. The envelope. The illegal search.

"Go on," he said calmly, although he wasn't sure how he would react.

"About Ricky Havers," Andi said, "I've been helping someone."

"Who?" Jim said, surprised. He wasn't expecting this.

"Sandra Havers," she said.

"Sandra Havers?" Jim echoed. "What do you mean?"

"She came to me after the police couldn't find Ricky and had no clue where he'd gone. They didn't close the file, but you know what happens. The file just sits in a box somewhere, and every so often they make an appeal for information. Sandra . . . well, she wasn't happy about it, and nobody would be. I mean, Ricky Havers was a bit of an asshole, even she says that, but she's his mother. She's not going to give up on him. Even if it means the worst-case scenario. So . . ." Andi took a breath as if about to make a confession. "I've been helping her. At least, I've been trying. So far, I haven't found anything, and she's losing hope."

"Did she come to you, Andi?" Jim asked. "You didn't go chasing her for a story?"

Andi shook her head. "She said if I could solve the Sarah McIntosh murder, I could help her find out what happened to Ricky."

"I see." It was making sense to Jim now. "So, all this obsession with Ricky Havers . . ."

"Sorry, Jim. I know I should have told you, but Sandra wanted everything confidential. You see, she thinks Dennis Havers has something to do with it."

"Her own husband?" Jim said incredulously. "I know Dennis is . . . well . . . slimy. But to abduct his own son? Why on earth would he do that?"

'Well . . . here's the thing," Andi said slowly, "and we have to keep this to ourselves, Jim — Ricky isn't Dennis's son."

"Shit," Jim said, stunned.

Andi nodded. "I know. Sandra has never told Dennis, but she thinks he may have found out. He was acting weird before Ricky went missing. Sandra said even the Smoke Room thing was strange. Dennis was always complaining Ricky was lazy and useless, and then he suddenly invests thousands of dollars into a business for Ricky. And it's weed. Dennis hated weed."

"Hmm. I thought Dennis was trying to buy the trailer park. The weed shop was a ploy to get the property value down. Smoke 'em out."

Andi smiled at Jim's weak joke.

"Sandra originally thought that too. But now she thinks Dennis had an ulterior motive. Maybe he didn't mean to hurt Ricky, but . . ."

"Something went wrong?" Jim finished for her. "Sounds harsh, though. He raised Ricky. I mean, even if he wasn't Dennis's flesh and blood . . ."

"Sandra says it would have humiliated Dennis. He wouldn't have been able to stand being deceived all these years. She thinks he was furious. She thinks it's all her fault and now all she can think of is finding Ricky. Alive or dead."

"Seems hypocritical," Jim said. "All these years Dennis had his affair with Nadine Dagg. Surely Sandra should be the one who feels humiliated. Has she confronted him about Ricky?"

Andi shook her head. "Not really. She tried when Ricky first disappeared. Dennis didn't seem concerned. He denied knowing anything about it. But now she's convinced he knows something. She's afraid and distraught."

"So if Dennis isn't Ricky's father, who is?"

Andi sighed. "I asked that. It might have been a potential lead. Maybe Ricky found out somehow and went looking for his biological father. It's a bit of a stretch, and Sandra claims Ricky had no idea. She doesn't know how Dennis found out either. But she says the identity of Ricky's father doesn't matter and can't be connected to the case. So I had to take her at her word. And I promised to keep it to myself, although I said if you helped me, I'd have to tell you."

Jim nodded. "You know I'll keep that confidence. What else have you got so far?"

"Not much. Sandra's given me a lot of information about Dennis's business dealings, but I haven't had a chance to look at it yet."

The envelope, Jim thought. Now it made sense. He was relieved. It was one thing for a source to hand Andi sensitive material, quite another for her to break the law to get it.

One thought came to him. "Do you still think the Thompsons are involved? Has Sandra shed any light on that?"

Andi shrugged. "I still think they're both hiding something. Sandra seems to think Summer Thompson and her husband have some history. I haven't got that far yet." Andi smiled suddenly, her face lighting up. "It'll be good to have your help."

Jim couldn't help grinning back. "Sure. Go do this interview with Madam Mayor, and we'll get on with it. Off you go," and he made a shooing gesture towards the door.

"Just one other thing, Jim." Andi hovered for a moment.

"What? More secrets?"

"No, I need my cheque."

"What cheque?"

"My cheque for last week's articles."

"Article, singular," Jim corrected her, "and you can have it when I get a thousand words about the Heritage Festival by 5 p.m. today."

* * *

When Andi left the office, she felt like a weight had been lifted from her shoulders. She hated keeping secrets from Jim.

He'd been her saviour when she needed help and she owed him a lot. Andi had taken the job at the *Coffin Cove Gazette* because it was her only option. She'd left her old job at a national media company in disgrace, and her married lover — who also happened to be her boss — had dumped her.

Andi felt no heartache for the ruined relationship. She had known for a long time that Gavin would never leave his wife, and she had hated the lies and deceit and sneaking around. It had just about finished her as a journalist until she hammered that nail into the coffin of her career all by herself. Once a rising star on the investigative reporting team for a large newspaper, where Gavin was the deputy editor, her upward trajectory had come to a crashing end when she had failed to corroborate a tip-off from a source. She had gone ahead and written the article, sure that everything was fine and assuring Gavin that the source was solid. Neither would turn out to be true. The tip-off had been bogus, and a prominent businessman had threatened to sue. It had been a horrible mess. The newspaper had had to rescind the article and print a full-page apology.

Andi's face still burned with anger as she remembered being called into the editor's office. Gavin had stood there, stony-faced and furious, as the editor fired her and issued him a warning.

He didn't look at her when they were out of the office, just muttered, "We'll talk later." They never did.

Eventually Andi stopped calling and texting and focused her attention on what to do next. Having been publicly disgraced, she knew that no media outlet would even accept a restaurant review from her.

Getting frantic, and with her bank balance dwindling, she saw an advertisement for a position at the *Coffin Cove Gazette*. In desperation, she applied, hoping Jim Peters, the owner, wouldn't find out about her humiliation

He already knew.

He'd offered her the job anyway, warning her not to screw up or lie to him ever, and then he said, "You know, there are more than just bake sales in this town. Give it a chance. It might surprise you."

His words had been prophetic.

Andi rubbed her face. She was tired of feeling sorry for herself.

This morning, Andi had felt the first spark of energy in a long time when Jim promised to help her investigate Ricky's disappearance. Andi had been touched when Sandra approached her. She had felt so sorry for the broken woman, begging Andi to help. Andi didn't have the heart to say no, but the pressure to find something, anything tangible was getting to her. But now, Andi smiled to herself, her old mojo was coming back.

She got out of the car and decided to walk to City Hall. Fresh air would do her good, she thought. It would give her a chance to think through all she had discovered so far and get it straight in her head, before she presented her investigation to Jim. She'd better be ready for his interrogation.

For once, the sun was shining.

As Andi took the scenic route towards City Hall via the ocean front, she thought about Mayor Jade Thompson. She was glad Jim had assigned this interview to her. She was convinced Mayor Thompson played some part in this unfolding story. Andi had interviewed the mayor when she was running for office, and she'd thought then that Jade kept her most interesting personal facts to herself. Jade Thompson was an enigma. She played everything close to her chest. Andi both admired her and was intrigued by her. Until Jade's candidacy, Dennis Havers had been mayor of Coffin Cove for ever, it seemed. Nobody seemed to like him, but nobody ran against him either. Jade was the first female mayor that Coffin Cove had ever elected, and she had also ended Dennis Havers' reign. Overall, Andi decided, it was a good thing. Jade had new ideas and seemed dedicated to serving the community. Andi had only just started digging around about Dennis Havers, but already she'd found out that the previous mayor had been more interested in helping himself than helping Coffin Cove.

Andi had first met Jade Thompson around the same time Ricky Havers disappeared. Andi didn't believe in coincidences. She had been convinced right from the start that there was some sort of a connection between Jade Thompson and Ricky Havers.

As she passed Hephzibah's café, Andi remembered that first encounter. She and Jim had been enjoying an afternoon coffee. Andi had immediately noticed the tall, serious woman at the counter. Andi had lived in Coffin Cove long enough to recognize most faces, and she was sure she hadn't seen this lady before. Yet Hephzibah not only seemed to recognize the woman, she also knew her coffee order.

Andi and Jim had been discussing Ricky Havers and the Smoke Room, the first ever legal marijuana store in Coffin Cove. Ricky was the proprietor. He was forty-two years old, and according to everyone Andi spoke to, he had never held down a job for more than a few weeks in his entire life. Still, most people agreed that if Ricky were suited to any kind of work, it would be running a marijuana store. Apparently Ricky had perfected the art of smoking weed. Most people assumed Dennis had fronted the cash for the store. Sandra Havers had always spoiled Ricky, but Dennis made no secret that he was ashamed of his layabout son. Dennis had acquired the deserted Coffin Cove strip mall, with its empty stores and overgrown parking lot, and paid for the renovation of the Smoke Room.

Not everyone in the community was happy about the Smoke Room. The legalization of weed was a hot topic, and Andi was planning a series of articles around the subject. She had only just got back to work, and Jim had thought it would be easier to meet at the café. Andi had still been using a cane, and there was a long narrow staircase up to the office.

Andi had been aware of the woman thanking Hephzibah and moving towards the back of the café, with the low comfy seats by the wood stove and the bookcases. She didn't like to stare and so turned back to Jim. She couldn't remember exactly how their conversation went, but she knew she'd said "Ricky Havers" just before she heard a slight gasp followed by the sound of china smashing.

The woman was white and shaking. The mug of coffee had fallen from her hands and shattered over the floor. For a moment, she seemed unaware she was splashed with hot coffee, and only moved when Hephzibah came rushing up to help. Jade had denied being startled in the coffee shop, making some excuse about cramp, but Andi had seen Jade's face. She'd been in shock. Completely white.

Andi couldn't help thinking that mug of coffee hitting the floor had signified the start of some very strange events in Coffin Cove.

Andi stopped walking and took a moment to take in the view of the ocean, as her thoughts remained with Jade Thompson.

A few days after the strange meeting at Hephzibah's, Andi interviewed Summer Thompson. Summer was Jade's mother. She was organizing a petition against the Smoke Room. It wasn't going anywhere. Dennis was mayor, and the planning committee had already approved the application. The only chance to get rid of the Smoke Room was if Ricky really screwed up, or quit. It was a decent story, but Andi's real motive was to probe a little further into Jade's strange reaction to hearing Ricky's name.

That interview had been weird too. Andi came away with more questions than answers. Summer had presented herself as an eccentric artist, all flowing skirts and arty knick-knacks everywhere. But it felt like an act, as if Summer wanted everyone to think she was a bit flaky. She couldn't quite put her finger on it, but Andi was certain Summer and Jade were hiding something.

The next day, Ricky disappeared.

The local police investigated, but as Ricky was a grown man and there was no sign of a struggle or foul play, there was little they could do. Sandra Havers was distraught and persuaded a relative in the RCMP to dispatch an inspector from the mainland to re-examine the Smoke Room and try to shake out some new leads. But there had been none. Several people, Andi included, had seen the neon "OPEN" sign of the Smoke Room turned on during the day of Ricky's disappearance. When Sandra and Dennis first looked for him, they found the sign turned off and the door unlocked. But the cash remained in the till and the inventory was untouched. It looked as though Ricky had gone out for a smoke and never come back.

One thing Summer and Jade had both revealed: neither of them liked Dennis Havers. But then, few people had a good word to say about him.

And now his own wife suspected he was involved in Ricky's disappearance.

Andi realized she'd been gazing at the ocean for a while. She checked the time. She was still early, but the gunshot wound still hampered her walking at times, so she needed to get going if she was going to be on time for her interview with Jade.

As she turned to walk up the hill, Andi's musings turned to the election battle between Dennis Havers and Jade Thompson.

Dennis had never had a serious opponent before, despite the fact Andi couldn't find anyone who had a good word to say about him. "Only in it for himself" seemed to be the consensus. But he'd been elected for multiple terms. Nothing in this town was straightforward, Andi thought as she struggled up the last incline towards City Hall.

Jade's announcement that she was running for mayor that August had come as a complete surprise to everyone. She'd quit a good job on the mainland and moved in with Summer. Andi had been astounded. She'd grilled Jade as soon as she could about her reasons.

"Coffin Cove has been in the shadow of crime and economic depression for too long," Jade had said simply. "I want to make it a better place for people to live. People like my mother. They deserve better."

She sounded sincere. And Coffin Cove believed her. Jade Thompson won in a landslide.

Andi arrived at City Hall a few minutes early. She waited in the visitor's area and flicked through a glossy community magazine all about Coffin Cove. It was impressive, she supposed. The mayor and her newly formed Tourism and Economic Development Committee had been working hard. Jade Thompson had leveraged grants and private investment to develop the boardwalk and open a new museum and heritage centre. The plans included improving the marina, hoping to attract sports fishermen and charter companies, grants and tax breaks for new businesses, and some much-needed repairs to the high school. It wasn't everything the town needed, but it was a start.

The atmosphere at City Hall was upbeat. The receptionist had greeted Andi with a wide smile. Jade had replaced some staff to fill the vacancies left by Dennis Havers' sycophants who didn't see their long-term future working for Mayor Thompson.

Mayor Havers had enjoyed being important. He'd surrounded himself with people who reminded him daily of his power and significance in this little town. Jade apparently didn't need constant validation, and all her team genuinely seemed to be focused on serving the community.

Well, nearly all, Andi thought as she watched Nadine Dagg appear in the foyer and lean over the receptionist's desk. Nadine whispered something in the receptionist's ear, and then leaned back and gave a loud tinkling laugh. Andi couldn't hear what she said, but the receptionist frowned and tilted her computer screen away from Nadine, not joining in the hilarity.

Andi had heard the rumours about Nadine Dagg and Dennis Havers. Their affair was an open secret. Why hadn't Jade Thompson got rid of this woman? Her loyalty would be with her lover, not Jade. Every chance she got, Nadine would be running back to Dennis with snippets of information.

For a fleeting moment, Andi wondered if Sandra Havers wasn't using her and the *Gazette* to get back at her husband. It would snowball any chance of Dennis getting re-elected, that's for sure.

Watching Nadine, in her cheap, inappropriate clothes and heavy make-up, Andi couldn't entirely blame Sandra for wanting to hurt her husband. Sandra might feel guilty about Ricky, but she didn't deserve the years of humiliation heaped on her from this very public affair.

It made Andi think of her mother. She had endured much the same thing from Andi's father — a man who loved attention, especially from younger women. When he'd made a name for himself as a writer and journalist in Ottawa, he'd celebrated his fame by having one tawdry affair after another. When Andi was old enough to understand what was going on, she asked her mother repeatedly why she didn't leave.

"Because I love him," she would reply, and Andi would stand back, helpless, as her mother starved herself thin, bleached her greying hair and went under the surgeon's knife in an effort to remain young and desirable for her philandering husband.

Andi realized she was staring at Nadine and dropped her eyes to the magazine she was holding. She felt sorry for Nadine too. After all, Andi knew what it was like to be the "other woman". Who was she to judge? God, relationships were so complicated. Better to avoid them for a while. At least until she'd got her life straightened out a bit.

"Miss Silvers?"

Andi had been so lost in her thoughts, she hadn't heard Mayor Thompson approaching.

If Jade Thompson was surprised to see Andi instead of Jim, she didn't show it. She welcomed Andi into her office and invited her to sit down.

She seemed relaxed and cordial, and happy to talk about the progress she'd made in the last few months.

"It's been harder than I thought," she admitted. "Not everyone in the community is happy with the tax dollars being spent. But I believe the new developments will boost real estate values and business revenues for everyone. And we will recoup the initial investment and loans in extra tax dollars."

Andi was scribbling notes.

"Can you tell me about the Heritage Festival?" Andi asked. "What are you hoping to achieve?"

Andi watched Jade talk animatedly about increased tourism and community participation.

If Jade was hiding a terrible secret, Andi thought, it wasn't hindering her dedication to Coffin Cove. She really was committed to fulfilling her campaign promises.

Andi was beginning to think she was wrong. Maybe her instincts were off. Maybe Jim was right, she needed more time to heal.

"I do have one question," Andi said, when Jade finished talking, "about the scheduled events for the festival."

Jade screwed up her face. "I think I know what you're going to ask," she said, and giggled.

For a second, Andi stared at her. It seemed out of character for this serious, almost humourless woman. But then Andi laughed with her.

"Yes, Mayor. Er . . . belly dancing?"

Jade cringed a little. "I know, Andi. But I encouraged community participation, and I understand Nadine and her dance troop are very professional." She said the last bit with a straight face, so Andi just nodded and made a note.

Jade's desk phone rang. She frowned but picked it up.

"I'm in an interview . . . oh . . ."

Andi waited. Jade swung her chair round and faced away from Andi.

There was a knock at the door, and it flew open.

"Mayor!" Nadine Dagg stood gripping the doorframe. "Mayor, I have to go . . ."

Andi found herself staring at Nadine for the second time that day. Even under that thick make-up, Andi could see Nadine's grey pallor. She seemed to have aged twenty years since Andi saw her less than thirty minutes ago. Her swagger was gone, and she clenched her hands together as she stepped forward and opened her mouth again to give the reason for her departure.

Jade Thompson clicked her phone down and didn't wait for Nadine's explanation.

"Of course, Nadine," she said quietly. "I just heard. Go."

Nadine left in a hurry, leaving the door open.

Andi looked at the mayor. She was white-faced.

"You'll know soon enough," she said, "so I might as well tell you. A body, that is . . ." Her voice faltered. "They've found human remains near Nadine's home. Her daughter Katie found them this morning."

"That's terrible news, Mayor," Andi said, horrified. But her brain was working overtime.

"Yes, it is." Mayor Jade Thompson stood and gestured towards the door. The interview was over.

Andi was certain she and the mayor had the same question: had Nadine's daughter found Ricky Havers?

CHAPTER NINE

Inspector Andrew Vega looked at his watch. *Old-school, that's what I am,* he thought. *Just an ordinary watch that does one thing — tells the time. Not my sleep patterns, or blood pressure, or how many steps I've taken today — just the plain old time of day.*

He was trying to simplify his life, and one thing he'd have loved to do was disconnect from the damn internet.

Vega hadn't slept well the night before and he was irritable. His eyes felt gritty. He knew his mind was wandering away from his work and he tried to force himself to focus.

How much information does one man need? he thought, annoyed again as his smartphone buzzed with a new notification.

He gazed at the files piled on his desk and avoided looking at his computer screen. He knew how many emails were in his inbox. Most of them were marked "urgent". So many that the designation was meaningless to him now.

So much of his job was form-filling. Statistics, reports, targets. He sighed. He knew the importance of data — he was a man who believed in the power of science — but some of the forms he was required to fill in every month seemed trivial.

He knew that he was procrastinating, and he needed to get on. He didn't have much time before the meeting with his boss. But instead of tackling his pile of overdue tasks, he pushed back his chair and went in search of coffee.

Then perhaps he would be able to make progress.

As Vega stood by the microwave waiting for a sludgy cup of old coffee to heat up, he thought about the meeting Superintendent Sinclair had called for this morning, just before he left the office the night before. It must be something important. Their weekly meeting was scheduled in a few days' time.

He'd arrived at E Division a little after 6 a.m., just as the sun was high enough to reflect off the building's tinted windows and early enough for the bullpen in his department to be deserted. He'd settled behind his desk, hoping to make the most of an early start. There never seemed to be enough hours in the day for Inspector Vega, one of the youngest inspectors seconded to IHIT, the specialist Integrated Homicide Investigation Team. IHIT investigated British Columbia's worst crimes. Its motto was *Justice for Those Who Have Died Unfairly*. Vega led seven investigative units comprised of the best and the brightest officers he had ever worked with. Usually his job was desk-bound, which he hated, but because of cutbacks, he was now working two roles — heading up one investigation team and supervising the rest. He loved being back in the field, but often felt overwhelmed by the extra load.

Vega checked his watch again and drained the last of the terrible coffee. He went back to his desk and made a concerted effort to clear up the boring administrative tasks he'd been ignoring for days.

Finally, he shuffled the last of his paperwork into a neat pile and headed to Superintendent Sinclair's office on the top floor.

His meetings with Sinclair were usually updates on the cases he and his team were working. She expected her staff to be concise — able and prepared to answer all her questions.

Andrew Vega was always prepared.

He liked Sinclair. She was direct. Spoke her mind. She was a shrewd politician when she needed to be, but not at the expense of the RCMP members under her command.

Their meetings were always brief. Sinclair didn't waste time with small talk. Not usually, anyway. They always worked through the list of investigations, Vega explaining the status and continuing lines of enquiry and Sinclair listening, taking notes and interrupting occasionally with a question.

When Vega entered her office, he was surprised to find her standing at the window with her back to her desk. After greeting him and gesturing for him to sit down, she was quiet and seemed lost in thought for a few moments.

Vega was surprised when Sinclair rested her elbows on her desk, leaned forward and asked Vega if he enjoyed his work.

"Yes, ma'am," he answered without hesitation. He loved his job. But where was this conversation going?

For a few minutes more, Superintendent Sinclair probed Andrew Vega about his career history before RCMP E Division and his promotion to inspector in IHIT.

Vega wondered why they were having this conversation. It was all in his personnel file. On paper, it looked like he was lacking ambition, he knew that. He'd taken a few sideways moves instead of promotions because the opportunities looked interesting. He'd even spent two years in Singapore on secondment with Interpol.

Many of his colleagues were constantly looking for the next leg up the career ladder, but Vega had never been motivated by that. It might be different, he often thought, if he had a family. Then the pay grade would be more important. But until then, he assessed every career move by two criteria: *did it look interesting* and *could he make a difference*?

Maybe Sinclair was looking for a successor? Vega knew he didn't want her job, spending most of the day pushing paper around a desk and bending to the political will of the higher ranks. More likely, she was watching over her shoulder.

There were some police officers who disliked reporting to a woman.

Not Vega. He knew that Sinclair must have worked twice as hard as her male counterparts to have the RCMP superintendent insignia on her shoulder. Vega thought it ridiculous that some men felt insecure about that. But Vega had grown up in an all-female household and was used to strong women.

He answered Sinclair's questions and figured that she would reveal her reason for this gentle interrogation soon enough.

He was wrong.

Instead, Sharon Sinclair sat silently after Vega answered her questions. Her brow was furrowed, and Vega thought she looked like she was struggling with a decision. For a moment, he wondered if he was in trouble.

But then she seemed to gather her thoughts and she smiled at Vega.

"Very good, Inspector," she said, "I have an assignment for you," and she handed Vega a file. "You remember the missing person incident from last year?"

Vega nodded and frowned. "Yes, ma'am, I do. The mayor's missing son." His derision was palpable.

Vega was still irritated at being dispatched to Coffin Cove to help the local detachment with a missing person's enquiry. The local cops were perfectly capable of dealing with the incident. It was purely a PR exercise, thanks to Dennis Havers' string-pulling, and a complete waste of his time.

"This came across my desk yesterday," Sinclair said, gesturing to the file. "The decomposed body of a male was discovered yesterday in a derelict chapel in Coffin Cove. Forensics are out there now with the coroner, but as yet we don't have an ID on the body, and we don't know if it's a homicide." She paused and looked at Vega. "But a preliminary report suggests the body has been there for a while. They've recovered several items which fit with the description of Ricky's clothing."

"A derelict church?" Vega asked. He didn't recall any buildings like that, and the search teams had done a thorough examination of the area. Supposedly.

"Apparently, it's hidden in dense woodland, and it's on private land. The local historical society were on a field trip or something and one of them found the body."

"Ah, nasty." Vega pulled a face.

"Yes, and although the local guys asked them to keep it all quiet . . . well, it seems the local gossip factory has been working overtime, hence a call to my office. And now you're here."

Shit rolls downhill, Vega thought, but kept his face expressionless.

"Should we get a team out there, ma'am?" he asked.

"I'd like you to go first, Andrew," she said.

Vega was surprised. Superintendent Sinclair rarely dropped formalities and used his first name. Before he could answer, she asked another question.

"You're familiar with Coffin Cove, right?"

He nodded. Apart from the visit to follow up on Ricky Havers' disappearance, Vega had led a team investigating the murder of a controversial environmentalist. The investigation was complex and was eventually linked to two other murders — one of them a cold case from decades ago. Although two arrests were made, and the results considered a success, a journalist had been shot and seriously wounded. Vega had warned her about interfering with the investigation, but like all journalists, she considered it her God-given right to ferret around in things that didn't concern her. "Uncovering the truth," she'd called it. "Taking unnecessary risks," he'd told her.

Despite his annoyance, Vega half smiled at the thought of Andi Silvers. He had to admit that some of her investigative journalism had been useful. Details she had managed to uncover had helped with the court cases which came afterwards. Also, he liked her. Well, maybe *more* than liked her . . .

Vega dragged his attention away from Andi Silvers and back to the superintendent.

"I've never been to Coffin Cove. But Emma knows the town quite well," she was saying.

Vega was amazed but didn't dare let it show on his face. Superintendent Sharon Sinclair lived with her partner, Emma Ross, who'd retired from the RCMP a few years ago. Sinclair never mentioned her private life. So this must be important.

"When Emma first joined the force, she was a member at the Nanaimo detachment and covered Coffin Cove. She was out there regularly. It's an unpleasant little town, apparently," Sinclair continued.

"Can't argue with that, ma'am," Vega said with feeling.

"Emma's recollection is that Coffin Cove had a horrible drug problem. Not just weed, either. For about five years in the late eighties, there was some kind of acid going around. LSD was pretty rare outside of the cities, but somehow it reached Coffin Cove and started a trend up and down the island. The Nanaimo team were sure that Coffin Cove was ground zero for the supply, but they could never get to the bottom of it. Because there's only one road in and out, and it takes an hour to get there from Nanaimo, they were never quick enough to respond to any tips that could have helped. And the acid was lethal. Several kids died. Emma says they were certain a gang of bikers were organizing the distribution network, but they intimidated anyone who spoke out, and they could never infiltrate the gang. It was such a small community, and they were suspicious of new faces. It was really bad while it lasted."

Sinclair paused, and it looked to Vega as though she was weighing up whether to continue. Then she started talking again.

"But that's not what prompted Emma to give me this file. Some cases stay with you, don't they? Back in those days, Emma had a call-out to Hope Island. It's a tiny island just off Coffin Cove. Back then, Hope Island used to be home to what the locals called 'The Commune'. It was an all-female 'alternative living' experiment, I suppose that's how we'd refer to it now. Back then, it was quite famous — well, infamous, I suppose. Women used it as a refuge of sorts." She hesitated, as if choosing her words carefully. "Back then, violence against women wasn't taken seriously." She sighed. "Even now, we need to do far better, but then . . . well, let's just say that domestic violence was seen as a *normal reaction to a disobedient woman.*" She spoke the words slowly and pressed her lips together in an angry line.

It was a rare display of emotion for Superintendent Sinclair. Vega waited for her to continue.

"On the way out to Hope Island," Sinclair said, "Emma remembers quite clearly the sergeant joking with the boat owner about dirty lesbians getting what they deserved." She continued without looking at Vega to see his reaction. "When she got there, they found one older woman who had a black eye and other bruises . . . and a young girl. God, Emma says she was really roughed up. It took a while, but the girl did start to open up. Emma believes, to this day, she knew something about the new drug we were trying to get a handle on, but it was no good. She was absolutely terrified."

This time she did look up, and Vega could see that she was furious. He waited, wondering what all this had to do with Ricky Havers.

Sinclair continued, "The commune women themselves were too frightened to talk much, but the woman who originally called in the attack alleged that a few drunk men in the pub — the Timberman's, it was called then, I think — they got it into their head to go over to the island and 'teach those bitches a lesson', as they put it. One name that came up was Dennis Havers. But nothing stuck. In the end, the women were too afraid to give names and they had to let it go. The details are all in this file."

"Ma'am . . ." Vega began.

"Inspector," Sinclair said firmly, "I am sure that the human remains they just discovered and an incident which took place over thirty years ago are likely not connected. However—" she took a deep breath — "one of the lasting regrets of Emma's career is leaving those women on that island, knowing that someone — or some people — were abusing them. I won't let that happen again. Emma's opinion is that Dennis Havers is a smug, obnoxious bastard, and I trust her judgment."

"I was going to say, ma'am," Vega said gently, "it seems that given the . . . er . . . climate back then — well, Emma did the best she could."

"I'm sure she did, Inspector," Sinclair said, and carried on. "Normally, I wouldn't let anyone's personal feelings about people connected to an investigation cloud my judgment. Or yours. But it's Emma, and well . . . I wanted you to have all the information available."

"Dennis Havers isn't Coffin Cove's mayor anymore," Vega noted.

Sinclair smiled. "Sometimes fate intervenes, Inspector. The older woman with a black eye I mentioned? Her name was Summer Thompson. Her daughter, Jade, beat Dennis Havers in the election. Wasn't even close."

"Maybe the good people of Coffin Cove share your opinion of Dennis Havers," Vega commented.

"Maybe. Still, we owe the Havers family the same consideration as any other victim's family—"

"If the remains are definitely Ricky's and if he is a victim," Vega interrupted.

"Yes, quite. If it *is* Ricky Havers, just . . . well, tread carefully, Inspector, when it comes to Dennis Havers. That's all."

"I will, ma'am." Vega gathered up his files and stood up to leave, but he had one more question. "Ma'am?"

Sinclair looked up. "Yes?"

Vega hesitated. "Did you ever get the impression Dennis Havers was somehow mixed up with the drug problem? Thing is, when I was over there last, someone suggested to me that Dennis has friends in high and low places."

Sinclair looked at him thoughtfully. "I'll ask Emma, Inspector. I'll get back to you."

As Vega left the superintendent's office thinking over the surprisingly candid conversation with Sinclair, he recalled something Andi Silver had said the last time they met. She clearly had suspicions about Dennis Havers. When Vega and Andi had coffee together, Andi had let slip that she was digging into Dennis Havers' past. She claimed it was all about the election — this was before he lost to Jade Thompson — but Vega knew Andi better than that. She sensed a story.

Vega made a mental note to have another coffee date with Andi. He told himself it was just work-related, but he couldn't help an unfamiliar but pleasant feeling of anticipation at the thought of seeing Andi again. He just wished she wasn't a journalist.

He checked his wristwatch again. Better get home to get his bag packed.

* * *

Three hours later, Vega grabbed a quick sandwich at the Flying Beaver Bar and Grill as he waited for the floatplane to dock. The bar was quiet. It was early in the tourist season, but soon the pub, which also served as the terminal for the floatplanes to Vancouver Island, would be full of holidaymakers.

"Andrew Vega?" a young man called, just as Vega heard the throaty roar of a floatplane landing and idling up to the dock. Within ten minutes, he'd clambered aboard the six-seater de Havilland Beaver floatplane. The small aircraft was pushed away from the dock and the engine spluttered and chugged before the pilot gave it full throttle and it was skimming along the water. One final thrust of speed, and within minutes, Vega looked down to see the brackish water of the muddy Fraser River meet the ocean. The twenty-minute plane ride was the quickest way to get to the island. If the grim discovery turned out to be Ricky Havers or some other poor soul who'd died "unfairly", then Vega would summon Sergeant Diane Fowler and a small team of specialist officers and the investigation would begin. Maybe it was an accidental death, or perhaps there was some other perfectly good reason for human remains to be found where they were. It was a derelict church, after all. Maybe Vega would be on a floatplane back to the mainland tomorrow morning, and Superintendent Sinclair's theories would come to nothing.

But as the plane descended sharply, and its floats brushed the ocean's surface just before slowing and then docking in Nanaimo, Vega was feeling anything but hopeful.

CHAPTER TEN

The rocky beach was deserted. It was too early in the year for holidaymakers and too late in the day for dog walkers. The tide was still out, leaving rock pools and clumps of seaweed, and the strewn driftwood pushed up against the thin strip of sand which separated the dense forest from the beach. A breeze was whipping in from the ocean, buffeting the yellow-and-black tape that cordoned off the trail leading to the ruined chapel and its deceased occupant. Andi could see it in the distance. It meant an RCMP officer was probably guarding the trail.

She had taken a gamble, thinking she might get to the chapel from the beach. She'd got directions from Hephzibah.

"It's part of Dagg's property, I think," Hephzibah said. "The easiest way is to follow the trail from the gravel pit. There's a path from the far beach, but that'll be impossible to access when the tide comes in."

It had been a frustrating morning, following an equally unproductive afternoon and evening. As with most bad, scandalous and just about every other kind of gossip, the discovery of a dead body somewhere in the woods near the Daggs' home did not stay a secret for long.

The day before, after leaving City Hall, Andi had gone straight to the detachment. Sergeant Rollins and the new constable were nowhere in sight. So Andi had rushed back to the office.

"They've found a body. It must be Ricky Havers. And Jade Thompson nearly fainted when she heard the news." The words spilled out of her.

Ignoring Jim's startled look, she ran to her desk and started frantically rummaging through the drawer.

"Whoa, whoa, calm down, start from the beginning." Jim threw his hands up in the air and waited until Andi composed herself.

She took a breath and told him what she'd heard at the mayor's office.

"So Katie Dagg found a body?" Jim started taking notes immediately. "Poor girl, what a shock. And she was out in the bush somewhere?"

Andi nodded. "Yes, somewhere near her parents' house. Looking for the site of an old church or something? She was there with Clara Bell, whoever she is."

"She used to be the museum curator, but never mind that. Has the body been officially identified?"

"Well, no. I don't know yet. But who else could it be?" She felt a little defensive.

Jim put his pen down, exasperated. "Just about anyone, Andi! A homeless person looking for shelter, maybe, who died of exposure. It isn't like you to jump to conclusions. Come on, now."

"I wasn't the only one," Andi said. "You should have seen Jade Thompson's face. She was terrified."

Jim didn't react. He thought for a minute.

"OK, you know the procedure. They'll get the coroner there first. Then we'll know more. Have you been to the detachment?"

Andi sank down into her chair. "Yes. Nobody there."

Jim nodded. "Charlie Rollins is probably as impatient as you to find out if it's Ricky. He was supposed to have searched everywhere. Won't be good if they missed this."

"You're right," Andi said, and then a thought struck her. "Jim," she asked, "should I tell Sandra?"

Jim shook his head. "There's nothing to tell yet. We're just speculating. This is the worst news anyone can ever get, Andi. We can't get it wrong."

He and Andi had called everyone they could think of, but the day ended with no more information.

Andi had hardly slept that night.

As soon as Andi's alarm rang at six o'clock in the morning, she was up and showered and out of her apartment as fast as she could. She made her way to the tiny two-man detachment. When she got there, it was already swarming with RCMP officers. From Nanaimo, Andi guessed.

She knew the basic police process. She figured that if the body was found the day before, then the coroner would have visited by now, but nobody was giving her any information. Andi didn't know what the official identification procedure would be, but there wouldn't be a public announcement until next of kin had been notified.

First Andi tried to phone Nadine. Nobody at the Dagg residence was answering the phone. George Gomich wasn't at home, and Andi heard at Hephzibah's that the mysterious Clara Bell had threatened police officers with her shotgun when they drove out to take a statement. They'd calmed her down, but Jim advised against driving out to talk to her.

"Don't worry about Clara. I'll talk to her. You camp out at the detachment and wait for a statement," he'd said, when Andi met him at the office just before noon.

Andi didn't like waiting for anything, so she took a drive up to the gravel pit, but there were almost as many officers camped up there and zero chance of her sneaking down to the site. Forensics would take a while, she supposed.

Sandra had not phoned her, and Andi was relieved. She hoped Sandra hadn't heard anything yet, but given the efficiency of the gossip network, and the obvious police activity in the town, she doubted that would last.

After a fruitless morning, Andi had headed back to Hephzibah's, the hub of all information, but tired of sitting around and unable to drink any more coffee, she had decided to chance the beach.

"You'd better get going," Hephzibah had said, after giving her directions. "High tide's in a couple of hours."

As soon as Andi saw the police tape in the distance, she knew it was unlikely she'd get anywhere near the scene today. But even so, it would only take half an hour to check.

Andi hunched her shoulders against the afternoon breeze, which had turned chilly, and tried to stave off her own sense of rising dread. She wasn't usually perturbed like this. It was the thought of being close to death once more, she realized. It reminded her of her own mortality, and she couldn't shake off this morbid feeling.

She trudged down the beach, scrambling over the rocks to avoid getting wet, and headed towards the trail entrance.

Andi could see two figures on the beach. One was a police officer and the other a woman.

As she got nearer, Andi could hear the conversation was animated.

"Please tell me if it's him," the woman was almost screaming at the police officer, who was holding out his hands in a dual attempt to calm her and stop her going up the trail.

When Andi got closer, she could see it was Sandra Havers, Ricky's mother.

Before Ricky went missing, Andi had only met Sandra Havers once. It had been some kind of business function. Sandra was with her husband Dennis, who was still the mayor. She was in her sixties, but Andi remembered a slender vivacious woman, immaculately made-up and with a healthy glow that suggested regular yoga classes and spa days. Since Ricky vanished, Andi had met Sandra several times. She'd aged. Her hair was thin, as if it were falling out, and Sandra didn't bother with make-up anymore.

The lady in front of Andi now had deteriorated further. Her skin, once radiant, sagged into a multitude of wrinkles.

She was stooped, as if she needed a walking stick to steady her. It shocked Andi. She thought Sandra must have lost thirty pounds since they had last met.

Sandra had been shouting at the officer, but now tears were streaming down her haggard face. She sank to the ground, kneeling in the sand, her bony hands covering her face. Her body shook with uncontrolled sobs, and Andi hurried towards her.

The officer was crouched down, patting Sandra's shoulder, looking around wildly.

"Ma'am, I've radioed for the officer in charge, he's on his way," he said to the shaking figure.

He looked up, saw Andi and gestured for her to come over.

"This lady will look after you, won't you?" He looked hopefully at Andi. "I'll run up the trail and see if Inspector Vega is on his way."

"No need, Constable."

Andi heard a familiar voice behind her.

"Mrs Havers?"

Andrew Vega hovered above Andi and the distraught Sandra Havers.

"Mrs Havers, I'm so sorry. I don't have any news for you yet. I can tell you that a body has been discovered, but my team has a lot of work to do before we will know anything. I can only imagine how hard this is for you, but I promise you this: as soon as I have any information at all, I will tell you myself."

His voice was gentle and firm, and Sandra Havers became visibly calmer.

"Mrs Havers, the tide will be in soon. Let one of my officers take you home."

Sandra Havers raised her head. She had stopped crying, and Andi could see she was trying to regain her composure.

"No," she whispered. And then stronger, "No, that's won't be necessary. I'll walk back. There's plenty of time before high tide."

"Why don't I walk with you?" Andi asked. "I can make sure you get home safely."

Sandra looked at Andi as if seeing her for the first time.

"Andi? Do you know anything? Have they told you anything yet?"

"No, absolutely nothing," Andi said quickly, aware that Vega was looking at her. "Right now, I'm not a reporter, I'm just Andi. And I'll happily walk you back to the boardwalk. Maybe you need a strong cup of tea at Hephzibah's?"

Sandra struggled to her feet. She looked at Vega. "You promise you'll tell me if it's Ricky?"

Andi thought she sounded like a small child.

"Of course, Mrs Havers, you have my word." And then to Andi, "You'll be OK?"

Andi heard the warning in his voice. She nodded at him. "Don't worry, Inspector Vega. We'll both be fine. I'll look after Mrs Havers." The last words were said pointedly, and Inspector Vega nodded back. He flashed a smile at Andi, and she felt her spirits lift a little. She'd forgotten how handsome he was.

He reached out and squeezed her shoulder. "Thanks, Andi. It's good to see you."

Andi held out her arm for Sandra Havers. The heart-broken mother took it and leaned on Andi a little as they made their way back along the beach. She hardly weighed anything, Andi thought, like a frail bird.

But Sandra's grip was strong.

"Andi. I know it's Ricky. I feel it. I'm his mother, and I know he's dead." Her voice was stronger. She sounded angry. "Why didn't they damn well do something? Why didn't they search for him when I asked? I begged them to. My boy would still be here now." And she broke down again, sobbing and leaning against Andi.

"Sandra, I'm so sorry." Andi didn't argue with Sandra. She thought the same. Why hadn't they searched more thoroughly? It was a question needing an answer.

They reached the boardwalk and Sandra disentangled her arm from Andi's.

"Will you promise me something, Andi?" Sandra asked.

"If I can."

"Promise me you'll do everything to find out what happened to my son? Even if it leads you to Dennis? I have to know, Andi, I just have to."

"I promise I will do that, Sandra."

Slowly they walked to Hephzibah's. Dennis stood in the doorway and beckoned to Sandra. She held out a shaky hand and patted Andi on the shoulder before walking over to her husband's side.

"Thank you," she whispered.

Andi watched Sandra walk away with Dennis, his arm firmly around her shoulder. She wondered if Sandra was going home with a murderer.

Because one thing was certain. If it was Ricky they'd found, he'd definitely been killed. Why else would Inspector Andrew Vega be in Coffin Cove?

CHAPTER ELEVEN

Coffin Cove gravel pit.

Muscle cars, old beaters and souped-up trucks idled and revved up on one end of a stretch of road behind the disused gravel pit, just a mile out of town. There had been plans for an airport right here back in the day, but now there was only this tarmac strip that led nowhere. At the other end, bikers lined up their beasts in perfect symmetry. There was no rivalry. This was no stand-off. There was simply no place else to go.

Here, the testosterone and sweat of Coffin Cove's bored youth mingled with diesel fumes and the stench of weed. It was sweltering. The bikers had already discarded their leathers and were burning up and down in T-shirts.

Hanging out at the gravel pit was one of two alternatives for Lee Dagg. It was either this or the drive-in movies. But there was some fuckin' chick flick on and his girl had blown him off, so here he was, hanging out with the usual losers, as they fussed over Harry's piece-of-shit Chevy. Everyone knew everyone here. They all hung out, sitting on tailgates, swilling cheap beers and smoking home-grown weed. Occasionally a couple of the muscle car boys would race, spinning tyres and kicking up dust and rubber, sometimes competing with the bikes. Then drunken assholes would start a fight. Sometimes a cop car would drive by, slowly, reminding them to keep the noise down. No one really bothered them. There was fuck-all to do in Coffin Cove, and besides, generations of youth had congregated here. Where else would they go?

Lee took a drag on his cigarette and flicked the ash away.

It was a sticky evening after a hot sultry day, and the heat hung down in the pit, unmoved by any breeze. Lee reached into the back of Harry's Chevy and found a cold beer.

He was bored.

Bored with this evening, bored with Harry and Walt, bored with his job. He was sick of his old man riding his ass about apprenticeships and carrying on the family business. He didn't want the fucking business. He wanted out of here. Out of Coffin Cove, and off the island. He wanted to make some real money. Maybe he would go up north. Or go to the oil patch. Make a shitload of cash, and buy a decent truck, buy a house on the mainland, get a girl . . .

He was broken out of his daydream by the low throaty growl of an engine.

He looked around.

A Mustang crunched over the gravel. Low-slung, tinted windows, red shiny paint job.

Unheard of in Coffin Cove, a town of rust buckets and reclaimed beaters from the scrapyard.

Even the bikers moved to get a closer look.

The car came to a stop, and a girl got out the passenger side.

Fuck.

Nadine.

Lee ground his cigarette into the gravel, looking down long enough to get his emotions in check.

"So you got a better offer, then?" he called out to Nadine.

She flicked her hair and smiled at Lee, unconcerned.

"I guess," she answered.

A slim figure got out of the driver's side. Lee didn't recognize him. He had almost white blonde hair and pale skin, as if he had been shielded from sunlight his whole life. As if to confirm this, he reached inside his pockets and put on mirrored sunglasses that covered most of his face.

In contrast to the redneck uniform of scuffed blue jeans and grimy sleeveless T-shirts, the newcomer was wearing immaculate chinos, suede boots and a chequered short-sleeve shirt.

"Holy shit!"

Harry stood at Lee's shoulder.

"You know who that is?"

"Some asshole who moved in on my girlfriend?"

"Nope. Well, yeah, but it's also Art Whilley."

"I don't give a fuck who it is . . ." Lee pulled out another cigarette, lit it and walked over.

"Hey Nadine, what the fuck . . . ?"

Before he could finish his sentence, another car pulled into the pit. Lee groaned again.

Dennis Havers was driving. He stayed in the car and Lee's older brother Wayne got out of the passenger side.

"This your car?" he sneered, indicating the Mustang and addressing Art Whilley.

"Yep. You got a problem with that?" His voice was high-pitched, like a young boy.

"No. I've got a problem with that . . ." Wayne nodded at Nadine.

Lee said, "Wayne, leave it."

"No fuckin' way, he's screwing your girl!"

A small crowd had gathered round the Mustang. Tension was in the air. A fight was coming.

Nadine, playing to the crowd, leaned against the Mustang, her shirt undone a little too far.

"Hey Wayne, how's it going?" She smiled at the older boy, not caring about his angry expression.

Lee watched, first in disgust, and then more intently, as Art reached into the Mustang and tossed a piece of card or paper to Wayne with a small nod of his head.

"That what you want?" Art Whilley asked, not appearing intimidated at all.

Wayne's demeanour changed.

"Sure. We just stopped by to say hi. Have a nice evening."

Lee stared as his older brother got back in the car and Dennis accelerated out of the gravel pit, churning up enough dust to choke the disappointed crowd.

"What the hell was that?" Lee asked Nadine angrily.

She didn't answer, just shrugged and tossed her hair again before she and Art left in the Mustang, leaving Lee looking bewildered.

"Don't sweat it, Lee. She's just trying to fuck with you. Ignore her." Harry patted him on the shoulder.

But Lee wasn't listening. He walked over to where the Mustang had been parked and crouched down. He spied what he had been looking for, a piece of card Art had dropped when he was talking to Wayne.

"How the fuck do you think he can afford that Mustang?" Walt was asking.

Lee stood there for a minute, fingering the piece of cardboard in his hand.

"I don't know. But I bet it has something to do with this."

CHAPTER TWELVE

PC Matt Beaufort had never been involved in a major crime case before.

Coffin Cove was his first posting as a fully-fledged member of the RCMP, Canada's national police force. Initially, Matt had been disappointed at being sent to this quiet backwater. After twenty-six weeks of basic training in the middle of Saskatchewan, followed by six months' on-the-job instruction in Whitehorse, the capital of Canada's Yukon territory, Matt had applied to join the Surrey detachment on mainland British Columbia. He needed the experience of a metropolis, he thought. He needed gangland shootings and drug cartels to replace road traffic collisions with moose and illegal whiskey stills. But the Surrey detachment was in an uproar as the residents had voted to create their own municipal police force, so they diverted Matt to Coffin Cove.

Matt Beaufort wasn't the type of man to sulk. He'd joined up to serve, and even if Coffin Cove couldn't give a rat's ass about the RCMP, as Sergeant Charlie Rollins informed him on his first day, he would still dedicate himself to the RCMP mission: preserve the peace, uphold the law and provide quality service to the community he served.

Charlie Rollins had been the sergeant at Coffin Cove detachment for over thirty years. He'd seen constables come and go. He was waiting for retirement, and now that Mayor Jade Thompson was shaking things up — unnecessarily, in Charlie's view — his pension cheque couldn't come quick enough. He'd preferred Dennis Havers, who often dropped off a bottle of Crown Royal, Charlie's favourite tipple, and clapped him on the back for a job well done. After all, turning a blind eye was Charlie's expert skill.

When Matt Beaufort reported for duty, Charlie looked him up and down, amused at the young man's enthusiasm.

"There's only three types of criminals we have to worry about in Coffin Cove," he told the new constable, "draft dodgers, dopeheads and drunkards. The draft dodgers are all old hippies eating their granola, we don't have to worry about the dopeheads anymore now that weed's legal, so you'll mainly be cleaning up after the drunks."

He was right. In the first week, Matt spent most days hosing down the RCMP cruiser, cleaning off the vomit from another inebriated "client".

Lily, Matt's wife, encouraged him to use his initiative.

"Just because old Charlie sits with his feet up all day, doesn't mean you have to," she told him. Matt knew she was right. So he "patrolled" the streets of Coffin Cove, popping his head into businesses and shaking hands with the fishermen down at the docks. He might not be catching Canada's most wanted, but he stopped a teenager grabbing a kid's bike from an open garage and the wharf manager was happy that diesel theft was down.

But yesterday was different.

First, they got the call from a frantic Mr Gomich, who said he and his hiking companions had found a body. It was all a blur of activity after that. Charlie Rollins, visibly agitated, wanted to look at the remains for himself, to make absolutely certain it wasn't a dead bear they'd found. Matt thought they should call in backup from Nanaimo right away, but he deferred to his sergeant.

They left the detachment and headed up to the gravel pit. There, Mr Gomich, an elderly woman with silver-white hair who refused to talk to him, and a younger lady, who identified herself as Katie Dagg, were waiting. Katie looked shaky. Charlie told Matt to wait while he and Mr Gomich disappeared down a trail. Nearly an hour later, the two men emerged. White-faced, the sergeant told Matt not only was the body human, he was sure it was Ricky Havers.

"There are bits of clothing still there," he said, wiping beads of sweat off his face after the hike in and out of the woods. "I'm pretty sure they match the description of the clothes Ricky was wearing when he vanished."

Matt hadn't been at Coffin Cove when Ricky Havers went missing. But he heard about it when he arrived. Apart from a murder investigation a year ago, the disappearance of Ricky Havers was the highest-profile case the small detachment had dealt with in recent years.

There wasn't much the RCMP could do. Ricky Havers was forty-two years old. There were rumours he'd been selling more than just legal weed. Maybe he'd strayed onto someone else's patch? Pissed off the wrong people? Or maybe one day he'd just woken up and decided there was more to life than selling weed to dopeheads in this tiny backwater.

Matt Beaufort thought it was probably drug dealers who had abducted Ricky. Nanaimo, the nearest big town to Coffin Cove, was in the midst of a drug crisis. Opioids were bad enough, but for months the Nanaimo detachment had been besieged with calls about crazed teenagers attacking people with knives or attempting to "fly out of windows". Four deaths had been attributed to a new street drug called "Duke". It was a hallucinogenic, according to the circular sent to all the detachments. It was similar to LSD but caused extreme paranoia and psychotic rages. Matt read and carefully filed all the information he could find and kept an eye out on his daily patrols. Nanaimo officers were also reporting a new street jargon associated with the drug. Dealers required a "tithe" rather than a "payment" and referred to themselves as "Knights". Matt had heard nothing like that in Coffin Cove, but he wondered if Ricky Havers had sold Duke from the Smoke House. Maybe he hadn't paid his tithe? The dates fit. Ricky had disappeared around the same time as Nanaimo officers noticed the new drug.

Matt put his theory to Charlie.

Charlie Rollins dismissed it immediately. "Ricky was a layabout his whole life. Dennis was giving him a last chance. I bet he realized he couldn't even run a weed store and disappeared in embarrassment. He'll be back, you'll see."

And now Ricky was back.

In fact, Matt thought, he hadn't ever left.

As Charlie Rollins panted from his exertion and the small group at the gravel pit processed the horror of their discovery, Matt mentally calculated that Ricky Havers' corpse was less than ten kilometres away from where he'd disappeared. And numerous search parties had missed it.

"Shit," Sergeant Rollins said, as the enormity of the discovery and the possible implications for his imminent retirement started to sink in.

Matt saw that Charlie wasn't just shocked, he was scared. He wondered if Charlie had ever really conducted "extensive searches" for Ricky. Had the lazy, complacent officer just put up a few posters?

"Maybe the body was moved there, sir," Matt said evenly. There would be time enough for blame. "Forensics should be able to tell."

His sergeant nodded slowly, as if weighing up this possibility, and said, "You're right, son. The things those crime scene guys can find out, it's amazing," and he seemed to cheer up a little as he and Matt taped off the scene and waited for the coroner and backup from Nanaimo.

Soon after the coroner began her work, she appeared, looking grim, and made a call to the Integrated Homicide Investigation Team stationed on the mainland. She didn't know yet if it was a homicide, but it was more than possible the remains were Ricky Havers', although more work would need to be done before final confirmation. As the case of the missing man was already flagged as something IHIT had an interest in, she explained, she was calling in a team from the mainland.

Matt was in awe. IHIT was legendary. Only the most talented officers joined this specialized unit. They'd created IHIT back in 2004, after a catalogue of failures allowed a notorious serial killer to evade the RCMP long enough to murder over twenty women. After that, the RCMP made sure IHIT had access to limitless expertise and resources to investigate the worst crimes in British Columbia and bring the perpetrators to justice.

They didn't take long to arrive. Ahead of the IHIT team arriving in Coffin Cove, Inspector Andrew Vega had joined the coroner at the scene earlier today, just twenty-four hours after the remains had been discovered. The forensics team were hard at work. It was clear to Matt that Inspector Vega was a man used to being in charge, as he quickly assessed the situation and assigned Matt to guard the trail leading to the scene of the discovery. The coroner would continue working with forensics, and when (and if) she deemed the death a homicide, the rest of the IHIT team would arrive and set up base for the investigation at the Coffin Cove detachment. Vega was quiet but had an air of authority which made even Charlie draw himself to attention when taking directions from this polite man.

For the entire day, the scene was invaded by ghostly figures in white suits, gliding around, examining, bagging and labelling the smallest items from the scene, anything that might help the investigating officers determine without doubt that this poor dead soul was indeed Ricky Havers, and the precise nature of his death.

Confirmation came later that evening. There was no doubt. It was definitely Ricky Havers, and Matt was now working his first homicide case.

Matt listened as Inspector Vega informed local officers. The mood was sombre.

"Forensics will continue at the site for another night, at least," Vega said. "I will inform the family after this meeting. We will make a public announcement to the press tomorrow morning. There is nothing more we can do tonight, so please go home. Tomorrow my full team will arrive. Get some sleep because it will be a long day tomorrow. And—" his voice sharpened — "I shouldn't have to tell any of you: do not divulge any information to anyone, got it?"

There were nods and murmurs from the listening men and women as they dispersed, leaving PC Matt Beaufort to lock and alarm the detachment.

A tragic day for the Haverses, he thought, as he remembered the distraught mother from earlier. He watched Charlie Rollins walk away from the detachment. He had a dejected air about him and almost shuffled along. Charlie had hardly said a word since they left the gravel pit. Matt had seen him talking urgently into his cell phone just before the briefing, but Charlie wouldn't even meet Matt's eyes. He didn't even say goodnight as he left.

Matt felt sorry for Charlie. His days were numbered, Matt was sure. But he was at the beginning of his career. And tomorrow would be the start of some proper police work, he thought as he backed out the parking lot and drove home.

CHAPTER THIRTEEN

Inspector Vega arrived at the Wilson Motel after ten. He'd made time earlier in the day to collect a key from Peggy Wilson, who greeted him like an old friend.

"Welcome back to Coffin Cove, Inspector. Sorry it's in such sad circumstances," she said, fishing for information.

Vega didn't bother to point out most people only met him in tragic circumstances. It went with the job.

Now, Vega sat on the bed in his small room. He wanted a shower but didn't have the energy.

It seemed a lifetime ago he'd boarded the floatplane.

The forensics team had taken several hours to conclude the remains were likely those of Ricky Havers. They had found a belt buckle and scraps of fabric which matched the description Sandra had given them when Ricky disappeared. It would take days for DNA testing to confirm Ricky's identity conclusively, but Vega felt he had enough information to speak to Sandra and Dennis Havers.

After the briefing, he went to the Haverses' home. Joanna, their housekeeper, let him in. She was red-eyed and subdued. Despite Vega's efforts to keep a lid on all information flowing around the town, he was sure Dennis and Sandra had surmised the bad news. Joanna led him into the living room. It was dark, and Coffin Cove's night lights twinkled through the magnificent picture window.

Vega had thought about all the families in Coffin Cove that night. Some of them slumped in front of the TV or shouting at their kids. Getting ready for work the next day or eating a late meal. Normal people doing normal things. But there, in that room, it had been Vega's job to take away any hope of these two people being "normal" anymore.

Logically, it wasn't him who'd ruined their lives. It was the person who'd killed their son. But Vega knew from experience it would be him who endured their initial grief and anger.

The meeting was harrowing. Sandra Havers had obviously tried to pull herself together since their previous encounter. She'd put on some make-up and changed her blouse. She sat in silence with Dennis's arm around her shoulder, as Vega gently laid out the few items in clear evidence bags for the Havers to identify. Dennis just stared. Sandra broke down. Dennis nodded.

"Yes, the buckle is from Ricky's belt," he said. "Inspector, how did Ricky die?"

"We can't be certain yet," Vega replied carefully, "but we can't rule out foul play at this time." Vega needed to keep that information to himself as long as possible.

"I see." Dennis nodded and gripped his wife a little tighter. "When will you be able to do that, Inspector?"

"We have a full investigative team on the way, sir. I don't know when we'll have answers, but I promise you we won't rest until we find out how and why your son died, and who else, if anybody, was involved."

Sandra's crying abated a little. Dennis held her arm but she pulled free and screamed at Vega.

"This is your fault! I told you something was wrong! I told you Ricky wouldn't just leave . . . this is all your fault!" She crumpled to the floor, her withered fists pounding on the rug, her body heaving with sobs.

Dennis knelt down beside her, but Sandra fought him too.

"It's your fault too. You never loved Ricky, not like me!"

Gradually, she calmed enough for Dennis to coax her back to the couch.

"I'm so sorry, Mrs Havers," Vega said, and reiterated his promise to do the best he could.

"Too late, Inspector!"

Dennis shook his head in apology and asked Vega to leave.

When the door closed behind him, Vega thought Sandra Havers had a point. They had failed Ricky. Vega remembered Charlie Rollins' pale face at the briefing and wondered how much searching for Ricky Havers had really taken place. Not much, thought Vega grimly, given Ricky had never left Coffin Cove. At least, that was how it seemed. Although it was highly unlikely Ricky would be taken out of Coffin Cove, dead or alive, just to be dumped back there again.

There would be time to find out exactly what Charlie Rollins had done. And he, Vega, should not be feeling self-righteous. Sinclair had sent him to Coffin Cove just after Ricky disappeared, when Sandra Havers was causing a stink with the higher-ups and Sinclair wanted to make sure they'd crossed every "t" and dotted every "i".

Vega groaned. What a shitshow. He'd been as complacent as Charlie Rollins. He'd been satisfied to assume a forty-two-year-old dopehead would amble away from his hometown of his own accord. He'd taken at face value the eye-rolling and shrugs about flaky Ricky who'd always lived on handouts. Only Andi Silvers had suspected foul play. Vega remembered how he'd dismissed her theories as conspiracies or the product of her overactive imagination.

Well, he couldn't afford to ignore anything now. He had to check every detail, no matter how small.

Vega had watched Sandra and Dennis closely. This was the worst part of his job, and also the most important. Murder victims almost always died at the hands of someone they knew, and Ricky most certainly had been murdered.

On the face of it, they behaved as he would have expected. Shocked and grief-stricken. Vega had left them both huddled on the couch, Sandra cradled by Dennis as if she were a small child. He wondered if it was the most affection the couple had shown each other in a long time, if ever. Vega had heard the rumours of extramarital affairs, and Superintendent Sinclair's information was fresh in his mind.

He would have to consider the couple as suspects until he could eliminate them.

Vega drove back to the detachment to find the small building deserted and locked. He cursed. He wanted to sift through the preliminary information and set up the murder room the way he liked it. It was his ritual at the beginning of every investigation. He made a mental note to tell Charlie and his young constable his team would need 24-hour access to the detachment during the investigation. Not only that, the two of them would be on call. Charlie would not coast to retirement, Vega thought. He was still angry.

He sat in the parking lot, not wanting to go to the motel just yet but knowing he should get some sleep. His team would arrive in the morning and he needed to be fresh. He turned his phone over in his hand, and on impulse, called Andi Silver's number. He told himself he should at least thank her for helping Sandra Havers.

"No problem," Andi said, less than a minute later. "Fancy meeting for a drink?"

Vega smiled into the phone. "Because you've been missing my company or because you want a scoop?" he teased.

Andi hesitated and then started to say something.

"Too late!" Vega laughed. "That told me everything I need to know."

He heard Andi laugh too. "Seriously Andi, thanks for helping me out with Sandra Havers, I appreciate it. I'm sorry we can't get together, but I promise you a large glass of wine when this is over."

"Is it Ricky?" she asked quietly.

Vega sighed. It wouldn't make any difference if she knew now. "Yes. I'm afraid so. There'll be the usual press briefing tomorrow morning. But that's all I can say, Andi."

"You've told Sandra?" Andi asked.

"Yes, I've just come from the Haverses'."

"Oh God, Andrew, that must have been awful for you."

Andrew Vega felt an unexpected surge of emotion. It *was* awful. His job meant he shared the darkest moments some people would ever experience, and although he knew how valuable his work was, there were times when it weighed heavily on him.

"It was worse for them," he managed to say.

"Poor Sandra," Andi said. "I can't imagine what she's going through." She paused for a moment. "Andrew, look, there's something you should know."

"OK," Vega said slowly. "What have you done?"

"It's not what I've done, it's what I'm going to do."

"Go on," Vega said, his tone sharper.

"Sandra thinks Dennis had something to do with Ricky's disappearance. She asked me to help her after . . . well, after you guys stopped looking."

"The case was open, Andi." Vega felt defensive, but he knew she was right. "Have you found anything?"

"Not yet, Andrew. But I will not stop looking. I promised Sandra."

"Damn it, Andi, you know that woman is grieving. She's looking for someone to blame. Who knows what damage you'll do to their marriage, their lives? Whatever you think of Dennis, Ricky was his only son. You can't destroy a man just because you're looking for a story."

There was silence at the other end of the line.

"The damage was done, Andrew, when you — or at least, Sergeant Rollins — failed to do his job. And now you're closing ranks."

Vega exploded. "How dare you, Andi? I'm here to investigate the death of Ricky Havers. If — and only if — there's evidence of foul play, we'll find it. And if anyone has been derelict in their duty, then we'll find that out too. Let us do our damn job."

"You do your job, Inspector, and I'll do mine."

Vega sighed. "I can't stop you, Andi. I don't want to stop you. But if you get in the way of my investigation or hold back any information . . ." His voice tailed off.

There was another silence at the other end. Vega wished he hadn't lost his temper and opened his mouth to apologize.

Andi said, "Good night, Andrew," and the phone went dead.

He put his cell down after the call. He regretted his outburst. Why did he let Andi Silvers get under his skin? At least Andi sounded more like her old self, he thought ruefully. He remembered visiting Andi in hospital after she'd been shot. It was a wake-up call for the intrepid journalist. The last time they'd met — just after Ricky's disappearance — he'd thought she seemed subdued. He sighed as he thought of Andi's disguised probing for information a moment ago. He was used to getting rid of journalists. But Andi was different. He really hoped their separate investigations wouldn't clash this time because he knew she would already be looking for that all-important story and wouldn't rest until she got it.

Vega looked at the clock on the bedside table. It was after midnight. He only had a few hours to get some sleep before he was up and back to the detachment. But instead of heading to bed, he opened his laptop and grabbed files from his briefcase.

The first hours of an investigation were usually the most crucial, but this investigation would be different. Ricky had been missing for months. Any evidence at the scene would surely be compromised, and the killer or killers were, most likely, far away.

Vega knew what he had promised the Havers. His team would not rest, but a definite conclusion to this investigation — well, it seemed unlikely. He cursed himself and Charlie Rollins again. If only . . .

But he checked this train of thought. It wouldn't do Ricky any good now. Besides, whoever killed Ricky Havers probably did so at the time of his disappearance. There wouldn't have been a reason to keep him alive unless they wanted a ransom — and nobody asked for one.

He mulled over what Andi had told him. Sandra suspected Dennis. Hopefully, he'd bought himself and the team some time. All the Haverses knew at the moment was that their son was dead. And that was a hard enough burden to bear.

He shook his head. Facts first, he told himself. And there was one major fact in this case: Ricky had seriously pissed someone off.

Vega groaned and finally fell back on the bed. He rolled over and closed his eyes and slept fitfully until his alarm rang.

CHAPTER FOURTEEN

Andrew Vega was an early riser, but he always programmed the alarm on his phone just in case. He hated being late. Plus, he'd stayed at the Wilson Motel in Coffin Cove before and knew that Peggy Wilson walked her dog in the morning. He did not want to bump into her.

She was a gossip.

Peggy had probably already broadcasted Vega's arrival and booking to her network, and his every move from now on would be the subject of speculation.

Vega wasn't about to give away any gossip fodder, but he still didn't want the distraction, so he rose as soon as the alarm sounded, showered and left his motel room.

He stood outside the door and looked around. Peggy had done some long-needed renovations. The entire building had been repainted. Outside every door was a hanging basket and there were new room numbers on the wall.

Vega had noticed the new sheets, comfortable mattress and fluffy towels, in sharp contrast to his last stay.

The upgrades must be working, he thought, as he saw a brand-new Mercedes parked in the bay next to his room.

Vega hadn't had time to see the rest of the town, but he'd heard the new mayor was determined to make Coffin

Cove a tourist destination and had implemented improvements. He'd also learned about the plans to demolish the old fish plant and thought it could only be a good thing. Apart from being an eyesore on the waterfront, the derelict building had been the scene of a murder just a little more than a year ago. It was a reminder of a traumatic time, and pulling it down would mark a fresh start.

Vega hoped he could put this investigation to bed as soon as possible. The most probable theory, given Ricky's chosen career and his associates, was that he had made some unfortunate choices and enemies of the wrong people. It was tragic, but these things did happen. But Superintendent Sinclair's "bad feeling" about Dennis Havers bothered Vega, especially now that even his own wife suspected him. If Andi was helping Sandra, then she must think there was some substance to whatever Sandra was telling her.

Andi also had her own suspicions, Vega remembered. She'd thought Jade Thompson, the new mayor, and her mother, Summer, were hiding some connection to Ricky Havers.

Vega hated relying on "bad feelings". Chasing down dead ends based on somebody's pet theory or gut reaction wasted so much time.

But Coffin Cove was a small town and its residents didn't like outsiders. They talked among themselves and shut everyone else out. News and gossip spread like a fanned fire. Vega was sure someone knew something about Ricky's disappearance. He just needed to find them and persuade them to talk.

In the meantime, he and the team would gather as much evidence as possible and make this case watertight. Then, when they found Ricky's killer, he or she wouldn't get off on some technicality.

He'd left his car at the detachment the night before because he'd wanted to clear his head with a walk after talking to Andi. It was also another way he could slip in and out of the motel without being noticed, and besides, he needed the exercise. A stroll from the motel to City Hall and the adjoining RCMP detachment took around twenty minutes, a few more if he stopped at Hephzibah's café to pick up a morning coffee.

He decided to do just that. The coffee out of the dispenser at the office was terrible, and he could also pick up one of Hephzibah's famous Morning Glory muffins. That would be a reasonably healthy start to the day. Vega knew he had long days ahead, full of hastily consumed junk food if he wasn't careful, so starting off on the right foot would be a good idea. He needed his wits about him and a full quota of energy.

The café was empty except for two fishermen, who nodded at Vega but paid him little attention.

"Good morning, Inspector, large coffee? To go or for here?"

Andrew Vega was happy to see the tall woman with wavy grey-brown hair pulled back into a ponytail, and blue eyes which crinkled at the edges when she smiled. From his previous time in Coffin Cove he knew that Hephzibah did more for the community than just sell excellent coffee and delicious baked goods. The café was a gathering place, a refuge, and often, the only place in town where someone facing financial hardship could get a free meal. She also provided a willing ear for everyone's troubles and a shoulder to cry on. Vega was pleased to see evidence of repairs and upgrades here too. A fancy new commercial coffee grinder and percolator sat on a new countertop.

"To go, please, Hephzibah, and one of those muffins too," he said, pointing to the fresh batch she'd just pulled out of the oven.

"You've got it. You'll be here to investigate what happened to Ricky Havers," Hephzibah said, in the form of a statement.

Vega nodded. It wasn't a secret. He watched Hephzibah as she poured his coffee into a paper cup and remembered his conversation with his superintendent and with Andi the night before. Maybe he could do a little digging before this morning's briefing. He checked his phone for the time. It was still early.

"Hephzibah," he said, as she handed him his coffee, "do you have a minute to chat?"

"Sure, just a sec!" She hurried over to the two fishermen and topped up their coffee, then smiled at Vega. "Let's sit outside and enjoy the morning sun, Inspector."

They both sat and watched the silver-grey morning tide wash against the shore.

Vega decided to start with Emma Ross's old investigation and the information he'd got from Superintendent Sinclair. "Hephzibah, what do you know about Hope Island and the women's commune?"

She looked at him in surprise. "How do you know about that?"

"Oh, just doing some research," Vega answered carefully.

"Well, as it happens, I practically grew up there," Hephzibah said, taking a sip of her coffee. "My mother, Greta, took me to the commune to escape my father, who was — and still is, sadly — a drunk. He's not violent now, but he used to knock Greta around. The commune was a refuge of sorts, I suppose. There wasn't much protection for women back in those days."

"And you grew up there?" Vega asked in amazement. "What about school?"

"We were homeschooled, I think you'd call it now. I left when I was sixteen, just after Greta died. Turns out my education was better than the one I would've got at the school here," she laughed. "Greta was a stickler for homework, and she loved to read."

"How did it work?" Vega asked curiously. "I mean, how did you get supplies?"

"We grew most of our food, and once in a while, Greta or another of the older women would head out and get flour and stuff." Hephzibah stopped for a moment and screwed up her forehead, trying to think. "You know, Inspector, we must have had some money, but I've no idea how we got it. Greta left my dad with just the clothes she stood up in, and most of the women on Hope Island were trying to escape from something."

Vega asked her a direct question: "Do you ever remember Dennis Havers from those days?"

Hephzibah thought for a moment, and then shook her head. "No, I don't. We had problems with some men from the town getting drunk and taking a boat to the island to cause trouble." She sighed. "You have to remember, Inspector, Coffin Cove was backward when it came to women's rights. Most men felt humiliated when their wives left. They wanted to teach them a lesson. Either that or they called them filthy names. Or lesbians." She smiled at the inspector. "And some were lesbians, of course. There was nowhere for women to be safe or be themselves if they deviated from what was considered the 'norm'. Especially here."

Vega nodded in understanding. In many ways, small-town life had changed little. "Was there a big drug problem in Coffin Cove?"

Hephzibah nodded. "I was too young to be fully aware, but yes, drugs were big business in Coffin Cove. There was a biker gang who used to run it all, I can't remember what they called themselves, but they ended up as part of the Hell's Angels, I think. You know what, Inspector?" Hephzibah got up as a customer arrived for coffee. "Why don't you talk to Summer Thompson? She lives in town. She's the mayor's mother," she laughed. "Isn't it funny? Summer was a leader of a commune, running away from Coffin Cove, and now she's part of the establishment."

"I'll do that — thanks for your time, Hephzibah."

"No problem." She called after him as he walked down the boardwalk, "Don't work too hard, Inspector. Make some time to spend with Andi."

Vega raised his hand in acknowledgment but didn't look around. Good grief, you couldn't sneeze in this town without everyone pulling out a tissue.

CHAPTER FIFTEEN

PC Matt Beaufort watched Sergeant Diane Fowler issue a statement to the waiting press.

"Sadly, our investigation has concluded that the human remains found yesterday morning were in fact those of Richard David Havers, known as Ricky, who was reported missing from Coffin Cove approximately nine months ago. We've identified several items belonging to Ricky, which were found at the scene. At this time, we are unable to answer any further questions about his death as we are conducting a thorough investigation, including DNA testing. His family have been notified and have asked that you respect their privacy during this very difficult time." Sergeant Fowler paused and looked up. "We will not be taking questions today. We will issue another statement in due course." She nodded at the small gaggle of reporters and walked back to join Inspector Vega.

Matt noticed Andi Silvers. He'd been so relieved when she'd shown up yesterday and helped calm Mrs Havers.

Andi looked up and made eye contact. She smiled and moved over to him.

"Was it a very late night for you?" she asked.

Matt nodded. "Yes. First of many, I imagine," he said importantly. "Forensics are still out there," he added, as if he were running the investigation. "Thank you for helping me with Mrs Havers."

"Oh yes, poor woman. I can't imagine how she is this morning, now her worst fears have come true," Andi said sincerely.

Matt nodded. "Yes, it's going to be hard."

"Hard on the town too," Andi mused. "Tourist season underway and all that. And now a murder."

"Yes," Matt agreed. "Who knows how long these investigations will take?"

He didn't notice Andi's head snap up and her staring at him. He looked over to see Inspector Vega frowning and gesturing at him.

"I'd better go. Thanks again for your help yesterday." And PC Matt Beaufort hurried off, but not before he heard her say, "No, *thank you*, PC Beaufort."

He had a sudden uneasy feeling.

* * *

Vega observed the small crowd while Diane was issuing their prepared statement. Nothing out of the ordinary. He'd spotted Andi Silvers and nodded to her. She smiled back. He wondered if she'd taken offence at his tone last night.

The media melted away — disappointed, Vega thought, at the brevity of their press release. But he needed time and space. He needed to go back to the beginning, right to the day Ricky Havers went missing. And he didn't need the added complication of media scrutiny, especially as they'd be asking some tough questions. Could they have done more when Ricky went missing? Would he still be alive now?

It would be up to Sinclair to run the PR on this one. Sergeant Charlie Rollins had a lot of explaining to do. His eyes fell on the young PC who'd been eager to help out the day before and hoped Charlie hadn't been passing on his lazy habits.

He frowned as he saw Andi greet the young man like they were long-lost friends. They chatted for a minute before he managed to catch the constable's eye and gesture for him to join the rest of the team. But it was too late. He saw Andi grin and snap her notebook shut. What the hell had that PC told her?

"Damn her," Vega muttered under his breath. Never mind if she were offended or not. He would not allow her to impede his investigation.

Sergeant Diane Fowler had done well. She'd taken the very first ferry from the mainland and arrived in Coffin Cove before nine. She and Vega had a quick briefing to bring her up to speed, and they'd agreed on the press statement. Then Diane had taken charge of the largest room available in the Coffin Cove detachment and made it ready for the team's arrival. The old building was like a maze, tiny rooms with rickety desks and worn files. There were three small interview rooms and Sergeant Charlie Rollins' office, which could be used at a pinch.

In the murder room, everything was now arranged the way Vega liked it.

In the corner was their own expensive computer equipment. At the front of the room was a large whiteboard. They set the room up for the most efficient information flow. Vega liked structure and routine. Every investigation was complex, and if things were chaotic, information would easily fall through the cracks.

He was ready to address his team. Officers were seated at their desks, sipping coffee and chatting. There was tension in the air. It was the same at the beginning of every case. Officers existed on adrenaline and coffee. The trick was to not let the case burn out, Vega knew. Keep the momentum and energy going. It was his job to keep these highly skilled members of the force motivated and disciplined.

Vega stood at the front of the room. He knew most of the officers by sight. Apart from Diane Fowler, his trusted sergeant, he hadn't worked with any of them before, but he knew the team was experienced and solid. The five officers in front of him had come from major crime units. They were motivated, highly skilled and all dedicated to their work. They were also young, Vega thought. That was OK. Sometimes, officers with decades of experience had trouble thinking outside the box.

He'd hoped for some more manpower. Sinclair had been brisk.

"I'll try to get some officers from Nanaimo, Inspector. But don't count on it. They're stretched to the max with a drug problem. You must do the best you can."

PC Matt Beaufort and Sergeant Charlie Rollins were also in the initial briefing. Vega noted the dark smudges under Charlie's eyes.

A guilty conscience interrupting his sleep, maybe? He'd have to put some hours in now, whether he liked it or not, Vega thought. He needed every single officer working at full capacity.

Vega spent a few minutes introducing everyone. Then he started.

He pointed to the whiteboard behind him, where he'd written one name: *Ricky Havers*.

"Ricky Havers was murdered. That is why we are all here, of course. For the time being, I've withheld that information from Ricky's parents, Sandra and Dennis Havers, and the press. I expect the media will be all over us soon and we'll be under scrutiny, but I want to buy us some time." He hoped Charlie Rollins was taking notice. "Ricky was shot in the back of the head. Executed, in fact. You all have a package of information — it includes some preliminary data from forensics. Their team will be at the scene for a long time. At the moment, we don't know if Ricky Havers was killed at the chapel or if he was killed elsewhere and brought to the site. What we do know is that he was not killed at the Smoke Room."

Vega had spoken to the senior technologist at the RCMP Forensic Laboratory Services after his conversation with Superintendent Sinclair.

"Gunshot wound," the technologist had told Vega on the phone before the meeting.

"Suicide?" Vega asked.

"Not unless he was double-jointed and able to tie himself up afterwards," the crime officer said.

"Explain." Vega knew gallows humour was part of the job, but he was impatient for answers.

"The victim's hands and his feet were bound with plastic cable ties," the chastened officer explained. "We're running tests, but it's likely the cable ties are a common make, available at any hardware store. But we'll confirm. Some of the victim's bones are missing from the scene, probably taken by animals, but we can say that the victim sustained a broken ankle and a broken clavicle. There is a hole in the skull, made by a bullet fired at close range. We must do more tests, sir," the officer said, "but at this stage, it looks to me like the victim was kneeling when he was shot."

"An execution?" Vega asked, almost to himself.

"Maybe. There's a lot more work to be done before we can say for certain."

"Can you tell me if he died at the scene?"

"Not yet, sir."

"And the broken ankle and clavicle?"

"Most likely from a fall. The clavicle is most often broken when pressure is placed on the shoulders or when the arms are stretched out, as if trying to break a fall," the technologist explained. "So it's likely the breaks occurred three or so weeks before the victim was killed, because although there are signs of healing, they're not very far along."

He assured Vega he'd get more information just as soon as it was verified. Vega knew it was a long process. Even after the remains were removed, the forensics team would take hundreds of samples to help them narrow down a time of death and how long Ricky Havers had been at the chapel site. The two findings might not necessarily be the same, Vega knew.

There was a murmur around the room as the officers digested the information. Some of them had been involved in gang killings. An execution-style killing was rare even for violent gang members. Only a cold-blooded killer could hold a gun to the back of a defenceless man's head and kill him. This was a deliberate act.

Vega looked around the murder room and waited for the noise to die down.

"You have a copy of the original case file of his disappearance. Despite extensive searches—" Vega looked pointedly at Charlie Rollins, whose face was stained red — "Ricky was not discovered at the ruined chapel. So we're working on the theory his body was dumped some time between the date of his disappearance and yesterday."

"Lucky those hikers found him," someone commented. "Much longer and the remains most likely would have been scattered by animals."

Vega nodded. Lucky? He didn't know.

"We'll be interviewing—" he looked down at his notes — "Katie Dagg, the museum curator, plus the other hikers." Vega continued, "The original investigation into Ricky's disappearance turned up nothing. Nothing untoward was found. Nobody saw him leave the Smoke Room. Nobody we interviewed at the time knew anything of his whereabouts. So, we re-interview, we dig deeper, we rummage around in the Havers family secrets *and* the Dagg family's — was it coincidence he ended up on their land or is that significant? Let's find out every last piece of information about Ricky Havers' life and those around him, so we can get justice for his death."

Vega paused. "In short, people, we start right back at the beginning."

CHAPTER SIXTEEN

Summer Thompson hung a dreamcatcher in her window, where it could twist and turn in the morning breeze.

Maybe it really would keep away bad dreams. She'd had another bad night. She was used to not sleeping. But she wished the sleep she did have was not beset with nightmares. Over the last weeks, Summer had woken up most mornings with her sheets twisted and damp with sweat.

Jade had risen early, as usual. Summer waited in her bed until Jade had left for work. She worried about her daughter on a normal day. Many of the Coffin Cove residents had been excited when Jade was elected. They were weary of the potholed roads, boarded-up businesses and crumbling facilities. They wanted Coffin Cove to be revitalized, like other small coastal towns on Vancouver Island. And they had put their faith and their vote behind Jade Thompson to create a future for the community. Summer had never doubted Jade would win. The campaign wasn't the hard part, it was just the beginning.

There were supporters of the previous mayor who were furious their self-serving cartel of private favours and lucrative contracts would cease. Summer knew that these people would not just accept the new normal. They would attempt to undermine Jade at every opportunity and do their best to make sure her tenure as mayor would be short.

And now that Ricky Havers had been found, Summer worried even more.

Jade disliked Summer fussing over her and preferred to have a quick coffee and leave in the morning. So Summer kept out of her way and only slid out of bed after she heard the front door click shut and the engine of Jade's car fade down the hill.

As Summer showered, the dark cloud of worry wouldn't leave her. She'd always been able to shake off bad dreams, but these days the past festered in her mind. She wished she could just wash it away, flush the stains and dirt of old secrets down the drain. Should she have just left Coffin Cove? Followed Jade to the mainland when she had the chance?

The answer always came back the same. She'd stayed because she had no choice. She'd made a promise to herself and the memory of all she had lost. She wanted justice. And Jade wanted that too — not for the same reasons as Summer, but with the same fierce intensity. It was one of the few characteristics they shared.

Despite her eccentric appearance, her tiny cottage jumbled with art supplies and half-finished paintings, Summer had a purpose. It burned deep down within her.

She was restless and didn't feel like making coffee this morning. So she gathered up the rest of the dreamcatchers she'd been making and decided to go to Hephzibah's for coffee. Hephzibah always let Summer display her arts and crafts in the café. Summer made a small amount of cash that way. Not only that, it would be a good way to gauge the mood and the gossip in the town.

Summer was a shrewd observer of people. People in Coffin Cove wondered if Summer had psychic abilities, and she allowed them to think that. In reality, Summer had no use for superstitious nonsense. She often told Jade, "If you listen hard enough, and watch closely, people will always tell you what they are thinking and doing."

Summer opened her front door and let the fresh ocean air waft in. She loved this cottage. When her daughter made Coffin Cove her permanent home again, Jade had purchased this tiny miner's house, perched on the hillside overlooking the ocean. It had needed extensive repairs, but Jade paid for everything, and soon the original hardwood floors shone, the wiring was safe and the old galvanized plumbing was replaced. Best of all, it came with a large lot. Summer and Jade had built a small art studio and there was still ample room for a garden. Summer was already growing seedlings in the glass-covered back porch.

Summer walked to the front gate. In her mind's eye she envisaged garden beds full of lilies, hostas and irises. Despite her worried mind, she smiled to herself. They'd have to build higher fences or the deer would soon be munching on their plants, and if the apple tree produced as much fruit as the blossoms promised, it wouldn't be a surprise to get a visit from a black bear. The wildlife was an upside of living in Coffin Cove.

The tiny house was idyllic, Summer thought, as she walked down the hill. But as much as she loved her new home, and living with her daughter, she wished Jade would find a partner, a soulmate to share her life.

Summer had had a soulmate once. She saw him every time she looked into Jade's eyes and was grateful. For a long time, she'd been consumed with her pain and anger. She knew she hadn't been the best mother. Sometimes, just the tilt of Jade's head or an insignificant gesture would bring all those memories flooding back, and she would be back in that dark place. All alone. Those emotions hadn't been productive, and she tried to keep focused on her purpose.

Things were different now between her and Jade. Still, it was no future for a young woman to be living with her mother, Summer thought, and she'd told Jade the same, when Jade first proposed moving Summer out of the run-down trailer park which used to be her home.

"I've missed living with you," Jade had said simply, and there was no changing her mind. So Summer had accepted the offer. At least she could keep an eye on her daughter and support Jade through her early weeks and months as mayor.

When Summer arrived at Hephzibah's, the café was quiet. The early wave of customers heading to the mill or the dock had already had their flasks filled and cleared out Hephzibah's first batch of Morning Glory muffins.

As Summer walked in, she could smell fresh baking, and Hephzibah was pulling out her second batch of muffins.

"Grab a seat, Summer, I'll be with you in a sec," Hephzibah called out.

Summer took one of the easy chairs at the back of the café with a view of the beach. She settled in and waited for Hephzibah to join her. The smell of baking took Summer back to her days living in the commune on Hope Island. Women had come from all around Canada to live in the virtually self-sufficient community. Summer's mind flooded with memories of Greta, Hephzibah's mother, who had fled from her abusive husband to Hope Island with her baby daughter. Greta had been an expert baker, Summer recalled. When they could get their hands on flour and sugar, usually via a sympathetic fisherman who would drop off supplies, Greta's baked goods were famous in the commune. Hephzibah had inherited her mother's talent, Summer thought, as the younger woman joined her with a tray of coffee and freshly baked muffins.

Hephzibah was one reason Summer had stayed in Coffin Cove. Greta died years ago, and just before she did, Summer promised her she'd always watch over Hephzibah. In latter years, it had been the other way around. Hephzibah had supported both Summer and Jade.

She was quite the mother figure to many of the townsfolk, and Hephzibah provided a friendly ear for anyone's problems. She also heard all the gossip. And that was why Summer was here this morning.

"So the body was definitely Ricky Havers'?" Summer didn't waste any time with small talk. If Hephzibah was taken aback, she didn't show it.

"Yes, the police issued a statement. Andi Silvers was in here this morning, heading up to the Daggs' to get more info from Katie. But I doubt she will. Apparently, the place is crawling with cops."

"Must be murder," Summer said flatly.

"Yes. Andi says so. Not official yet, but why would all these police be here?" Hephzibah said. "They informed Dennis and Sandra before the press conference. Can't imagine what they're feeling."

"Guilt?" Summer remarked cynically, and then, "Sorry, totally unfair. Nobody deserves that pain."

But a place in Summer's heart remained hardened towards Dennis Havers.

Like all of Coffin Cove, Summer had believed Dennis Havers was corrupt. But there was little that anyone could do to stop the shady real estate purchases, the awarding of city contracts to his inner circle for a price and the collection of extra repair fees from his commercial tenants which amounted to a protection racket. But Dennis owned so much of Coffin Cove and had been one of the major employers for so long, it went against most people's financial interests to oppose him.

If Dennis had been elected once again, Summer would have been one of his tenants in the trailer park. Dennis was just waiting for the sale price to decrease, as the owner grew more desperate. It had been part of Dennis's plan, Summer believed, to drive out as many tenants as possible, and squeeze the owner's cash flow until he could negotiate the sale price he wanted. Setting Ricky up in the marijuana store wasn't outside the law. Weed was legal. But Dennis had known that Ricky would never be content with selling his official inventory.

Summer had organized a petition against the Smoke Room. It was nothing more than a gesture, really. The city council gave her a few minutes to make a presentation, but Summer could see by the bowed heads and embarrassed squirming that Dennis had "persuaded" the council members to reject her proposal to close the Smoke Room.

Summer was making her own arrangements to move when Jade came to visit. She knew her daughter had been miserable in Coffin Cove. Undiagnosed dyslexia had blighted her early school years. She'd never been part of the in-crowd during her teenage years. It had been difficult for Jade, a quiet bookish girl, and she'd made her escape to college, intending never to return. Summer hadn't known, until the previous summer, the trauma her daughter experienced at the hands of Ricky Havers.

The thought of it now made Summer clench her fists in rage. Her beautiful daughter. Defiled by that entitled piece of scum. Jade had been strong enough to confront Ricky. Summer remembered that night. But even in death, Ricky was still making Jade pay.

Jade had been very quiet when she came home the previous evening. She'd told Summer about the discovery. She hadn't mentioned where Ricky was found, except it was on Dagg's property. When Summer heard that, she felt as if an icy hand was clutching her heart. She said nothing to Jade, except to squeeze her hand and whisper, "Don't worry. It's all over now."

Jade had nodded, but Summer could see the anxiety in her daughter's face. And she didn't believe it herself.

Having been lost in her thoughts, Summer lost her appetite for muffins and finished her coffee in silence when Hephzibah hurried off to serve her customers. Summer watched the ocean transform from pewter to blue as the morning clouds scuttled across the sky, and wondered what she could do to protect her daughter.

Even though the sun was out, and the half-hour walk home usually made Summer perspire, she shivered in the breeze, unable to shake a sinister chill. When she reached the gate to the cottage, she stood for a moment looking out over the bay. The ocean was so pretty and calm in the sunshine, but all Summer could see were scenes from the past, playing out in her mind. She and Coffin Cove shared a dark, menacing history.

Summer tried to enjoy the blue sky. She took a few slow, mindful breaths of cool air.

The dark clouds of the past were rolling in.

* * *

As Summer lifted her face to the sun and stretched her palms outwards and upwards, as if worshipping Mother Nature, a man watched her from a distance. He'd been watching the cottage for hours. He'd seen Jade Thompson, the mayor, leave early. Her face was drawn and tense as she drove past him, oblivious to his presence. He'd even lifted his hand in greeting, as if he was just an early-morning walker. But he need not have worried. She was preoccupied. But still beautiful, he'd thought. He'd then seen Summer Thompson walk down the hill. He wanted to follow her but stayed hidden near her home. He didn't need her recognizing him yet. As he gazed at her back as she walked away from him, he thought she too, like her daughter, looked like she had the weight of the world on her shoulders. Still a handsome woman, the man thought. Thicker round the waist, and she still favoured that bohemian look. He snorted to himself. Summer had never been a hippie. It was just a convenient part she played. It must still work for her, he supposed.

He hung around a little longer hoping Summer would return. He was taking his time, getting reacquainted with his old stomping ground. He'd reveal his presence soon enough. In the meantime, he'd gather information on some of his favourite people. He was getting ready to leave when Summer walked up the hill, her head down. He turned away from her and bent over, as if picking something up or tying a shoelace. She walked straight past him. She stopped at the gate and looked over the bay for a long time. He was fascinated. Could she sense him? Summer had always been very astute.

He watched her turn and walk back indoors. Long after she disappeared from view, he watched for her, hoping to catch just one more glimpse.

CHAPTER SEVENTEEN

"Let's start at the beginning," Jim said.

"Right, then." Andi felt a buzz of anticipation. She lived for this, teasing out the threads of stories, chasing down leads and exposing the truth. This time she had extra motivation. Andi had looked into Sandra Havers' eyes and seen raw pain. No mother deserves to live like that, not knowing what happened to her son. Andi had made a promise and intended to keep it.

Earlier, Jim had raised his eyebrows when he saw the brief article Andi had written, but nodded his approval. She pressed "send". On Friday morning, the residents of Coffin Cove would know they were in the midst of a murder inquiry. Thanks to PC Matt Beaufort and his loose tongue, Andi had her first scoop in a long while.

Andi felt a small pang of guilt but pushed it aside. The police should be held accountable. Charlie Rollins barely moved from his desk to put up a "Missing" poster to help find Ricky, and even Vega had swept aside any suspicion of foul play. Now it was too late for Ricky Havers. The best Andi could do for him and Sandra was to find out what happened.

Andi smiled at Jim, grateful for his support.

They pushed two desks together and spread out the contents of Andi's file.

Andi had cleared a wall. She liked to have a visual representation of her investigations. It helped her "see" connections. And so she created a story wall. Jim didn't mind it either.

"All right. For the moment, the start of all of this is Ricky's disappearance."

She pinned a picture of Ricky in the middle.

Jim looked at her with raised eyebrows.

Andi explained. "His disappearance wasn't the start. Like all good stories, we've joined in the middle. The plot started way before then."

Jim nodded. "Fair enough. So what have we got? Facts first — we'll go over the theories in a minute."

As if she were telling a story, Andi walked Jim through the known facts of Ricky's disappearance. She pinned pictures and their own articles on the wall to illustrate her points.

There wasn't a lot of material.

"Nobody saw anything, nobody heard anything, there was no evidence of a struggle. Ricky didn't have a car. If he left of his own free will, he didn't take any clothes. He didn't take any money, and he hasn't used a credit card or his bank account since. It's as if he just vanished about nine months ago, and then turned up dead in an old ruined chapel."

Jim said, "OK, what about the theories? What have we missed, what have the police missed?"

Andi laughed without humour.

"For a start, Charlie Rollins was in charge of the investigation. I talked to him a few days after Ricky vanished, and all he said was, 'Ricky's a grown man. He can leave Coffin Cove when he wants.' He put up a few posters in the end, but basically did nothing until Sandra started rattling cages and they forced him to. Even then, he just made an appeal for people to come forward if they knew something. He still, to this day, has *done* nothing."

Jim nodded.

Andi carried on. "And you know what I find strange about all that? Dennis Havers was the mayor. You'd have thought Charlie Rollins, however lazy he is, would have put some effort into finding the mayor's son. Don't you think?"

Jim shrugged. "It looks like a complete dereliction of duty. But we have the benefit of hindsight. Charlie didn't know there was anything to worry about at that point. It was a reasonable assumption that Ricky had left for personal reasons and was just fine."

"What if . . ." Andi stopped. She walked over to the wall and taped up a piece of paper with Charlie Rollins' name on it. "What if Charlie Rollins did nothing because he knew there was nothing to worry about? Maybe someone told him not to waste his time looking."

"You think Charlie Rollins was complicit in Ricky's death?" Jim dismissed that. "No way. Charlie's an idiot, but he's not a killer. I don't buy that."

"No, I'm not saying that. I'm saying maybe someone told Charlie not to worry, Ricky was fine, he just didn't want anyone to know where he was?"

Jim took a deep breath. "I guess it's possible. I assume you're going with Sandra Havers' suspicion of Dennis?"

Andi said, "Let me put it this way. If Ricky hadn't been operating the Smoke Room, don't you think he would still be alive and well and smoking dope in Dennis's basement?"

Jim shook his head. "Uh, no. You'll have to do better than that, Andi. These are conspiracy theories at best. A more plausible explanation would be Ricky dealing illegal drugs through the Smoke Room and stepping on someone's toes."

"Then why not just beat him up? Why spirit him away and kill him in the bush? Drug dealers don't usually plan elaborate crimes, do they?"

Jim didn't answer.

Andi carried on. "I think Sandra's right to be concerned about Dennis. And I also think there's a connection between Ricky Havers and Jade Thompson. Or Summer Thompson."

"Wait here." Jim left the office and went into a small storage room. He came out carrying a cardboard box. He set it down on the table and looked at Andi.

"Now, I'm not saying I agree with you — yet. I think you have a lot of theory and not enough evidence — hardly any, in fact. But I know you have good intuition for a story, and I know you read people well. I'm inclined to think the simplest explanation is usually the best. Ricky pissed off another drug dealer. They dragged him off and for whatever reason, he ended up in the woods, and because Charlie Rollins is an idiot, nobody found him until now. But—" he held up his hand to stop Andi interrupting — "but . . . I did some digging. I checked in Dad's archives to see if there were any stories linking Summer Thompson and Dennis Havers. And I also did a search on Art Whilley and Daniel Ellis."

Andi's eyes widened. "The company documents! You snooped," she said accusingly.

"I supervised," Jim said calmly. "I'm your supervisor and it's my job to supervise you and your . . . er . . . source documents. Did Sandra give them to you?"

Andi nodded. "I thought she must have persuaded some friend in the RCMP to do a search or something. I didn't know how to use them — if I could use them without getting her into trouble. Or me."

"Or us," Jim said. "Well, thankfully, you exercised good judgment. You've benefited from excellent supervision. Now, let's see if we can approach this from another direction."

He pointed to the box. "Let's go through this and get everything relevant up on that wall. Ready?"

They worked until Jim's eyes hurt and they had filled the wall with a visual timeline of Ricky Havers' disappearance. They'd made connections between persons of interest and identified gaps in their knowledge and questions that needed answering. They had a list of people to interview.

But it still looked chaotic to Jim. He grabbed a blank piece of paper and a marker pen and scribbled down five words. Then he held it up for Andi to see.

"We have to answer these questions before we can write anything," Jim said.

Andi read aloud, "Who, what, why, when, where." She gestured to the wall. "The 'who' part of this is somebody up here, I'm certain. The 'what'? What killed Ricky? Only the police and forensics can answer that."

Jim shook his head. "No, you're confusing the 'what' with the method of killing. I'm thinking more about the connection between the 'what' and 'why'. What was the motivation? Why Ricky? What motivates people to kill?"

Andi held her hands up and counted off her fingers, "Love, sex, money, power, anger, revenge."

Jim nodded. "And why Ricky? Because of drug dealing? Then it would be money and power. But we know they left the cash in the register at the Smoke Room, and as far as we know, the inventory was left alone as well. Also, why not kill him on the spot? Why take him? And — this is the one question which bugs me — why did Ricky end up at the chapel site, a few kilometres away? If someone wanted him dead, why dump him in Coffin Cove?"

"It's remote," Andi pointed out. "It's not a well-known trail, and it's on private land." She guessed where Jim was going with this but was playing devil's advocate.

"Exactly. It's hard to get to. The person or persons would risk being seen. I know it's just the Daggs and one neighbour up there, but there's plenty of old logging roads around here and lots of places in the bush to dump a body. Including mineshafts. If a body was dumped down a mineshaft, it would never be found."

"And that also brings us to 'when'," Andi said. "Surely if a body was dumped months ago, there would be nothing left. What about bears? Cougars? So Ricky was either killed recently, or his body was kept somewhere and then left at the chapel."

Jim nodded. "Either way, I believe the chapel is significant. And another thing, Andi — I think it blows up your theory about Dennis having anything to do with Ricky's death. Why leave his body right here in Coffin Cove?"

Andi nodded. "I guess so. I still think Dennis is connected, but maybe it's got something to do with his past? Someone getting to Ricky because of some shady deal that went wrong. Leaving Dennis or someone else a message?"

"Possible, for sure. But I think the location is the key. So I'm starting there." Jim rubbed his eyes and looked down the list. "I'll take Clara Bell," he said. "She's eccentric, but she liked my father, so she'll probably talk to me. She knows local history and the entire area. And first thing tomorrow, I'll have a coffee with Charlie Rollins. See if I can pry something out of him. But he's waiting for a pension, so I doubt he'll confess anything."

"OK. I'll take Katie Dagg. I couldn't get near her today, but I'll try again. I'm curious why she took a hike out there in the first place. If the location is significant, or the killer wanted a message sent, then he or she had to be confident the body would be found."

"Good point. Not many people go traipsing through the woods, there are too many old mineshafts. You have to know where they are."

"OK, boss." Andi yawned. "I'm bushed, so I think I'll call it a day. I need an early night. Tomorrow night is the belly dancing display and Cheryl's expecting a crowd." She pulled a face.

Jim laughed. "As senior reporter for the *Coffin Cove Gazette*, I expect you to attend."

"I thought you were the senior reporter?" Andi retorted.

"No, I'm supervisor to the senior reporter, remember? And you'd better get off. You'll need an early start. As soon as your inspector sees the headline tomorrow, he'll be trying to shut you down."

Andi grimaced. "I know. Still, all is fair in love and war, right?" She gathered up her purse and said goodnight.

* * *

Andi didn't usually worry about a story after she'd submitted it. But although she was tired, she couldn't sleep that night.

She flung back her bedcovers, padded over to her kitchen area and drank a large glass of water.

Damn it, she was concerned about Andrew Vega's reaction to her short article. If she was entirely honest with herself, she'd written it in a fit of self-righteous pique after their phone conversation the other day. Andrew had been so patronizing. She hated being talked down to, as if she was naïve about the potential impact of her investigation.

As Andi sat in the darkness, she had to admit she'd used Constable Beaufort's inexperience for her own ends. Just to get back at Andrew. And that wasn't right.

What was wrong with her? Why did she care what he thought of her? Hadn't she had enough of trying to please men? She'd spent so much energy — to no avail — to get Gavin's attention, and that had ended in disaster. She couldn't make that mistake a second time. Problem was, she really liked Andrew Vega, and she was certain he liked her back. But that would likely change when he read her article tomorrow.

Andi put down her glass and went back to bed. As she pulled up the bedcovers, she decided this was one more sign she wasn't ready for another relationship. Not for a long time.

CHAPTER EIGHTEEN

Kevin Wildman sniffed. Something was wrong. The smell had intensified. He'd ignored the unpleasant odour in his apartment for how long? A day? Maybe two, he thought. Yeah, two days. He'd been too busy checking forums and blog sites on his laptop, and there were so many now, it was hard to keep up. So much important information the government was hiding from everybody. He had to be ready. There would be a revolution. A day of reckoning, he was sure.

Daylight was showing through the threadbare curtains Kevin kept closed at all times. When he'd found this apartment, it was the perfect place to crash. But now he was worried he was being watched. He *knew* he was being watched. The red light on the camera attached to the Smoke Room at the end of the strip mall was always glowing.

It was hard to see, because Kevin's apartment was all the way at the far end of the strip mall. Kevin's "apartment" was a ramshackle affair built over the Coffin Cove Bookstore. All the other stores had flat roofs, but at some time in the past, someone had tried to make a little living space above this one. At first Kevin had been delighted with the clear view of the Smoke Room and the parking lot from the small side window, like a sentry guard in a tower. But now he wasn't so sure. If he could see everybody, maybe everybody could see him? He felt exposed. And now, the red light seemed to be angled towards him. Kevin tried to keep out of view, making sure the curtain was always pulled closed, and crawling around the two rooms on all fours. He'd stopped leaving the apartment unless it was absolutely necessary. When he had first noticed the red light, he'd investigated at different times during the day, running down the stairs at the back of the apartment and along the overgrown parking lot to the Smoke Room, gazing up at the camera to see if the light was still on.

Now Kevin knew that was a mistake. He'd given away his location. Now they knew where he was. Ricky had vanished ages ago. But they were still watching him.

Kevin had spent many hours fixated on the small red halo. Whenever the Wi-Fi signal from the nearby trailer park dropped out, Kevin would crouch down below the grimy window, making notes of his observations. He was sure the red light blinked at him sometimes. He just didn't know what it meant.

Kevin stood up shakily. It was possible the smell was coming from him. He'd smoked a lot of weed, popped some pills. He must have eaten. There were pizza boxes scattered on the floor. But he wasn't certain how long they had been there. And it was hard to keep clean here. The water was still on and the toilet could flush, although it had been blocked for some time. It had overflowed, and all his piss and shit and the pages he'd ripped from the old books downstairs and used to wipe himself had spread over the wooden floor of the small two-piece bathroom. Kevin had just shut the door.

Kevin had noticed this potential living space back when he was working for Ricky. These stores in the strip mall were abandoned. Some had plywood in the windows and large padlocks on the doors. But the old bookstore had an outside metal staircase leading up to the second floor. At the top of the stairs was a rotting weather-beaten door that to his delight wasn't even locked. Inside he'd found two rooms, empty save for an old orange flowery couch and a plastic table and fold-up chair. Kevin tried out the couch. A cloud of dust billowed up when he sat down, and there were mouse droppings everywhere. But Kevin didn't care. He couldn't believe his luck when he flicked the light switch and the single light bulb glowed. There was running water too.

A fuckin' palace. Close enough to keep an eye on Ricky too. Kevin trusted no one. And besides, he knew Ricky was stupid enough to fuck up a good thing. He wasn't serious about the business.

When Ricky opened the Smoke Room, Kevin hung out there all the time he wasn't working. Ricky had a trailer in the park, but Kevin wasn't welcome there. Ricky did too much entertaining, and the girls complained about Kevin watching.

Stupid bitches jiggling and bouncing up and down on Ricky, pretending he was some big fuckin' stud. He'd seen Ricky's limp dick. No way he kept it up.

Kevin rubbed his own crotch absent-mindedly. Nothing. Pills and weed did that to you, eventually. Women were a distraction anyway. He'd tried to warn Ricky. Women would be Ricky's ultimate downfall, Kevin was certain of that.

The new boss didn't like Ricky "entertaining". He'd promised Ricky fuckin' bricks of cash if he'd run the Coffin Cove patch for him.

And the dude definitely had cash.

Kevin had seen the fancy new car when the boss came to visit. It glided to a halt outside the Smoke Room one evening, the engine hardly making a sound. The boss wore the same clothes as the men at golf clubs who left their laptops and wallets in full view. The boss entered the Smoke Room. Kevin hadn't been invited to the meeting. Didn't matter. He hurried to the back of the building, scaled the rusty fire escape to the flat roof and ran across to the Smoke Room. Being as quiet as possible, Kevin opened the wooden hatch and tiptoed down the staircase, as far as he dared. Ricky kept the inside access to the roof hidden behind a door marked "Staff Only". He liked his privacy, and it was handy for Kevin when he needed to know what Ricky was up to.

This was the third business meeting Kevin had spied on. The first two were with the boss's lieutenants. They arrived on bikes, noisy throbbing engines and gleaming chrome. The two large men removed their old-school crash helmets, not caring who saw them, and met with Ricky in the store.

Ricky always told Kevin he wasn't intimidated by bikers. His old man, Dennis, had "connections", he used to boast. If ever he needed protection or a little "work" done, he'd said, tapping the side of his nose, he knew who to call.

On this day, Ricky was pissed. He'd been told how to operate, what to sell and how to sell it. They'd left him with an assortment of "shit", he said. They wanted to test him out before the boss trusted him with the new product.

Kevin shrugged. Seemed fair enough. Ricky was arrogant, being the son of the mayor and all, but that also made him a potential risk. Plus, Dennis Havers dropped in at unscheduled intervals to check the inventory and cash, and just to see if Ricky had bothered to turn on the "OPEN" sign.

Dennis was bankrolling the Smoke Room. He'd paid for the licence, filled in all the forms and purchased the order of government-sanctioned supplies.

Ricky was overjoyed. He loved weed — considered himself an expert in the various strains — but had no intention of selling weed from his new shiny store. He and Kevin discussed this many times. Since legalization, there was no money in weed. Everyone was growing their own now. Sure, there were some consumers who paid a little more for their favourite flavours and the oils and edibles were a hit with the girls. Their business model, Ricky decided, would focus on opioids.

Kevin had agreed. Opioids were easy. Easy to get and easy to sell. He liked them too. The intense feeling of warmth and euphoria as he sunk into oblivion — much better than a joint.

Ricky had banged on about "bread-and-butter revenue" and "wide customer demographics" for opioids, but Kevin tuned him out. He found Ricky annoying when he got like this. He loved the sound of his own voice, got all high and mighty, as if he were going to build some fuckin' empire by selling asshole junkies a handful of fuckin' painkillers.

Kevin sighed. Ricky could never keep his mouth shut. That had got him killed.

Kevin had sold Ricky's first consignment of shit for the new boss. The goons on the bikes seemed pleased and promised Ricky a meeting with the boss.

Ricky had been excited but evasive. Kevin sensed he was being dumped. He could tell Ricky didn't want Kevin involved in this extra money-making venture. Kevin smirked to himself. Ricky needed him. Ricky wasn't a salesman. For all his big words and fancy business talk, all he'd done was rely on Daddy for handouts. Kevin said nothing and watched and waited, pretending not to notice as Ricky called on him less and less.

The new boss was older than Kevin had imagined. Kevin strained to hear the conversation, as the boss was quietly spoken. He could hear Ricky's arrogant tone as he showed the boss around the premises. As they got nearer the door to the staircase, Kevin shrank back, ready to scoot back to the roof if he saw the door handle turn. It didn't, and the two men in the store carried on their conversation, near enough for Kevin to hear every word.

Kevin was puzzled. The boss seemed more interested in Dennis Havers than anything else. He asked pointed questions about Dennis's involvement in the Smoke Room. Kevin nearly laughed out loud as Ricky blustered some bullshit about being his "own man". *Tell that to Daddy when he comes to collect the rent and balance the takings*, Kevin thought.

The boss changed tack and started grilling Ricky about loyalty. Again, Kevin wanted to laugh. Loyalty was not a concept Ricky grasped. But then Kevin didn't rate it highly either. But the boss banged on about it. He'd been betrayed before, he said. He was a patient man, though. His voice got lower, and for the first time, Kevin shivered, and hoped he wouldn't be discovered. The man was fuckin' nuts. He wondered if he was holding a knife to Ricky's throat or something, because Ricky remained silent while the boss described exactly what would happen if Ricky screwed him over.

Finally, he heard Ricky speak. His voice was shaky, as he promised absolute unconditional loyalty.

Then the boss seemed to lighten up. The voices faded a bit and Kevin slipped down one step to keep listening. This was the important bit. What was the product? From what Kevin could make out, it was some kind of psychedelic. He hoped it wasn't mushrooms. He fuckin' hated mushrooms. They were finicky to grow and hardly anyone could get it right. They were either mouldy or dried out, and instead of a hallucinogenic out-of-body experience, all you got was a mouthful of expensive dung. But it wasn't mushrooms. Something like LSD, but better.

Kevin liked the idea. LSD was old-school. It wasn't found much on the island, most people preferring shrooms. But the market was saturated with crap products and people were restless for something new.

Kevin had heard enough. He slowly moved his body round to creep upstairs. The voices grew louder, and the boss said something about "night". Operating in the night? Kevin hesitated. No, it wasn't "night". He was asking Ricky to join his "knights".

Kevin didn't chance it. As quiet and quick as a rat, he scuttled up the stairs, closing the hatch behind him, and descended the fire escape before running across the waste ground behind the strip mall and entering his secret hideout, just as the boss left the Smoke Room. Kevin watched from the window, just peeping over the sill enough to see the top half of the boss as he bent to open his car door and then disappeared from Kevin's view as he got into the driver's seat. Then Kevin heard the low purr of the engine fade into the distance.

Kevin waited for Ricky's call. He kept looking at the cheap pay-as-you-go phone Ricky had given him. No text, nothing. Ricky didn't call him the next day or the day after that. Kevin wondered if Ricky was being tested. Maybe the boss was making sure of Ricky's loyalty. Maybe there was some kind of initiation for the new "knight".

Kevin watched and waited. He wanted in on this new venture. Maybe he'd wait and approach the boss himself? He could be an asset. He knew several customers looking for a new high, something more exciting. The new product, whatever it was called, could fill a gap in the market, as Ricky would put it.

A couple of nights later, Kevin got excited as he watched Ricky smoke his usual joint on the roof of the Smoke Room. This had to be it — the test. Kevin watched as a woman climbed the fire escape and stood looking at Ricky. It wasn't one of Ricky's prossies, she was dressed different. She didn't look like she was coming on to Ricky either.

Kevin saw Ricky reach out, as if he were going to shake the woman's hand . . . *What the fuck?* Kevin saw a flash of light, and Ricky fell backward, seemed to right himself and then fell and collapsed like a rag doll on the ground behind the Smoke Room. Kevin was on his feet, clutching his head. What had the boss done? What had Ricky done to piss him off? Kevin realized he was standing in the window. He ducked down and waited for what seemed like hours. Then he straightened up and dared to look out the window. It was dark. Kevin could see the glow of the neon sign on the shop, but nothing else.

This didn't make any sense. Why would the boss send a woman to shoot his new knight?

Kevin paced the room. What to do? Maybe this was a way to get in, he thought. If Ricky was dead, then maybe he could take over the operation? And if Ricky wasn't dead, and Kevin helped him, then maybe they'd both be so grateful, they would cut Kevin in?

Kevin made up his mind. He left his lair and stood in the night air for a moment until his eyes adjusted. There was enough light from the trailer park to cast shadows, and as Kevin made his way carefully through the debris, he could see the outline of Ricky's body. Kevin waited. Ricky wasn't making a sound. Kevin inched closer and saw Ricky's chest moving slightly. He was breathing. One leg was bent at a weird angle, and Kevin could just about see a dark patch under Ricky's head, which he assumed was blood. Unconscious, but not dead.

Kevin knelt down beside Ricky's inert body. He felt around in Ricky's pockets, pulled out his phone and grinned. It was still intact. He sat back on his haunches and opened the phone. He knew Ricky's four-digit password and tapped it in. He scrolled down the recent calls. There was only one number without a contact name. Ricky had called and received a couple of calls in the last two days, so Kevin took a chance and pressed the phone icon. The call was connected, and Kevin breathed out with relief as he heard the same man's voice he'd heard a few days ago.

"Yes?"

Kevin hesitated.

"What is it?" the man said.

"Your knight is down," Kevin said and quickly ended the call. He pushed the phone back into Ricky's pocket and hurried away into the night.

That had been months ago. Ricky had disappeared. Kevin had watched Dennis and Sandra and then police cars come and go. He never saw the boss again. Maybe Ricky had been spirited away to another patch? The new psychedelic had made it to the streets of Nanaimo. Kevin asked around, but nobody had seen Ricky. He wasn't one of the knights in Nanaimo, at least.

Kevin kept his head down, dealing in this and that, stealing and selling, and waiting in his tiny hideaway for word from Ricky.

Nothing. But Kevin knew he was being watched. The red light blinked on and off. It had to mean something.

CHAPTER NINETEEN

Jim's truck trundled up the rutted logging road to Clara Bell's home. She lived in a small trailer, a good twenty minutes beyond old Ed Brown, Harry's father. As Jim passed, he raised his hand in greeting to Ed, who was sitting on his porch. It was a little after ten in the morning, but Jim suspected Ed would already be sipping his second beer.

Poor Harry, Jim thought. He took the brunt of looking after his father. Not that he owed Ed anything. It was his vicious drunken temper that drove Greta, his wife, to take Hephzibah and live on Hope Island, leaving Harry behind. A strange decision, Jim thought. Harry rarely talked about his childhood. He'd been married once and had a grown-up daughter, but he was a bit of a loner.

Harry has an eye for Andi, Jim thought. But Andi, did she have feelings for Inspector Vega? There was certainly a spark between those two. It might be a rocky road, given their chosen professions, though. In fact, Vega would be cursing Andi right about now. Jim smiled to himself. He supported Andi and her article, even though she hadn't held back. He wondered how it would affect her relationship with Vega. But that was by the by. For decades now, the RCMP had paid lip service to Coffin Cove, choosing to let Charlie

Rollins mark time until his retirement. Things needed to change around here.

Charlie had walked the other way when he saw Jim earlier that morning. Jim had let him go. For now, he thought, only for now. He was inclined to believe Charlie was guilty of laziness and incompetence rather than conspiring with Dennis Havers. Still, Charlie's failings might have cost Ricky his life. They were right to publish the article, even if it ruffled a few feathers, Jim decided. Let it all play out.

Jim laughed out loud. Why was he worrying? Andi could take it. Last night at the office, she looked just like the old Andi, ready for battle.

The logging road climbed and narrowed. On either side, tall firs shaded the trail. Clara Bell had lived out here alone as long as Jim could remember. He couldn't remember a spouse or siblings, although there was talk about a brother who'd left to look for gold up in the Yukon.

The road swerved abruptly to the right, up to Clara's home. Jim tried to avoid the bigger potholes.

"What the hell . . . ?" Jim slammed on his brakes as a horse appeared in front of him. A cloud of dust obscured his view, and when it cleared, he saw that the horse hadn't moved a muscle. Jim got out of his truck and slammed the door. What was wrong with the damn animal? He heard laughing and saw Clara Bell standing with her hand on her hip.

Jim thought Clara looked like a pioneer woman in an old sepia photograph from the 1800s, with her shock of white hair and long dark skirt.

"Fools everyone, does my Trigger," she called out. "Better than a guard dog."

Jim laughed too. "Where did you get this, Clara?" He walked over to the horse, a life-size plastic model, complete with real horsehair for a mane and tail.

"Oh, I got it at one of those auctions," Clara said, waving her hand. "Looks real, don't it?"

"It does. How are you, Clara? Got over your shock?" Jim walked towards the old woman, thinking she'd hardly changed all the time he'd known her. Even thirty years ago, her hair had been white and wild, spilling over her shoulders. Her face was weather-beaten but smooth. It was hard to say how old she was. Eighty? Ninety? It was possible.

She'd always been intense, fixing you with those dark watchful eyes as she listened to what you had to say. People in town said she was fierce, and when she was curator of the museum, children had been afraid of her. But get close to Clara Bell, do her a kindness, and she'd be a friend for life. A long time ago, Jim's father helped Clara, and every so often, she'd dropped off deer meat or a trinket from her collection, as thanks. Clara still hunted for her meat. She was an excellent shot, as many a poacher found out if they got too near to her treasures.

Ah, yes. Clara's treasures. Jim looked around in amazement. Clara had always collected . . . everything. He supposed she was a hoarder. But all her "things" seemed organized. There were piles of old bicycles and rusty parts, rows and rows of fishing rods propped up against an old shed, surrounded by buckets of fishing tackle, the glint of metal lures catching the light. A hundred or more ceramic garden ornaments, all in varying states of disrepair, and some gnomes with missing heads were gathered together. Old furniture, iron bedsteads, chainsaws. Jim stood and gaped.

Clara didn't seem to notice. "I'll make some tea, James." She had always called him by his full name. Clara disappeared up the steps into her trailer. Jim heard the chug of a diesel generator as he followed her. It was Clara's only source of power, and it kept her lights on and the water pumping from her well.

Once inside, he couldn't see her. There were boxes piled to the ceiling, and just one narrow walkway through the maze. Jim spied Christmas tinsel poking out of some containers. Others were full of books, as far as he could tell. Clara, or he assumed it was Clara, had written "History" and "Stories" and other categories in shaky handwriting on some boxes.

Jim knew a little about hoarding. When his father had been in the early stages of dementia, he refused to throw anything away. But Clara was a collector, Jim decided. Although the trailer was full, and undoubtedly a fire hazard, it smelled clean. Clara took care of her treasures.

Clara appeared from behind a tall mound of folded linen. She held two mugs of tea in her hand. Both mugs commemorated a royal wedding. She handed one to Jim.

"This way," she said, and she eased herself between two more piles of boxes and opened a door. They were at the back of the trailer. Tall fir trees shaded this side, but it was no less cluttered.

"The water feature collection," Jim murmured, as everywhere he looked were stone fountains and birdbaths: some shaped like cherubs and clamshells, some even had water burbling out of the mouths of concrete fish.

"Sit," Clara said, pointing to a stone bench, while she settled herself on a wooden Adirondack chair which had white paint peeling from the arms.

"You didn't answer my question, Clara."

Clara sipped at her tea thoughtfully. "I've seen dead bodies before, James."

"Still, must have been a surprise at least. Unexpected."

Clara nodded. "Bad business."

Jim pushed a little harder. "Why were you out there, Clara?"

Clara's face darkened a little. "George Gomich said the new curator wanted to know some local history. Said she'd heard about that silly old story and wanted to see the chapel for herself." Her voice had taken on a sneering tone.

Jim wondered and then asked, "Do you miss the museum, Clara?"

To his horror, a tear ran down the old woman's face.

"Clara, I'm sorry, what did I say?"

She brushed at her face. "Don't mind me, I'm a silly old woman. But I loved that place. Gave me a reason to get up in the mornin'. Hurts when you get cast off, James. You'll see when you get old. You young 'uns don't understand until it happens to you."

Jim hid his smile. It had been a long time since anyone referred to him as a *young 'un*. "I do understand, Clara. My father felt it when he left the *Gazette*. He said he had a lot more to give."

Clara nodded. "That's exactly it. Wise man, your father." And then she said, "That new mayor. She said I could move into some new housing they're going to build. Assisted living, she called it. Do you think they'll make me leave here?"

She sounded genuinely scared.

Jim reached across and patted her hand. "Nobody will make you leave your home, Clara. Not as long as I'm around, I promise you."

Jim thought it was best to change the subject. "Young Katie Dagg, she does love Coffin Cove. And she's a nice girl. She'll do a good job at the museum."

Clara sniffed. "She seemed nice, I suppose. For a Dagg."

"You don't like the Daggs?" Jim asked. "Why? Is it something to do with their property? Or the chapel?"

"Wayne Dagg stole that house from Arthur," Clara said suddenly. "Him and that Dennis Havers, they bullied him and stole from him. And got him mixed up in all that drug stuff with the bikers. He was a good boy, Arthur. Helped me with my maps."

"Art Whilley?" Jim asked, leaning forward. He remembered the company registration documents Sandra had given Andi. This was why he was here. "You knew Art Whilley?"

Clara nodded. "When he was a boy. Before he got mixed up in all that craziness. He used to visit me. To get away from that monster of a mother."

"You helped him, Clara?" Jim asked, not wanting her to stop and knowing now why Andi liked to record all her interviews.

"He helped me," she said. "We walked all over and he helped make all my maps of the old mineshafts. And so I taught him how to shoot, and how to skin animals. He was good with a knife. He was smart too, liked to read. I gave him some of my books."

"Well, you must have thought a lot of him," Jim said with feeling. He knew how hard it was for Clara to part with her treasures.

She smiled. "Didn't have a son of my own. He was good company. Told me a lot about my collection and helped me hook up the generator. That mother of his . . ." Her face darkened.

"Did anyone else try to help him?" Jim asked.

"Ann South, she did. And her boy, Douglas. He looked out for Arthur. But Wayne Dagg and Dennis Havers, they tormented him. Until they found out he was clever. Then they used him and then they killed him."

Jim sat back in his chair, shocked at what the old lady had said. Clara was odd and didn't live in the modern world, but she wasn't crazy. "Dennis Havers and Wayne Dagg killed Art Whilley? You sure about that, Clara?" he asked again.

She shrugged. "Arthur burned in that fire. That's what they told me. But he was too smart to get caught in some fire. So they must have burned him."

Jim leaned forward. "Clara, can you tell me all you know about Arthur and Hell's Half Acre?" He had no idea how it all fit with the death of Ricky Havers, but he was sure Clara knew something. Something important.

Jim was at Clara Bell's trailer for two hours. He listened carefully, hoping he could remember everything she'd told him. When he was ready to leave, he pressed a fifty-dollar note into her hand. For a moment she glared at him, but then stuffed it into a pocket in her skirt. Then she grabbed his arm and pulled him nearer.

"Come again soon, James. And next time, bring diesel."

Jim watched her in his rear-view mirror through the dust until he rounded the corner. He sped up until his phone dinged and he knew he was back in the range for cell phone service. He pulled over and punched in Andi's number. They were on to something now, he thought, as he waited for the call to connect.

CHAPTER TWENTY

"Ready for a top-up?" Hephzibah smiled down at the man.

"Sure, why not?" He held up his mug and smiled back.

Hephzibah was pleased. She'd been waiting for an opportunity to get a better look at him. Walter had been adamant he'd recognized this man, and now Hephzibah was really curious.

She sneaked a look at his face while she filled his mug. In his sixties, maybe? That made him older than Harry, but they might have been in school together, if he was from Coffin Cove. He looked like he took care of himself. His face wasn't weathered, like most men around here. His hands were smooth, his nails trimmed. Definitely not a man who worked outside.

Hephzibah said casually, "Are you visiting Coffin Cove? I don't think I've seen you in here before?"

The man said, almost teasingly, "I was just in here the other day, you don't remember?"

Hephzibah felt herself blush. "No, I meant . . ."

The man laughed. "I'm sorry, I know what you meant. I'm in town for a few days, looking at real estate. I'm a developer and I heard your new mayor has a plan for the old fish plant site."

"Oh, that's wonderful!" Hephzibah said. "It's time that old building came down. There was a murder there, you know, and it's time we got rid of that old monstrosity."

"A murder?" the man said and pointed to a stack of fresh newspapers on a rack. "Looks like it's a common occurrence in Coffin Cove."

"Oh, no, it's a very tragic case. Ricky Havers was the son of our previous mayor . . . but it's a really friendly town," Hephzibah responded, wishing she'd put the papers out of sight. The headline wasn't great advertising for the beginning of the tourist season, especially as the Heritage Festival kicked off this evening.

"Friendly? Is that right?" the man murmured.

"I hope it doesn't put you off. We need new blood." *God*, Hephzibah thought, *not the best choice of words to use!*

"Oh, bad things happen everywhere," said the man as he picked up his coffee. Hephzibah took that as a signal he wanted to be left in peace, but she hadn't yet got a name. She didn't recognize him at all, and only a name would satisfy Walter's curiosity.

"Have you been to Coffin Cove before?" Hephzibah tried.

"Long time ago. I had relatives who lived here once." The man focused once again on his coffee, in a way that told Hephzibah the conversation was now over.

* * *

Vega swore. "This is a damn hatchet job! Have you read this?"

Diane Fowler nodded. "It's unfair, sir."

He sank into a chair. It wasn't even nine o'clock, and already the day was going badly.

He reread the article on the front page of the *Coffin Cove Gazette*. The paper only printed once a week, on Fridays, and it was distributed to every household and business in town. But thanks to Andi, the *Gazette* also had an impressive presence on social media, and Vega was certain Superintendent Sinclair would hear about this soon enough. The RCMP monitored online media for every mention of their activity, and this article wasn't just reporting that Ricky Havers' body had been found, it was confirming murder. If that wasn't bad enough, the article questioned the police response to Ricky's disappearance. More than just question, Vega saw with dismay. It was an unbridled attack.

"If our Mounties had done their job, would Ricky still be alive?"

Andi's article was a methodical takedown of the entire investigation, from Charlie Rollins' fuck-ups to their own "inadequate" press briefing.

"Coffin Cove deserves better," the article concluded. *"Let's hope our new mayor will demand immediate improvements."*

Vega held his head in his hands. Andi hadn't mentioned him or his team specifically, but he'd got the message loud and clear.

"Has Charlie Rollins seen this?" he asked.

Sergeant Fowler shrugged. "If he hasn't, it won't be long before he does. You know what this place is like."

Vega nodded. "Keep him away from the front desk. I don't want him or anyone else talking to the press. Especially not Andi Silvers or Jim Peters. I'll talk to Sinclair and see what we can do to limit the fallout. To try and at least stop the rest of the media descending on us."

"Are you going to respond to this?" Diane asked, holding up the paper between her fingers as if it were a soiled tissue.

"Not sure. I must talk to the Havers."

If Dennis Havers was involved, Vega thought, he'd be on full alert. Damn Andi. She didn't know the damage she'd done.

"Sir, PC Matt Beaufort. He thinks it was him who tipped off the *Gazette*. He didn't mean to. He just let it slip, and now he's shitting a brick," Diane said.

"And so he should be," Vega said, annoyed.

"The thing is, sir, I've been watching him. He's not like Charlie. He's dedicated, and in the short time he's been here, he's made a good impression on the community. They like him and they talk to him. He could be an asset, if—"

"If I don't blast him for a silly mistake?" Vega finished.

"Yes, sir." Diane looked relieved.

Vega nodded. "OK, I'll talk to him later. You take him with you today. Get him out and away from the detachment. Now, I have to call Superintendent Sinclair."

Sergeant Fowler left him alone.

He took a deep breath and tapped in the number.

Sinclair seemed calm. She'd seen the article, but she'd endured many media attacks in her career, so was relatively sanguine about it.

"Nanaimo detachment is dealing with a high-profile overdose of that new street drug. Son of a minor celebrity, so the media is all over it. It should buy you a couple of days. As for Charlie Rollins—" she snorted — "I wouldn't waste much time defending him. His retirement is imminent."

"Sounds like a reward, not a punishment," Vega commented.

"There are some battles we can't win, Andrew," Sinclair said briskly. "Let's focus on the war. The Charlie Rollinses of this organization are fading away, and a good job too. I know you're irritated by that young constable's mistake, but I'm inclined to let this one go. Encourage him. Our new recruits are down by sixty per cent. We can't lose the good ones."

"Yes, ma'am."

"And progress so far?"

Vega told her. It didn't take long. Nine months was a long time, and they were having trouble locating anyone in the trailer park who might have remembered something around the time Ricky disappeared. It looked like they would have to rely on forensics to solve this case.

"Don't be so sure, Andrew. It's a tiny community. Someone knows something. Shake it out of them. Not literally," she added dryly.

Vega had to make another call. He couldn't put it off.

The phone was answered on the first ring.

"Mr Havers?"

"Inspector." Dennis sounded monotone.

"Mr Havers, you may have seen an article in this morning's *Gazette*," Vega started.

Dennis interrupted. "Joanna brought us a copy, Inspector. My wife is very upset. The doctor is with her now."

"I'm so sorry," Vega said. "The information should have come from me. I apologize."

"What difference does it make now, Inspector? Ricky is still dead. Do you know who killed him?" He sounded as if he were asking if Vega knew the weather forecast.

Vega said, "No sir, we don't. And that's the other reason for my call. We will have to ask you and Mrs Havers some questions."

Silence.

Vega continued. "It's routine, sir. We must talk to anyone who knew him, we'll have to look at his financial records too. Did Ricky owe anyone any money, sir? Someone . . . er . . . connected to the Smoke Room, maybe?"

He heard Dennis sigh. "Inspector, I paid Ricky's many debts throughout his whole life. My son wasn't an angel. He did things to people. I tried to make them go away — those I knew about — with money. But money doesn't always work, Inspector. I'm understanding that now."

"I see, sir. Can you come to the detachment, sir? Or would you like me to come to you?"

"I'll see you tomorrow, Inspector. Today, I must look after my wife."

The phone went dead. And then, immediately, it rang again.

"Yes, Vega here?"

It was a technician from the forensic laboratory.

"Sir, we can confirm now that your victim was not killed at the discovery site. There were traces of embalming fluid and evidence that the remains were kept in cold storage, maybe a freezer, before being transported to the site."

"Embalming fluid? The killer attempted to embalm the body?"

"Yes, sir. But embalming fluid, contrary to what you'd think, does not do a good job of preserving the body long-term. Our best guess is the killer tried embalming, and then freezing when the body started to decompose."

Vega was silent for a moment, processing the new gruesome facts.

"So two things I'm thinking right away," Vega mused, almost to himself. "The killer wanted the body to be found."

"Yes, sir. And given the lengths he — or she — went to to preserve the body, maybe it was important the body was identified? I mean recognized, without the lengthy process of DNA?" the technician added.

"Yes. And it also means the site, the chapel where he was found, was significant," Vega said. "Thank you."

"Er . . . that's not all, sir. And I'm sorry to complicate things . . ." the technician continued.

Vega gripped his phone a little tighter. *What now?* "Go on," he said.

"Well, most of the remains were recovered from the site, except for a few, because of wildlife we think. But we have identified some human remains that do not belong to Ricky Havers."

Vega closed his eyes. "You're telling me we have two bodies at the same site?"

"Yes, sir. We are attempting to extract DNA, but these remains have been there for a very long time. We may not get a positive identification."

Vega ended the call.

A second body. Another victim?

Vega got up and poked his head through the door of the conference room. "Diane? I need you to get the team together."

Then he sank back down in a chair. Coffin Cove and its damn secrets!

155

CHAPTER TWENTY-ONE

Andi was at a dead end.

First, she'd phoned Katie Dagg. She'd used Katie's cell phone number, but Lee Dagg had answered and refused her request to talk to Katie. She had spoken to the police and was taking a few days off, Lee said. She was still in shock. He'd been polite, but before Andi could thank him and end the call, she'd heard a woman's voice angrily telling him to "put the fucking phone down." The phone went dead. Andi guessed it was Nadine.

Next, she'd knocked on Mr Gomich's door. Initially, she'd been surprised when Peggy Wilson answered, but then it made sense. Peggy was the chief purveyor of gossip in the town, plus she had been the unfortunate person to discover a dead body in the fish plant a year ago.

She completely understood the shock, she'd told Andi, shaking her head, so she'd come straight over to give George and Margie Gomich the benefit of her support and counsel. She sighed. Only people who'd been through trauma would understand. George hadn't said much, but she had all day and would stay until he was ready to talk. Get it all off his chest.

Mrs Gomich had appeared before Andi could say anything and said she'd had enough of visitors — giving Peggy a meaningful look — and George just wanted to be left alone. He didn't get a good look at the body anyway. It was poor Clara Bell who'd found that Ricky Havers, and perhaps Clara needed support and counselling. (Another meaningful look at Peggy Wilson.) Andi had asked if she could include that comment in her article, and Mrs Gomich had told her she "didn't bloody care what she wrote, they just wanted some bloody peace and quiet."

So that was that.

Andi was sure she wouldn't be able to get close to the chapel site just yet, and anyway, she wanted to avoid any possibility of bumping into Andrew Vega. Her article had gone out that morning. She'd seen the headline when she picked up a coffee at Hephzibah's.

In black and white, it seemed stark. Andi contended that Coffin Cove had been let down by the RCMP and the community deserved better. Andi contrasted the tiny two-person detachment with the 200-strong force in Nanaimo, which was supposed to provide backup. She'd analysed crime statistics and population numbers and made the convincing argument (or so she thought) for at least triple the RCMP members, increased training and replacement of obsolete methods and equipment. She also dismissed Vega's press conference as "arrogant" and called for greater transparency.

"Despite repeated requests from the Havers family, the response to his mysterious disappearance was lacking, to say the least. No televised appeals, no search parties, no helicopters, nothing except a short public relations visit to 'quieten down the locals'. Even now, after the tragic discovery of Ricky's body, the inspector in charge of the investigation will not provide the community with the information they need: was Ricky Havers murdered? And if RCMP had responded immediately, would Ricky Havers be alive today?"

Andi had been careful not to name Charlie Rollins. But she'd felt the frosty reception to her article as Hephzibah poured her coffee. The fishermen, who usually waved and smiled, kept their heads down. There was a definite chill in the air, Andi thought.

"I don't understand," she whispered to Hephzibah. "They complain all the time about theft and petty crime, how Charlie should get off his backside and do his job, and now they're upset?"

Hephzibah shrugged. "You know what it's like. *We* can complain about our own, but an outsider — well, that's another thing entirely."

"I'm still an outsider?" Andi asked, surprised.

"Just down from my house a couple moved in back in the early eighties. Harry still calls them 'the new neighbours'," Hephzibah said with a smile. "Don't worry. You wrote the truth. It's your job. They probably secretly agree with you, and when you find out what happened to Ricky, you'll be the hero of this."

I don't want to be a hero, thought Andi, *I just want to give Sandra some closure.*

Standing in front of the Smoke Room at the small abandoned strip mall, Andi did not feel like a hero, and she knew she wasn't any nearer to finding answers for Sandra.

She wondered if she should call Andrew Vega. Explain why she'd written the article. He'd probably think she was trying to make a point after their argument on the phone. Was she? Why did it matter what he thought anyway? Better to focus on helping Sandra.

After striking out with both Katie Dagg and George Gomich, she'd decided to start again where the mystery had begun. She didn't expect to find anything to help her, but she thought the location might inspire some creative ideas. Maybe coming back to the start might shake something from her subconscious, something she'd overlooked.

Andi peered through the window of the Smoke Room. It was hard to see anything because the windows had some kind of plastic coating on them, which allowed people inside to see out but blocked the view from outside.

Andi could make out a long counter and a few tables and chairs. She assumed all the inventory had been removed.

Not for the first time, she wondered at Dennis Havers' motivation to set up a pot store right here in the strip mall. When Andi first arrived in Coffin Cove, two small businesses were struggling to stay open in the ugly low-slung block of storefronts.

They were all boarded up now. Dennis Havers had purchased the strip mall for pennies on the dollar. The previous owners had died with no heirs to take over. Gradually tenants moved out as the building fell into disrepair, and the lawyers in charge of probate stopped answering the phone. When property taxes were delinquent two years in a row, the City of Coffin Cove put the strip mall up for auction. There was only one bidder: Dennis Havers.

He didn't clean up the old site or make any repairs. The flat roofs on three stores sagged. The parking lot at the back was overgrown with weeds and brambles. Soon it became a dumping ground for old shopping carts, stained mattresses and rusting appliances.

The Smoke Room had been the first business to open in the strip mall with Dennis Havers as landlord. It was controversial. Behind the strip mall was Coffin Cove trailer park. Twenty-eight trailers sat on permanent rental pads, in a nicely landscaped four acres. There was a children's play area, a barbeque and picnic area, and from the east corner, a view of Coffin Cove bay. The monthly rental payments were inexpensive, and it was Coffin Cove's only option for low-cost family housing.

Dennis had been trying to purchase the park for years. The rumour was he wanted to replace a few of the older trailers and raise the rent for everyone — by a substantial amount. The problem was, he could only legally do that when new tenants moved in. Plus, the current owner was quite happy with the way things were. He wasn't selling.

Andi believed, along with several residents, including Summer Thompson, that Dennis intended to drive out tenants. The Smoke Room, run by his useless but predictable son Ricky, would soon attract an undesirable clientele. The ploy worked. Despite a petition organized by Summer Thompson, the Smoke Room opened, and immediately half the tenants at the trailer park gave notice to move out.

Andi could see a new "For Sale" sign at the entrance to the trailer park.

Dennis got what he wanted, Andi thought. But how did Ricky's disappearance fit into all this? Was Dennis involved at all? For the first time, Andi doubted Dennis had anything to do with Ricky's disappearance and murder. She thought of Jim's words: why dump the body right here in Coffin Cove?

Andi walked back towards the car. She'd go back to the office and do some research on Dennis's business activities. Maybe that would throw up some leads. And maybe Jim would get something from Clara Bell.

As she took one last look around the strip mall, Andi thought she saw a slight movement in the second-floor window of the last store on the block. She walked over and peered through the dirty window of the old bookstore. The owner had just left the store as it was, with books still on the shelves. Andi could see the books were curled up from damp and covered in dust and grime. Nobody had been in there for years. Maybe it had been the light, she thought. But then she heard a noise, like a chair scraping across a floor. Andi tried the door. Locked.

Frowning, Andi walked around the unit to the parking lot at the back. She hadn't noticed before, but behind the piles of debris was a narrow metal staircase leading up to the second storey of the bookshop, and at the top of the steps, there was a second entrance.

On closer inspection, Andi saw the grass and weeds had been trodden down around the foot of the rusty staircase. Looking around, she could see there was a small pathway, much like an animal trail, leading away through the over-grown parking lot, towards the trailer park.

Someone living here? Andi wondered. Squatters? She had to look.

Nervously, she climbed the metal steps and peered through the glass pane of the door. She saw a filthy couch on one wall of a small room. Pizza boxes and beer cans were strewn everywhere, and something that looked like a brown liquid was oozing under a small door at the far corner. She didn't want to go in.

Definitely squatters, Andi thought, and wondered how long they'd been there. Could they have witnessed Ricky's disappearance? Had Charlie Rollins missed this too?

Then Andi caught sight of a green light blinking from a box in the corner. She looked again. Was that a laptop? Was there power in this decrepit living space?

Andi had her face near the dirty pane. As she focused on the laptop, thinking it might be stolen, a man's face appeared, like a jack-in-the-box, right in front of her. She screamed and almost lost her footing. The man had wild eyes and matted hair. Andi didn't wait for introductions.

She turned and took the steps two at a time. The man had flung the door open and was screaming after her. Andi was fast, but then she realized the man was coming after her.

Tripping over the garbage, Andi kept upright and headed for her car. It was the fastest she'd moved in a long time, and she felt the scar on her thigh pull.

Not fit at all, she thought, as she panted and slowed. All at once, she felt a hand clamp on her shoulder and spin her around. She was face to face with the man, and all Andi could register in her mind was the stench. He was still screaming, incoherent words, as Andi struggled to get free.

"You killed him! Killed him . . . the night . . . the night . . ." He was almost chanting. Andi pulled free and ran to her car.

He followed her, still spewing obscenities and, as far as Andi could make out, accusing her of killing someone in the night. She fumbled for her car keys as the man loped towards her, his arms flailing.

"You're spying on me . . . watching me . . ." He was spitting and foaming from his mouth and getting nearer. But to Andi's relief, another vehicle screeched into the parking lot and distracted his attention.

The man ran in the other direction, to Andi's relief, but someone grabbed the man from behind and tackled him to the ground.

"Are you alright?" a woman's voice asked Andi, full of concern.

"Yes, thank you . . ." Andi saw it was Sergeant Diane Fowler.

"Oh, Miss Silvers, glad to see you are unharmed." The sergeant's tone changed from concerned to icy. "You're lucky we were doing a drive-by."

"Thank you, Sergeant, I appreciate your help," Andi said sincerely, realizing the sergeant must have read her article. She was trembling.

"Not at all, Miss Silvers," Fowler said, not bothering to disguise her sarcasm. "Always glad to be of service to a member of the free press."

Andi said nothing. She watched Sergeant Fowler walk back to her colleague, the young constable who'd inadvertently helped Andi get her scoop, and helped him restrain the squatter, who was now howling like a captured wild animal.

Andi got into her car and sat for a moment, letting the adrenaline subside and wiping her face with tissues. She fought an urge to cry. Then her phone rang. It was Jim.

* * *

Diane Fowler looked in disgust at the handcuffed man.

"Great. A babbling crackhead. We don't have time for this," she grumbled to Matt. But he wasn't listening.

"Did you hear what he said, Sarge?" he asked excitedly.

"A lot of nonsense, is all I heard," answered Diane, "and now we've got to put that filthy creature in the cruiser and take him back to the detachment."

"No we don't, Sarge," Matt said, with a big grin on his face. "He was talking about the 'knights' and I'm sure he said 'dukes'."

Sergeant Fowler looked at him, not understanding. "So?"

Matt explained how he'd been looking out for the new drug on the streets of Coffin Cove.

"The Nanaimo guys are picking up everyone they can find connected to this new street drug," Matt explained.

Diane nodded, her confusion clearing. "Good work, Constable. Give Nanaimo a call, this arrest is all theirs."

CHAPTER TWENTY-TWO

Jim pulled into the strip mall parking lot.

"What happened to you?" he asked, as Andi climbed into the passenger seat.

"Had a bit of a clash with a squatter," Andi answered and told him what had happened.

Jim whistled. "Wonder if he saw anything."

"That's what I thought," Andi said. "Something else Charlie Rollins missed. The man looked like a junkie. Maybe Ricky was selling more than weed. Maybe this is all to do with a drug gang killing." She sounded dispirited.

Jim snorted with laughter. "Don't sound so disappointed, girl. If you'd run into that junkie a day ago, I'd have said yes — sounds like Ricky pissed off some local drug lord, straightforward as that. But today, I heard an interesting story about Hell's Half Acre. And now, we're going to have a visit with someone who can verify some details. Leave your car here. We can talk on the way."

"OK, boss."

* * *

"Hello there, Jim. And you're Andi Silvers," a slim blonde woman said, before Andi could introduce herself. "I'm Terri South. Come in and sit down while I make us some coffee."

Andi and Jim followed Terri into the kitchen and looked around. The interior of the house was not what Andi had expected. It was a complete contrast to the exterior, with its old wheelless cars propped up on blocks and rusty junk piled up around the workshop.

"Doug South is a mechanic," Jim had explained as they drove up to the house. "He's lived here his whole life. Ann South, his mother, was a schoolteacher. They both knew Art Whilley when he was a child. Art Whilley's house, which is now owned by the Daggs, is less than half a click from here. And if Clara is telling the truth, Doug will be able to connect Art Whilley and Hell's Half Acre with Dennis Havers. You see, Andi," Jim was serious, "I don't think it was a gang killing. I believe Ricky's body was put in the chapel on purpose. I don't have all the answers, but I think Doug can fill in some gaps."

Doug South was not in the house. "He's off getting some parts," Terri explained. "He'll be back soon."

Jim explained why they were there. Terri's face clouded. "My poor Katie," she said. "What a shock. And terrible for the Havers."

Andi couldn't imagine Doug South sitting in this room, not with oily hands and stained work overalls. The kitchen was ultra-modern, with glossy dark granite tops and brushed chrome handles. It was spotless. The dining area opened up into a conservatory, with floor-to-ceiling glass windows. Tasteful wicker furniture was arranged to take advantage of the view. Although they were a few kilometres from the town, Andi could still see a peek-a-boo view of the ocean through the trees.

The conservatory was decorated with unusual carvings, which Andi suspected came from Africa. They looked authentic too, not a knock-off from a cheap art shop in a Nanaimo mall.

All around the room were touches of colour — yellow throw cushions and a patterned rug. It was like a room from a magazine, Andi thought.

Terri South guessed the gist of Andi's thoughts.

"Not what you expected from a redneck homestead like ours, eh?" She smiled.

"It's beautiful," Andi said. "I feel like I walked into a brochure."

Terri South looked pleased. "I love decorating. Doug tolerates it, but he thinks throw cushions are actually for throwing." She threw back her head and laughed at her own joke.

Andi immediately liked her. Terri had a pixie face and a twinkle in her eye.

Terri made coffee for the three of them and handed out little coasters for the coffee cups as they got seated in the conservatory.

"Have you and Doug always lived here?" Andi asked, knowing the answer, but wanting to start the conversation.

"Yes," Terri said, "this house belonged to Doug's mother. We lived with her when we first got married. She was ill, and Doug didn't want to leave her on her own — his dad died when he was young, so we moved right in after our wedding day. Doug was so good with her." She sighed. "He was heartbroken when she died. We always talked about moving, but Doug loves the workshop for his cars and the business. I knocked a few walls down and redecorated, and neither of us could see much point in leaving."

"Were you born in Coffin Cove?" Andi asked.

"We're both Coffin Cove born and bred," Terri said proudly. "You saw the gravel pit, right?"

Andi nodded.

"Doug and I met right there!"

"At the gravel pit?" Andi was confused.

"Back in the day, it was the place where we all hung out. We drank beer, smoked a bit of weed," Terri winked at Andi. "But I wasn't there for the booze or drugs. I was there for the racing. Right behind the pit is the Quarter Mile. Doug and I fell in love when we were racing."

"Racing? You mean cars?" Andi asked, still confused.

"Yep. Muscle cars, old beaters, trucks, bikes — you name it, we raced it. God, it was so much fun. I miss those days." Terri's eyes shone as she reminisced.

Andi looked at her, trying to imagine this petite, smartly dressed woman revving up a muscle car and tearing down a track in a cloud of dust.

"What? I don't look like a racer to you?" Terri laughed, seeing Andi's expression. "Anyhow, you haven't come to chat about the old days with me, have you?"

Jim shook his head.

"We're investigating the death of Ricky Havers. We think the community deserves answers," he said simply. "Answers we didn't get from the police. And we think the chapel where Ricky was found is significant."

Terri set down her coffee. "I didn't even know it was there until . . . well, until they found the remains. But Katie Dagg, my neighbour, found him. She was doing some research for her new job at the museum. She must have been terrified, poor kid. I used to babysit her when she was little."

"You know the family well, then?" Andi asked, sitting back and letting Terri talk. She knew from experience when to just let the conversation flow.

"Not really well. Just Katie. Doug and I couldn't have any children of our own, so we loved having her to make a fuss over. Katie was a sweet kid, and she's grown up to be a lovely young woman."

Jim steered the conversation back. "Do you remember the family who lived there before the Daggs?"

Terri nodded. "I remember Art Whilley. He was living alone at the old cabin when I married Doug. He was an odd man. A loner. Doug knew him well, and Ann, my mother-in-law, helped Art when he was a child. He was a very smart boy, she used to say. But the other boys at school bullied him terribly, and Ann was sure they abused him at home.

But back then, there was very little anyone could do. Folks turned a blind eye to that sort of thing."

Jim nodded. "I know. We let people sort out their own business, didn't we? Didn't think we should interfere with families. Goodness knows how many kids suffered."

"The parents died before I moved in. Art . . . well, things were wild at that house. We called the place 'Hell's Half Acre'. The bikers who used to race at the gravel pit hung out there. The parties got out of hand. And one day, there was a fire. Doug rushed over, but he couldn't save Art. The poor man died in the fire. Doug was cut up about it. I think he was Art's only friend growing up." Terri stopped and stood up. "I have some old photographs. I found them after Doug's mum died. Let me get them, and I'll make us some more coffee."

Andi's phone buzzed. She checked her messages and saw one from Andrew Vega. She didn't read it, just tucked the phone back in her pocket.

Terri came back with three more cups of coffee and an envelope.

"Ann, my mother-in-law, she never threw anything away. She was a schoolteacher in Coffin Cove and had hundreds of pictures of the children she taught. We had mountains of paperwork to go through when she died, but I never could bring myself to throw away photographs, especially if Doug was in them."

She pulled out some crumpled photos and handed them to Andi. "See, that's Doug there, and beside him, that's Art Whilley." The photographs were faded but in colour, and Andi saw a well-built blonde man standing with his arms crossed, leaning on a red car. He was grinning broadly at the camera. On one side of him was a thin, pale man, with almost white hair, looking in the photographer's direction, but not smiling, and on the other was a tall dark man with long hair. He was scowling. In the background was a younger man, laughing.

Andi peered closer at the picture.

"Is that Lee Dagg?" she asked, pointing at the scowling man.

"No, that's his older brother, Wayne," Terri said. "The blonde one, that's Art. And it's his Mustang. And that's Daniel Ellis in the background."

Andi saw Jim stiffen slightly. Probably because these were familiar names.

"I didn't know Lee had a brother," Andi said, handing back the pictures.

"Yes, Wayne owns the house. Lee and Nadine are just tenants, of sorts."

"I thought you said the Whilley family owned the house? What happened to Art?"

Terri sounded sad. "Oh, it's a tragic story. Art died in the fire, Wayne disappeared and Daniel died too."

"What?"

"OK, you have to understand that Coffin Cove back in those days was, well, lawless. There was a real drug problem, and we were overrun by bikers. Even Doug was in a gang. I put a stop to that nonsense when we got married, but some of them were involved in some nasty stuff. The cops didn't take much notice of the town, we didn't have a detachment back then, and they were an hour away. So we were basically left to fend for ourselves."

"Art doesn't look like gang material," Andi remarked, picking up the picture again and looking closely.

"Art was different. I mean really different. I told you Ann thought he was abused when he was little? His mother, Barb, was a monstrous woman, apparently. Ann couldn't abide her, and my mother-in-law rarely had a bad word to say about anyone. She said Barb never fed Art properly, so Ann would call him in to eat with Doug. That's how they became friends."

"What are you all talking about?"

Andi looked up and saw a man, with his arms folded, much like the photograph, stood in the doorway. He was older, with faded tattoos on his forearms. And unlike the photograph, he wasn't smiling.

He nodded at Jim. "You be careful what you say," he told Terri, "she's a reporter."

Andi inwardly groaned. *That damn article again.*

Doug sat down. Andi could see he was careful, making sure he dusted off his pants before sitting.

"What have you got there? Old photographs?" he asked.

"I was just telling Andi about Art Whilley," Terri said.

"Oh yes? What do you want to know about him? He's been dead for years."

Andi and Jim exchanged a glance. Doug sounded defensive.

Terri said, "I was just telling them what a dreadful childhood he had. And how you and Ann helped him."

Doug grunted. "His mother was a bitch. Art was neglected. He was dirty, and he didn't get enough food. My mum would have him in for dinner, but we could hear Barbara screaming at him after." He shuddered. "She was hideous. She never washed. She had this long greasy hair and she stank. She was enormous too. I remember one time, it was in the summer, she was sitting on the porch of their shitty cabin, and she wanted to go to the bathroom, but she couldn't get up. So she screamed for Art to help her. But instead of going in the cabin, he helped her down the steps, and she just lifted her dirty old dress and just peed. Right there!" He shook his head. "Best thing that ever happened to him when she died. Massive heart attack. Never woke up."

"What about Art's father?"

"Fred Whilley? Fucking spineless, that's what he was. Letting that bitch treat his son like that? It wasn't right."

Terri frowned at Doug.

"Sorry about the language, but who mistreats a kid like that? Anyway, he died shortly after his wife. Art was about sixteen or seventeen, I think. We were close friends for a bit — my dad passed away when I was young, so we had something in common. And Mum made sure he had food. He lived there for years on his own."

"He stayed in the house after his parents died?" Jim asked.

"Yep. Nowhere else to go. And no other relatives. I think he was happy on his own," Doug said. "Nobody worried much about that. He was nearly an adult, so . . ." He shrugged. "Art and I kinda drifted apart when he started hanging around with the Daggs."

"You didn't get on with the Daggs?" Andi asked. She was intrigued by this story. Terri had fetched a plate of cookies and was busy brushing up crumbs as Doug munched on them. His hostility seemed to have faded.

"Oh, I like Lee. He's OK. Wayne, not so much. He was in a biker gang."

"You were too," Terri interjected.

"For the love of God, woman, it wasn't a gang, we just rode together," said Doug, exasperated.

Andi laughed. She was starting to like this couple.

"As I was saying, Wayne was in a biker gang — high up in the ranks —and they were into selling drugs. Everyone was into drugs back then. Everyone smoked weed and some took those magic mushrooms."

Doug paused. "I didn't mind the odd puff, but I preferred a beer. Mind you, Coffin Cove, in those days, was full of hard drinkers. The pub back then, the Timberman's, you remember, Jim? It wasn't like it is now. No lounge or food or anything. Just about every week there was a fight. Either loggers against fishermen or bikers against everyone. There was a lot of booze and a lot of drugs, and everyone had a lot of money. Fishing was booming and so was forestry. You know, fishermen would come in and offload their catch and have rolls of notes on a Friday, and by Monday they'd be broke. But they didn't care, they'd just go out and do it all again. It was nuts. And you know, there were always enough assholes around to take money off the idiots. And Wayne Dagg was one of 'em."

He shook his head in disgust. "He didn't deal in weed. Wasn't enough money in it for him. He preferred the hard stuff. They — him and Art — were dealing this new kind of drug. I guess you'd call it a 'designer drug' now. They sold tiny crystals stuck on little strips of cardboard. Some kind of acid — you know, the stuff that makes kids think they can fly and they jump out of windows?"

"You mean LSD?" Andi guessed.

"Something like that. Except it was supposed to be really pure. Give better trips and all that." Doug snorted. "Everyone was raving about it. And Art was right in the middle of it. He was smart. He was always reading, and Mum used to give him books on chemistry and all kinds of stuff. He was always working on something in that old workshop at the back of Dagg's place."

"You think he was making the drugs?" Andi asked.

"I don't know for sure. He was definitely growing mushrooms for a while. All I know is Wayne Dagg and the bikers were at that place all the time."

Doug shook his head and rubbed his face with his large hand.

"I'm sure glad those days are over," he said. "My poor old mum used to say that place was hell on earth for Art when he was a kid. But when the bikers were there, we called it Hell's Half Acre."

"Can't have been pleasant living next door to Hell," Andi commented.

"No, it wasn't. Mum slept with a loaded shotgun next to her bed. And there were some nights we didn't sleep at all." Doug turned to Terri. "My lovely wife here didn't know what she was in for when she moved in, did you, dear?"

Terri gave a short laugh. "Wasn't any worse than where I was living. My dad was one of those drunk loggers. Coffin Cove wasn't a place for women back then. It was like the Wild West. Some women got tired of the Saturday night beatings and moved to Hope Island just across the bay. It was safer there — until the men got it into their heads to take a boat over and get their women back."

"Holy shit!" Andi was amazed. "What happened?"

"All those women knew how to use a gun. There were several black eyes and a few women got quite a beating and, well, there were stories of worse — but the men backed off when one of them started firing. It was one of those rare occasions when the cops showed up. Not that they did anything.

The cops were afraid of the bikers, mostly, and left them alone. But the women made a complaint, and I guess it forced the cops to follow it up. In the end they tried to charge one woman with disturbing the peace, but when she turned up in court with two black eyes, the judge dismissed the case."

Andi was so engrossed in Doug's stories, she'd forgotten to take notes. She leaned forward and pulled her notebook from her purse.

Doug put his hand over hers.

"I don't mind telling you these stories, but don't you go putting our names on anything, now. I wouldn't be happy about that."

His tone was friendly enough, but his face was hard.

Jim said, "We're not here to dredge up old stuff, Doug. And nobody's name will be mentioned. We're just trying to find out why Ricky Havers disappeared and why and how his remains turned up at that old chapel site."

Doug released Andi's hand.

"Can't see what it has to do with Art Whilley," he said. "He's dead now, and Wayne Dagg disappeared. He's probably dead now too. It's been peaceful here since Lee moved in. And I'd like to keep it that way."

"So do you think it's just coincidence that Ricky's body was found on Dagg's land?" Andi asked, opening her notebook with her pen poised, despite Doug's narrowed eyes.

Doug shrugged. "No idea. Why don't you ask Dennis?"

"Did Dennis Havers know Art Whilley?" Jim asked. Andi guessed he was thinking about the company documents Sandra had given her.

Doug's face lost any trace of friendliness. "Dennis hung around with Wayne Dagg," he said curtly.

Andi was scribbling. "Was Dennis a biker?" she asked.

Doug laughed. "Dennis? No. He was just a bully. He kept all the dirty work at arm's length. He and Wayne made sure they controlled Art. They even got rid of his only girlfriend."

"Who was that?" Andi asked.

"Nadine Dagg. Well, Nadine Turner as she was then."
Jim and Andi stared at him.

"To start with, she was Lee's girl—" Doug began.

"But she wasn't . . . let's say, the loyal type," Terri interrupted.

Doug nodded. "Back then she was a real looker. She was officially Lee's girlfriend, but she was a real flirt."

"Hmm." Terri glared at Doug.

Doug shifted in his chair. "I only ever had eyes for you."

"Right."

"Ok, so what happened?" Andi said hastily, sensing the chilliness.

"You've gotta know what Nadine's like. Even when she was young, she had her eyes on the prize. She liked money."

"Still does," agreed Terri.

"And she didn't care what she did to get it. Lee was an apprentice with his dad and was making a decent living. But Wayne and Art were in a different league. So Nadine starts hanging out with Art, and they hook up. Wayne warns him off because he's looking out for his little brother. Eventually Nadine went back to Lee. I think it was all too wild, even for her. It was the beginning of the end of Art and Wayne's . . . association. The fire was shortly after that."

"Can you tell us about the fire?" Jim asked.

Doug sighed. "It was bad. We were used to fireworks going off at all hours, but we heard an explosion and our house shook. It felt like a propane tank went up. Anyway, I rushed outside, and there's Art's cabin on fire. There were bikers all over the place, trying to get out. I . . ." His voice faltered. "I saw Art inside. It was so hot, though. There was no way I could get to him. It burned all night long and the next morning there was nothing but a pile of ash."

"No fire trucks?" Andi asked.

"No. Back then we were out of the fire protection zone. No fire trucks and no police."

The room was silent. It wasn't a pleasant story.

Andi frowned and sucked the end of her pen.

"So how did Wayne come to own the house? Or the land, I suppose?"

"Nobody knows," Doug said, and he stood up and stretched. "Wayne must have persuaded Art to sign it over, or maybe he bought it, I dunno. But the title was registered in Wayne's name. All I know is he wasn't around the night of the fire and nobody's seen him since. Lee never mentions him, and I don't ask."

Andi hesitated for a minute and looked at Jim, wondering how much she could push this. "You know, I do have a couple of questions."

"Alright, then." Doug stared at her.

"Did Summer Thompson have anything to do with . . . well . . . any of this?"

"Summer? You bet she did," Doug answered immediately. "Summer was going with Dennis for a while, before she went out with Daniel Ellis."

Andi felt a rush of excitement. Her intuition hadn't let her down.

"She was Dennis's girlfriend?" Andi repeated, just to make sure she had heard correctly.

"For a while," Doug said. "But then she started going out with Daniel Ellis."

Daniel Ellis. That name kept coming up.

"And what happened to Daniel?" Andi asked.

"Dead," Doug said. "Fishing accident."

"Was he part of the biker gang?" Jim asked. "Or involved in the drugs?"

Doug shook his head. "He was to start with. But Daniel wasn't like that. And when he and Summer got together, she didn't want him to have anything to do with Dennis or drugs. Art didn't like Summer at all. Daniel was nice to him, not like Wayne, but he never saw Daniel anymore after he took up with Summer."

Jim put down his coffee cup.

"Thanks for talking to us," he said and held out his hand. Doug took it and they shook.

Andi was still making notes. She finished and went to hand the old photo of Art Whilley and Doug South back to Terri.

"You keep it," Terri said, "if it helps."

Andi smiled and put it in her purse, and then turned to Doug. "Just one more question, Doug. What did the bikers call themselves?"

"The Knights," he said.

CHAPTER TWENTY-THREE

Katie Dagg gritted her teeth, and when that didn't work, she buried her head in a pillow. She was in her room with the door closed, but she could still hear them. It was just as bad as it had been during most of her childhood, when she'd sit in her bedroom while Lee and Nadine screamed at each other.

She thought she might go downstairs. Maybe she could get them to sit down and talk civilly to each other? They didn't belong together. They didn't love each other. So why were they still in this house making each other miserable? It couldn't be for her sake.

Deep down, she knew it was all about money. Lee earned it — most of it — and Nadine spent it. It had always been that way. Nadine wanted things. If someone at work had a new truck, she wanted a new truck. If a couple went on holiday, she wanted two weeks all-inclusive somewhere. And if she didn't get it, she screamed at Lee. Nadine had been obsessed with renovating the house when she saw Terri South's elegant home and had racked up Lee's credit card to the limit.

As far as Katie could make out, this particular argument was about a dress. A belly dancing outfit, to be exact. She didn't know how much it had cost, but the price tag had sent her normally reserved father completely over the edge.

"For fuck's sake, Nadine," she heard him bellow, "thousands of dollars on a dress that makes you look like a common hooker! Where's your self-respect? Or did you leave it in Dennis Havers' bed?"

Katie couldn't make out her mother's reply, she just heard doors slamming. She'd heard enough, anyway. She knew about her mother's affair. Everyone knew. Nadine didn't even try to hide it.

Katie stayed where she was. Her parents' relationship had deteriorated past the point where a nice civil chat mediated by their daughter would do any good at all. Especially as Nadine really seemed to dislike Katie.

Katie sat up on her bed and looked around her bedroom. It hadn't changed since she was last living here. She had a single bed with a patchwork quilt, a large chest of drawers and a vanity unit with a large oval mirror. None of the furniture was new when she got it. Even when she was a child, she liked old stuff. She and Lee had found everything in old antique stores and they'd both worked on restoring the furniture together. They'd had so much fun. She didn't remember her mother being involved at all.

Katie looked at the old photos she'd taped to the edges of her mirror. There were pictures of her and her friends from school, poking out their tongues and pulling faces at the camera, and all the photos her dad took of her at her graduation, her first car, every significant event in her life, but none of her and Nadine. Not one. There was one picture of her mother, a recent one, posing for the camera in her belly dancing outfit.

Katie winced. She was ashamed of her embarrassment. Maybe that was why Nadine was so hostile? She'd picked up on Katie's disapproval. Maybe she thought Katie and Lee were ganging up on her? Maybe she should show some support for her mother and go to the belly dancing display at the pub?

But she didn't want to. It had been an awful few days. She'd had trouble sleeping. Every time she closed her eyes, she saw that skull hanging in front of her. She shuddered. She wished she could turn back the clock and not go on that hike at all. There was only one positive thing about it all. A kind young constable said to her, when he came to take her statement, "I know it was awful for you, but now Mr and Mrs Havers will at least be able to grieve for their son. It is an end to it, even if we wished it could have ended another way."

Katie was trying to hang on to that.

She heard a car door slam and then another. Her father's car left the driveway and Katie sighed with relief. Her warring parents must have called a truce. It looked as if Lee was taking Nadine to the Fat Chicken.

The house was finally quiet. Katie pulled herself together and grabbed some laundry off her floor. She wandered into her parents' bedroom and picked up their laundry basket. If she did some housework it would help, and maybe keep the peace for a while.

In the laundry room, Katie sorted out clothes. She dug her hands in her jeans pocket, and her fingers closed around a piece of stiff paper. She pulled it out.

Damn. Another reminder. It was the business card that man had given her. The one who'd suggested she research that silly story. The man who started it all.

* * *

Andi was exhausted. She felt overloaded with information. Jim had dropped her off at the mall to pick her car up. Neither of them had said much since leaving Doug and Terri's home. Jim leaned over as Andi got out the passenger seat.

"Andi, I'm not sure where all this information leaves us. I need to think it over. I'm not certain Doug South told us everything. Let's talk about this tomorrow at the office. I have an idea, but I don't know. You'll think it's crazy. But for now, you concentrate on the belly dancing tonight." He'd grinned at her.

Shit. The bloody belly dancing. She'd forgotten.

But here she was, sitting at the bar, waiting for the festivities to begin.

Harry sat on a stool opposite her. He raised a beer glass. "Our intrepid reporter," he said — a touch sarcastically, Andi thought. She moved around the bar to sit next to him.

"Not you as well," she grumbled. "Everyone in this bloody place complains about Charlie Rollins all the time, but when I write an article, people act as if I've betrayed the town."

Harry nodded. "I know. Life's so unfair."

Andi rolled her eyes. "Seriously?"

Harry put his pint glass down. "Seriously, I agree Charlie's only one notch above useless, but he needs his pension, Andi. His wife is sick, and they're struggling."

Andi looked at him, her heart sinking. "Shit. I didn't know."

Harry shrugged. "Doesn't mean he shouldn't do his job properly. Forget it, Andi. The article is out there now. But the good news? If you write a scintillating piece about Nadine's belly dancing, everyone will forget." He grinned at her. "C'mon. Cheer up."

Andi managed a smile. Then she saw Hephzibah waving at her.

"I'm going to sit with your sister. Coming?"

"Nope. I'll get a better view here." Harry winked at her.

Nadine and her two fellow dancers shimmied and sashayed more or less in time with the music blaring from an old stereo system. The audience whooped and cheered, and the dancers shook and jingled their tassels for an encore.

"Good lord," Hephzibah said, "that's quite the outfit Nadine's wearing. Or nearly wearing. I wonder what the mayor thinks of her half-dressed assistant?"

Andi looked around the pub. "Doesn't look like she's here. You'd think she would make the effort for the first event of the Heritage Festival."

"Maybe it's for the best," Hephzibah said, as Nadine bent over an unsuspecting elderly man and jiggled her breasts, to the loud approval of the men in the crowd.

Andi felt a pang of sympathy for Nadine. She remembered how hard her mother had tried to get Andi's father to pay attention to her, in the end even starting arguments. Now Andi knew more about Nadine's past, the women seemed less of an evil adulteress and more like a woman trapped in an unhappy marriage, trying to capture some happiness. Why was it all so bloody complicated?

Andi remembered the message Andrew Vega had left. He wasn't angry, he just sounded tired and disappointed. *Why didn't you call me before printing that article, Andi? I thought we had a better understanding than that. Call me when you get the chance.*

"Hey, look over there." Hephzibah nudged Andi. "It's the mysterious handsome stranger."

"Who?" Andi looked where Hephzibah was pointing and saw a tall slim man wearing an expensive-looking jacket and looking bemused at Nadine's performance.

"He's a developer," Hephzibah said. "Walter's sure he knows him. He's deciding whether or not to develop the fish plant."

"Wonder whether Nadine's helping to seal the deal," Andi murmured. "He can't keep his eyes off her."

Hephzibah laughed. "Another drink?" she said, pointing at Andi's empty wine glass.

"God, yes. They've not finished yet."

Half an hour later, Nadine and her dance team ended their performance. Walter looked pleased as the bar emptied out slowly. Cheryl was cleaning down tables and chatting with the remaining customers.

Andi looked around for Harry and saw him leaving. She waved and he raised a hand in response. Hephzibah left too, and Andi promised to see her for coffee in the morning.

Andi just wanted her bed now. She saw Nadine sitting on a stool at the bar and hoped she had a ride, because she knew she'd drunk far too much to offer to drive her home. But Nadine's head was down and she seemed intent on texting someone, so Andi let it go.

At least the evening took everyone's mind off Ricky Havers, Andi thought, as she left the bar and walked around to the steps up to her apartment. Except Sandra and Dennis, of course.

Andi spent a few minutes on her laptop, making some notes about the belly dancing. Before she went to bed, she pulled out the photograph Terri South had given her.

Andi shook her head. Would any of this help her keep her promise to Sandra? She hoped so.

CHAPTER TWENTY-FOUR

Dennis Havers closed the bedroom door as quietly as possible. Sandra was finally sleeping. After Inspector Vega had brought Ricky's belt buckle and other items for them to identify, she'd held it together remarkably well. He, on the other hand, had been shocked enough to feel light-headed. But when the police officers left, Sandra was first inconsolable and then hysterical. When Sandra read the article in the *Gazette*, Dennis had been worried enough about her state of mind to call their doctor. He'd administered a sedative, and eventually, Sandra allowed herself to be taken to her bedroom, where Dennis undressed her and covered her thin shoulders with the duvet.

He'd sat with her, gazing at her frail arms and hands that clutched at the pillow, even as she slept. She hadn't been out of the bedroom since.

Before Ricky disappeared, Sandra Havers was an immaculate woman. She loved being the mayor's wife, and whatever other problems the Haverses had in their marriage, she'd never let Dennis down when it came to her public role.

She was good-looking too, Dennis thought. She'd kept her figure with hours and hours of yoga and maintained an expensive grooming regime, including weekly visits to the spa and salon in Nanaimo.

Dennis had bitched about it at the time, but over the last months, he'd seen Sandra disintegrate. She wore only jogging pants and sweatshirts. She rarely put on any make-up, and she only had her hair done when Dennis arranged for a lady to come to the house.

The first days after her son vanished, Sandra had been confident they'd find him. They were an influential couple. Dennis was mayor, he was a powerful businessman. They'd put out feelers, call in favours and find their precious boy. She made phone calls, drew up lists of places to search and cajoled members of the multiple committees she served on to spend hours putting up posters and knocking on doors.

It was her main — no, her only — topic of conversation. Where might her son have gone? Maybe he'd fallen, hit his head and lost his memory? Maybe he'd had a girlfriend who broke his heart, and he'd run away? Maybe he'd been abducted?

At first Dennis had indulged her. He'd even attempted to help her. But all along he'd fully expected Ricky to come back, his tail between his legs.

Dennis looked at the closed door and knew it was only a matter of time before she found out. Tomorrow, he'd have to answer Inspector Vega's questions.

He went downstairs and sat in his study. He looked around. Everything in this room was carefully chosen to reflect his status. Each leather-bound volume in the bookcase, covering one whole wall, was a book he imagined a powerful man would read. He'd never even opened one. The chair he sat in had been ordered from Eastern Canada and upholstered in the softest blood-red leather. The desk was handmade from first-growth fir, with yew inlay and just enough gold leaf to exude class. Dennis loved this room.

He especially loved gazing out the picture window. He could see the entire town. His 180-degree view took in the pulp mill at one end of the bay and the craggy cliffs at the other. He could look down on the roofs of his constituents when he was mayor and imagine them to be his subjects.

Sometimes, he stood smoking a cigar and counted each property and business he either owned or leased, calculating in his mind his net worth.

Now, he looked out at the ocean, still blue in the late afternoon sun, and wondered why he'd never gone fishing like other men in Coffin Cove. Daniel, his very best friend, had been a fisherman. He'd loved being on the water.

"There's nothing like it, Den. Being out on deck as the sun comes up, that time in the morning when the sea is calm. It's the most beautiful thing in the universe," Daniel had told him, with wonder in his voice.

Daniel had been like that. Unworldly. He loved the ocean. And he loved Summer Thompson.

Oh, why was he thinking about Daniel now? He'd pushed that memory out of his mind. Yet when he saw Jade for the first time, smiling and handing out campaign leaflets, he could hardly breathe. It was as though Daniel had risen from his watery grave and come back to mock him. At that moment, Dennis lost the will to fight the election. Oh sure, he'd gone through the motions, but when the results were announced, he didn't care. He was done with Coffin Cove. Or maybe it was the other way around.

Since Ricky had gone, his entire life had fallen apart.

He bent down and pulled out the bottom drawer. He found a bottle of bourbon, a cheap one. He kept it hidden, offering important visitors the limited edition single malt from the crystal decanter. Dennis looked at the bottle of Jack Daniel's, unscrewed the lid and took a gulp, straight from the bottle. Why the fuck had he done that? Pretended he liked the expensive booze, when really, he preferred cold beer and cheap liquor?

Everything in his life was a pretence. Especially over the last months.

Dennis reached into his desk drawer again and pulled out a manila envelope. He opened it and pulled out the single sheet of paper. It was the results of a DNA test he'd had done a year or so back. It proved Ricky wasn't his son. He'd always had an inkling. Ricky and Sandra were always close. Ricky irritated him. The boy was arrogant and self-centred. More than once, Dennis had to placate an angry father after Ricky had molested his teenage daughter.

"Just teenagers experimenting," Dennis would say, as he pressed an envelope of hundred-dollar bills into the man's hand, intimating his lawyer would drag the poor girl's name through the mud if the matter was taken any further. It usually did the trick.

Doris, Dennis's mother — a vinegary, mean woman, who'd always hated Sandra — first told Dennis she was convinced Ricky wasn't his biological son. The information gnawed away at him until he confirmed it once and for all.

He wasn't prepared for the rage he felt when he saw the results. The fury and humiliation were all-consuming. How dare Sandra deceive him? How dare she spend his money and spoil that lazy piece of shit who never worked a day in his life?

So Dennis laid his plans.

He set Ricky up with a business he knew the pothead would jump at. His very own weed store? It was like all Ricky's dreams come true at once. For all of Ricky's adult life, he'd only showed interest in two things: screwing and weed. And Dennis figured he would kill two birds with one stone. He wanted to buy the trailer park behind the strip mall, but the price was too high. A few months of the Smoke Room and Ricky's pothead friends partying day and night, and most of the decent tenants would leave. With substantially decreased revenue coming into the park, Dennis was sure he'd get a great deal. And Ricky? Dennis was certain of one thing: Ricky was stupid enough to think he could make some cash on the side with illegal drugs, probably hooking up with that scumbag Kevin.

Dennis was right. He had ears everywhere and knew Ricky was trying to muscle in on another patch. Dennis made a few phone calls, and it was all set up: two thugs for hire would snatch Ricky, smack him around a bit and teach him a lesson. When they dumped him back, Dennis would confront Sandra and Ricky with the DNA results.

Of course Ricky wasn't his flesh and blood! There was no way he, Dennis Havers, would father such a pathetic loser. Then he'd send them both packing.

They'd have to manage without their lavish lifestyle and access to Dennis's bank account.

At first, he'd thought the plan had worked. One day, Ricky disappeared. Even Sandra wasn't unduly worried. Then she started making phone calls to his friends and driving up to the Smoke Room to check every couple of hours. Dennis took no notice, expecting Ricky to be dumped on the doorstep any day soon. But another week went past, and then another. Then Dennis made some calls. But his thugs swore they hadn't touched Ricky. Couldn't find him, they said. He was already gone.

Dennis made more calls, but the answer came back the same. Nobody had seen Ricky. The word was he'd started doing business with a new organization, but nobody knew who they were, not even Kevin.

As Sandra intensified her search and involved the police, Dennis became paranoid. Had Ricky found out about Dennis's plan? Had he taken a once-in-a-lifetime business deal and just left? Dennis knew he wouldn't let Sandra suffer. Ricky loved his mother. There was no doubt in Dennis's mind. So he must have been taken against his will. Who took him? Why?

The rumours spread through Coffin Cove. Dennis heard the gossip — it was payback, some said, for all the shady deals Dennis had done over the years. That reporter, Andi Silvers, suspected him, he knew. She'd even asked him outright during the election campaign.

"Did you have anything to do with the disappearance of your son, Mayor Havers?" she'd asked in the middle of an interview, with all his staffers present. Dennis had just stared at her, too stunned to reply. Eventually the awkward silence became too much, and Andi was asked to leave, but Dennis saw the triumphant smirk on her face.

He took another swig of Jack Daniel's. The study was in shadow now. The sun had slid down behind the house, and Dennis could see the lights from Coffin Cove, turning his old empire into a fairyland.

He got up from his desk and staggered slightly as he removed a picture from the wall, revealing his safe. He made himself concentrate as he turned the dial. The steel door clicked and opened smoothly.

Steadying himself, Dennis emptied the contents of the safe on his desk. Without bothering to close it up or replace the picture, he sat back down again. He picked up a clean sheet of headed notepaper and started to write. When he was finished, he reached over to a roll of cash he'd just taken out of the safe and peeled off several bills. He stuffed them in the envelope, sealed it and wrote "Joanna Campbell" on the front. The housekeeper. She deserved it. He knew she'd find it tomorrow. He sat back in his chair and let his thoughts flow as his intoxication increased.

He thought again of that day with the reporter. When Andi Silvers left, his staff fussed over him, promising to make Jim Peters fire her immediately. But Sandra had surprised him most. She had flung her arms around him.

"You mustn't feel guilty," she sobbed. "It's not your fault! You've been the best dad and husband. Ricky loves you, wherever he is, and I'll always love you."

He'd rubbed her back and soothed her.

He'd been a shit of a husband. He'd been screwing Nadine the whole time they were married. Nadine. She'd been his mistress, his dirty, vulgar secret, for years.

They'd flaunted their affair. Dennis quite liked the rumours. Didn't all powerful men behave like this? Taking what they wanted, not caring what anyone thought, not even his wife?

God, what had he been thinking? Nadine rubbing up against him in the office or at official city functions.

Sometimes in front of Sandra. She'd behaved with dignity, never commenting, never causing a scene. Nadine, on the other hand, made no secret of her goal: to be the second Mrs Havers. Some nights, she'd phone, drunkenly screaming down the phone at him, threatening to destroy his marriage. Nadine even texted him the day after Inspector Vega confirmed Ricky's death. She'd invited him to go to her belly dancing night, for fuck's sake.

It was all over now. Nadine's last call was from the office. She'd been snooping around for him, keeping him updated on the new mayor's activities. She'd told him about a developer sniffing around the old fish plant. Dennis had wanted to get his hands on that, but he didn't care now. No, it was the name of the developer that made his heart skip a beat: Knights Development Ltd. Was it just coincidence?

Nadine had tried one last time.

"You know I always look out for you, Dennis. We're a good team. We go way back, don't we? We've known each other for ever, from the old days at the gravel pit and those crazy times . . ."

Crazy times indeed. Dennis tried not to think of them, but in his mind he saw the old gang hanging out.

"Hell's Half Acre. Now there's a place," Dennis grunted to himself, half laughing. He knew he was drunk, but picked up the bottle anyway. It was nearly empty. His vision was blurred, and he had a hard time sitting up straight, but he swallowed the rest of the bourbon in one go.

He thought he saw a man in the doorway. It looked like Daniel. He squinted, trying to focus. It couldn't be Daniel. Maybe it was Ricky, come back to haunt him from the dead. His eyes cleared for a moment. He saw who it was.

Dennis fumbled over his desk. Where was it? He'd taken it out of the safe — where did he put it?

"Is this what you're looking for, Dennis?" The voice came from beside him.

Horrified, Dennis swung his head to the side and saw the figure half crouched beside him.

"No . . . Sandra . . ." Dennis said, but the last thing he saw was a blinding flash.

* * *

Sandra Havers woke. She was very groggy. She didn't know what had woken her, but then she heard the click of the bedroom door opening.

"Ricky?" she said sleepily, then she remembered. Not Ricky. It wouldn't ever be Ricky.

"Shh . . . Sandra," a voice said. "Go back to sleep. You'll see Ricky soon."

Sandra curled herself under the duvet. Maybe if she slept, it would all be different tomorrow. Maybe she would see Ricky. With a sigh, she closed her eyes.

Sandra didn't see the light or hear the crack.

The bedroom door closed gently as a blood-red stain spread across the duvet.

CHAPTER TWENTY-FIVE

The morning sun woke Andi early.

It was only five o'clock. Hephzibah wouldn't be brewing her first pot of coffee for another hour, but Andi wanted an early start today. After yesterday's scuffle with that weird junkie at the strip mall, the meeting with the Souths and, to top it all, the belly dancing display, Andi needed to get her head straight.

She twisted out of bed, rolled her shoulders and pulled back the curtain, her eyes drifting to the alley below. Rats competed with gulls for scraps of greasy food that fell around the dumpster. It didn't matter how careful Walter was with the garbage or how many traps he put out, the rats kept coming. Once a year (apparently that was all he could afford), Walter called in pest control, but as the weather warmed up, the rats multiplied, and their population seemed impervious to any eradication method he tried.

This morning, as dawn illuminated the rats' activity, they seemed reluctant to scuttle back to their hiding places. The gulls landed in the dumpster too, and in the alley, pecking at the contents. Andi shuddered, closed the curtain and opened her laptop.

Might as well get an article drafted about last night. Jim would be impressed if she turned up with a thousand words and might even cut her a cheque. As much as Andi sensed there was a lot to investigate around Ricky's murder, she still had to pay her rent.

An hour later, she was pleased with her first draft. Reflecting on what she'd written about Charlie, and Harry's words last night, she was careful to be respectful of Nadine and the other belly dancers. If nothing else, they'd thrilled Walter. Andi suspected it was the best night they'd had at the Fat Chicken for a long time.

She stretched and checked the time and then took a quick shower. When she was dressed, she snapped shut her laptop and grabbed her phone. She noticed a text message from Andrew Vega and a voicemail. Both of them said the same. "*Phone me please, Andi. We need to talk.*" She groaned. Later. Coffee first. Then she'd face the music.

Going down the wooden stairs to the alleyway, she didn't notice at first that the gulls didn't lift into the air at her approach. She did notice the quick movements of the rats scattering and a piece of tinsel, she thought, waving gently in the morning breeze.

At the bottom of the steps, she could see that it wasn't tinsel at all. It was a piece of glittery material that had come adrift from a lifeless body.

As Andi stared into Nadine's open, unseeing eyes, she could hear a strange sound. It took a few moments for her brain to process it was the sound of her own screaming.

* * *

PC Matt Beaufort kissed his wife and left their new townhouse, turning once to wave before getting into his car for the forty-five minute drive to Coffin Cove. It was a bit of an inconvenience to live outside the town, and it was stretching the RCMP regulations to the limit, but Lily's heart had been set on the tiny two-up two-down, with the new kitchen cabinets and the balcony overlooking the park. They could afford it, with a bit of help from Matt's in-laws, his salary and Lily's part-time wages from the pharmacy, which was also within walking distance.

Life was good, Matt thought. He wasn't supposed to work today, but Charlie had called him the night before and asked Matt to cover. He didn't give an explanation, but Matt guessed he was feeling very low about the article in the *Gazette*. Matt didn't blame him. Charlie was lazy. But he wasn't a bad man.

On the positive side, Matt was feeling pleased with himself. Although he'd been the one to inadvertently give confidential information to the reporter, he'd redeemed himself yesterday with the arrest of that junkie. He hoped it would lead to some solid information Nanaimo detachment could use. They needed a break. The drug problem was getting worse, with another overdose just the other day.

He'd earned a pat on the back from Inspector Vega and approving nods from Sergeant Fowler.

The last day off he'd had, he and Lily visited his in-laws, Anthony and Doreen Dupre. Another advantage of this posting was the proximity to Lily's parents. His own family — what was left of it — was far away in Toronto. A car accident when he was only a baby had left him and his brother alone in the world apart from an aunt. She'd passed away just before he finished his RCMP training and his relationship with his brother had long since dwindled to a phone call at Christmas. But Lily and her parents had surprised him by turning up for his graduation and excitedly taking pictures of him in his ceremonial serge.

He'd felt part of a family at last.

Lily's father Anthony listened gravely as Matt described his job and his daily tasks. He hoped, he said, for something more exciting than just the petty thefts he was dealing with at present. They often sat on the back porch of the house, while Lily and her mother chatted for hours over tea or went shopping. Matt knew he could confide in Anthony.

When Matt finished talking, the older man got up from his chair and disappeared into the house for a moment. He returned with a wooden box and handed it to his son-in-law. Matt examined it. Around the sides and on the lid were First Nations carvings, depicting different animals. Matt turned it around in his hands, admiring the artwork.

"For me?" he asked.

Anthony nodded. "Yes. It's a bento box. Keep it in the hallway. When you come in from work, empty in your wallet, your warrant card, your badge, anything to do with your identity as an RCMP officer. With those items, empty your soul of the stress and hardships you've experienced in the day. Take on your role as a husband and partner with renewed calm." Anthony paused. "It doesn't mean you can't lean on Lily for support — she's a strong woman, like her mother. But if you bring home your workday — especially the horrific things you'll see and hear in your chosen career — it will wear away at your marriage and your heart, understand?"

Matt nodded. He did. Already, he'd had a few evenings when he couldn't shake off a melancholic mood after a particularly hard day. Lily and he hadn't argued, but he could see how the stress might affect their relationship.

"And one more piece of advice, if you'd indulge an old man." Anthony smiled, but then became serious again. "Try to see all the people you serve, both the victims and the criminals, as human beings. Even those who have committed terrible acts against others have a story to tell. They are all sons and daughters and have been loved by somebody at some time in their life. Everyone deserves a little dignity. See the humanity in your daily work life. What you see as excitement will mean tragedy for someone else."

Matt pulled into the parking lot, smiling at the thought of his father-in-law.

Within minutes of entering the detachment, he was on his way out again. A dead woman had been found by the dumpsters at the Fat Chicken.

Matt was the first on scene. He found Andi Silvers trembling in shock. He gazed down at the dead body of Nadine Dagg and tried not to gag.

As Inspector Vega and the IHIT team arrived, Matt recalled his father-in-law's words. He knew now that he disagreed with Anthony Dupre about one thing. This day in his career as a police officer, he failed to find any humanity at all.

CHAPTER TWENTY-SIX

He eased along the trail. It was dark, but there was enough moonlight filtering through the tall firs to guide his way. He was light on his feet and could recall the path enough to avoid gnarled roots and deep ruts.

When he got nearer, he saw a pinprick of light and smelled a cigarette.

That's good, he thought. When he'd asked for this meeting, he'd wondered whether the man would remember how to find this place. They hadn't been here since they were children.

Once, the place was a refuge, a sanctuary. Not anymore.

He was in the clearing now.

The full moonlight threw shadows across the mounds of stones, making them appear like crouched animals waiting to pounce. A hunched figure sat on the crumbling wall of the chapel with his back to him. The tiny glow of the waiting man's cigarette moved as he inhaled and then blew out smoke.

He moved quietly, stealthily, feeling with one hand around his belt.

It wasn't until he was close enough to touch that his prey jumped and jerked his head round.

With one swipe, he pulled the blade of his hunting knife neatly across the man's throat and watched as the expression of shock on the man's face dimmed and faded, as a cloud moved across the moon and the clearing was in darkness once more.

CHAPTER TWENTY-SEVEN

Andrew Vega sat on the end of Andi's bed. He wasn't sure how to start this interview. He looked around the tiny studio apartment. It was L-shaped, and around one corner was the small kitchen and dining area. In the middle, an overstuffed chair piled high with laundry, and against the wall, a bookcase which clearly wasn't big enough to house Andi's library, as there were stacks of books all over the floor. She also had an eclectic assortment on her bedside table. Vega smiled inwardly. It was one thing he and Andi had in common. His own condo was full of diverse reading material, but his living space was neat and orderly. He disliked chaos.

Andi sat hunched miserably on her pillows, hugging her knees. Vega could hear the hum of activity outside the apartment. There was so much to do, and they were still in the early stages of the Ricky Havers investigation.

Thankfully, the coroner was already on the island, so it hadn't taken long before she'd arrived and taken charge of the crime scene and the body of poor Nadine. She'd officially deemed the death as a homicide.

"Her throat was slit," the coroner said. "Competently too. One nice clean slice. No signs of hesitation or sawing."

She made a back-and-forth gesture across her neck, which made Vega feel slightly sick.

Now, the parking lot at the back of the Fat Chicken was full of highly trained forensic search specialists collecting evidence, taking photographs and bagging and tagging every fibre, fluid sample and anything else the scene could offer. Then they would send every exhibit to the Case Receipt Unit, where every item would first be logged on a computerized system and then distributed to forensic analysts. This was painstaking work. It took time, and although Vega was always frustrated as he waited for those important results, he knew it was vital to every investigation that nobody deviated from procedure.

Cutting corners now might allow a perpetrator to go free. Vega had seen how a clever defence lawyer could call into question the integrity of an entire investigation over the slightest administrative error.

Vega ran a hand through his hair. Lee Dagg had to be informed of his wife's death. It was the worst part of Vega's job — any officer's job — and made even more difficult because Lee Dagg needed to be questioned. Why was Nadine out here alone? Where had Lee Dagg been when his wife was killed? Until those questions and many others were answered, Lee Dagg was firmly on top of the list as the perpetrator of this heinous crime.

But Andi had to be questioned first. She'd found the body. She was also in the bar all night, so probably had vital information. He needed Andi to be on her game. He hadn't expected her to be in this state of shock.

He sighed. Andi was a talented journalist. She coaxed information from people who would never talk as freely in a police interview. She was observant and intelligent, and many of her theories proved correct. But often, she worked with her intuition and gut feeling. He, on the other hand, was trained to work with evidence first. His cases were driven by facts, and he rarely allowed his mind to be clouded with theories based on nothing but "bad feelings". And he was still really pissed about her article.

This wasn't a game. Andi's work was important, but if Vega made a wrong call, it could mean life or death for some poor soul. Like Nadine Dagg.

But now Andi had seen for herself the horrors of Vega's job. He didn't wish the experience on anyone, but maybe now Andi would understand he wasn't trying to thwart her search for the truth — he was trying to save lives and seek justice for victims. It was more than a story, more than an article for people to gossip over. It was the end of a human life, and a tragic life-altering experience for those left behind. These were the people Vega served.

Now wasn't the time for a lecture, Vega knew.

Andi was in shock, and Vega needed information. So as much as he felt a disconcerting urge to scoop Andi into his arms and at the same time blast her for the article, he needed to focus.

"Andi, I know you've had a terrible shock. But right now, I need you to think back to last night. You were at the belly dancing event, correct?"

Andi nodded, and for the next few minutes, Vega established a timeline for Nadine's movements before she met her killer.

"So you left the bar at eleven?" Vega asked. "Who was left in the bar?"

"Yes. The performance was over and the other dancers had gone, I'm certain. Harry left just after. The bar was empty. Cheryl was wiping the tables, so she'd be able to tell you more. But Nadine was sat on a bar stool, and I thought she was texting for a ride or she'd got a text. She was definitely looking at her phone. And then I left and came straight here."

"OK. And did you go to bed straight away? Or go out again?"

"No. I made some tea and made a few notes on my laptop about the belly dancing for my article, and then I spent a bit of time looking at some photos I got for my story . . ." She stopped. "I'm sorry about the article," she blurted out.

"I didn't mean . . . well it didn't come out . . . I, well, Harry told me about Charlie Rollins' wife. I had no idea."

Andi looked stricken, and Vega took her hand. "Don't worry about that now," he said, thinking he didn't know about Charlie's wife either. "I need you to help me now, Andi. So let's focus on the timeline. Did you save your work on the laptop?"

"What?" Andi looked confused.

"There will be a time stamp," Vega explained.

"Oh, I know what time it was," Andi said. "It was twenty past midnight. I heard some voices outside, and I thought it was late for anyone to be leaving the pub."

"You didn't look outside?" Vega asked.

"No. Oh God, if I had I might have . . ." Andi clapped her hand to her mouth. "I could have helped or scared him off or something."

Vega shook his head. "You don't know who it was, Andi. Let's go back to earlier in the evening. Was there anyone in the bar who was taking particular notice of Nadine? Or behaving oddly?"

Andi regained her composure. "Well, everyone was taking notice of Nadine. It was quite the show." She managed an eye roll. "I didn't notice anyone in particular, but you should talk to Hephzibah. She pointed out some guy who's been hanging around the last few days. She thought he might be interested in real estate. I didn't get a look at him because I was more focused on Nadine. But I thought it was more significant who wasn't there."

"Oh?" Vega looked up from his notebook. "What do you mean?"

"Well, Lee Dagg wasn't there. I didn't see him at all." Andi hesitated. "I know this is just gossip, but it wasn't much of a secret that Nadine and Dennis Havers were having an affair. They did kind of . . . flaunt it, I suppose. Even since Ricky went missing."

"Was Dennis there?" Vega said, interested. "And did Lee see him?" He wondered if this was a case of a jealous husband tired of being humiliated. It had happened before.

"No," Andi said, "he didn't show all evening. Not really surprising, given the news of Ricky, but I saw Nadine keep checking her phone. I thought she might be waiting for him and she could have been texting Dennis when I left, I don't know."

"We can find that out," Vega said, making a note to see if the forensic search team had found Nadine's cell phone. "Who else was missing who you thought should have been there?"

Andi shrugged. "Jade Thompson. She's mayor. It's the start of her festival. She wasn't very enthusiastic about belly dancing when I interviewed her — we had a bit of a giggle about it, actually — but she's been pushing this festival and attracting tourists since she got elected, so I was surprised she didn't at least drop in." Andi added, "And I made a point of looking for her throughout the evening."

Vega nodded. He agreed with Andi. It made little sense, and he couldn't see how Jade could be connected with Nadine's death, but he had to keep an open mind.

"Anything else?" Vega asked. He intended to get Andi to give a written statement at the detachment, but he knew how vital it was to get as much information from Andi when it was fresh in her mind. Memory was a weird thing.

Andi opened her mouth to reply, but there was a loud rap on the door.

"Inspector? Andi? It's only me." Walter walked in with a mug of tea in his hand.

Vega couldn't hide his irritation.

"We really need some privacy . . ." he started to say, as Andi took the mug.

"Plenty of sugar for the shock," Walter said, ignoring Vega. "Hey, would you look at that! Now I know who that guy reminds me of."

Walter was pointing to Terri South's photos of the bikers in the gravel pit. But he wasn't pointing to a biker.

Andi got off the bed and went over to Walter. "Who do you recognize?"

"Oh, it can't be the same person. Must just look like him. This guy's been dead for years," Walter said, jabbing at the picture with his finger. "Art Whilley. Used to live in Dagg's place, years ago."

Vega cursed under his breath. "Walter, thanks for the tea."

"Oh, sorry, Inspector, did you want one?"

"No, Walter, I don't—"

Before Vega could finish, Sergeant Fowler walked in.

"Inspector, could I have a word?" she asked.

"Sergeant, can it wait? I'm in the middle . . . Walter, please could you leave us?"

"No, sir, I need to speak to you now. Right now," Diane Fowler said emphatically.

"OK." Vega could see from Diane's face it was serious.

"Walter, go back to the bar and wait for an officer to take a statement. And please don't chat with Andi here or Cheryl, it's imperative we get your own recollection of events. And Andi, same for you. We'll talk again later." He gave Andi a brief smile and then ushered Walter out of the apartment.

"What is it, Sergeant?"

"Sir, that lady over there," Diane Fowler nodded to a grey-haired, thick-set woman who was talking to a uniformed officer. She was clearly distressed, Vega could see. She had red eyes and was clutching the arm of the officer, as if she had difficulty standing up.

"I see her, what's happened?"

"Sir, she's the Haverses' housekeeper, Joanna Campbell. When she got to the house this morning, she found Dennis Havers dead in his study, blood everywhere and a gun beside him — and, sir, I'm afraid Sandra Havers is dead too. She was shot while sleeping in her bed."

"Shit," Vega said, running a hand through his hair. "Shit."

CHAPTER TWENTY-EIGHT

The Haverses' house seemed untouched. There was no sign of forced entry. The only sign anything was wrong, Joanna explained, her voice cracking with emotion, was that the French doors to the patio were wide open.

"I closed them," she said in a whisper. "And then I put coffee on. I was going upstairs to knock and ask if Mrs Havers wanted some breakfast. She hasn't been eating since . . . since Ricky, and I was trying to get her to eat some eggs. I saw the study door was open and thought Mr Havers might like coffee. I pushed it open . . . and . . . and . . ."

"It's OK," Inspector Vega said, "take your time."

Joanna's voice was a whisper as she told him how she'd seen Dennis Havers and the pool of blood. She knew he was dead, so she ran upstairs shouting for Sandra.

Then she described how she'd found Sandra Havers curled up under the covers, the blood-soaked duvet the only sign anything was wrong.

"Did you touch Mrs Havers?" Vega asked.

Joanna nodded. "I hoped she was still alive. But she wasn't." The woman broke down in tears.

Vega called for an officer to escort Joanna away, and Sergeant Fowler directed officers to tape off the entire house as a designated crime scene.

Vega stood at the door of the study, careful not to touch anything. The metallic smell of blood filled the room, with something else. Vega sniffed. Booze? An empty bottle of Jack Daniel's sat on the desk beside Dennis Havers' head, which was resting on one side, with his arm stretched across the desk.

There's the answer, Vega thought, as he took in the gory scene. Splatter and congealed pieces of brain tissue obscured the view from the large picture window, while a pool of blood was turning brown as it soaked into a rug beneath the desk.

Suicide? Vega thought. Some kind of suicide pact? Was that why Dennis Havers didn't want to see him yesterday? Because he knew he was going to kill himself? But something was off, and Vega scanned the room again.

A crime scene technician stood beside him and must have been thinking the same thing. But he answered out loud.

"Not suicide, sir," he said, and pointed to the gun on the desk. "The gun would have fallen if he shot himself. Not been placed neatly on the desk."

Vega nodded. "Of course." He mentally kicked himself. He must be tired or overwhelmed. Usually, he'd have picked up on that immediately. Then he noticed something else.

"What's that?" he asked the technician. He could see a piece of paper poking out from under Dennis's inert arm.

"Looks like an envelope, sir."

"A note? Can you look, please?" Vega asked.

"I'm not supposed to . . ." the technician started to say.

"I'm not asking to take it," Vega snapped, "just look in the envelope and tell me what's in there."

The technician eased out the envelope. "Addressed to Joanna Campbell, sir. Just cash, I think . . . Oh, there is a note." He read it aloud to Vega, who thanked him and told him to put it back exactly as he found it. They would photograph the study and the bedroom next.

"Terrible day, sir. First Nadine Dagg," Diane Fowler said to Vega, appearing at his shoulder. She looked as stunned as he felt, Vega thought.

He nodded, "And now the Haverses."

These killings must be connected, he thought. But two different methods? *Damn it.*

"Where's the coroner?" he asked.

"On her way, sir. The house is sealed off, and I've got some officers coming from Nanaimo, they'll be here shortly. How do you want to play this, sir?"

"I'll speak to Sinclair, see if we can get another forensic team over here. If not, they'll have to do double duty. Speak to the team leader, please. Get some uniforms to round up everyone who attended the belly dancing night, including Andi Silvers, and get their statements. And Sergeant? Bring in Lee Dagg. Make him wait at the detachment."

"Does he know his wife is dead, sir?"

"That's what I'd like to know, Sergeant. As I see it, Ricky Havers was found on his or his family's property, and Nadine here was supposedly having an affair with Dennis Havers. That's a connection I need to follow up."

"Yes, sir. Anything else?" Fowler inquired.

"Yes. Get officers knocking on doors. I know this place is away from the town centre, but usually you can't fart around here without someone knowing. Someone must have seen or heard something. I don't want the community to panic, but if we can't find a connection between these victims soon, we'll have to assume we have a crazed gunman killing randomly in Coffin Cove."

"Not just a gunman, sir," Diane Fowler said. "Someone who knows how to use a knife."

CHAPTER TWENTY-NINE

Doug South stood in the doorway of his workshop. It had been a good morning, all things considered. He lit a cigarette and inhaled, letting his body cool down after working up a sweat underneath the car hoist.

Terri hated the smell of cigarettes and never let him smoke in the house. It was OK. He smiled. Terri and her throw cushions and "show towels" in the downstairs cloakroom. How many times had he repainted the interior of the house? He couldn't remember and he didn't care. He'd paint it a thousand times more for her if she asked him to. Terri had moved in when they got married and looked after his mother. She had never complained, never asked to move, even after Ma died. So small sacrifices like smoking outside and peeling off his oily clothes before he went in the house were fine by him.

He'd stopped smoking a pack a day years ago when Ma got cancer. Now, it was an occasional sneaky reward after a particularly productive day. And today was just that. The old Mustang was coming along. When he'd started, he'd had nothing but the rusted-out chassis. After years of sourcing parts from collectors and working on it between fixing customers' vehicles, it was nearly complete. Just the bodywork left now. Coats of glossy red paint, the exact shade of the original, and it would be ready to take Terri for their first ride.

It had been a labour of love. That's what he told himself, anyway. In solitary moments, leaning against the workshop door and looking through the trees to the dark shadow of Whilley's old net shed, he acknowledged this wasn't really about love. It was about guilt.

That's what he'd felt the day before when he found Jim Peters and that other reporter talking to his wife. When that woman looked at him, he felt sure she knew exactly how he was feeling. He'd been open and truthful about everything — why shouldn't he? He had nothing to hide. He hadn't been involved in that drug racket. He'd tried to help Art. He'd tried to do what his mother asked.

When he let himself, Doug could still remember every detail of that last night. The finale.

Something was going to happen, he'd felt it for weeks. Something bad. It had gotten wild and dangerous over at Art's place. More than partying, more than bikes racing up and down the trail and idiots performing burnouts and smashing beer bottles. There had been a tension in the air, a palpable threat. Doug's heart was heavy. They'd just buried his mother. Terri and he were wandering aimlessly around the house, unable to settle. Just as they were ready to go to bed, they heard a huge explosion, a split second before they felt the vibration. The force was powerful enough to rattle the windows.

Doug stood up.

Terri said, "Don't go, Doug."

He knew he had to. He'd promised his mother. She'd clasped his large hands with her fragile fingers, and with great effort lifted her head off the pillow.

"Look after Art," she'd whispered. "He has no one. Not like you. You have Terri." And she sank back, exhausted from the effort.

Doug had promised.

When he neared Whilley's place, it was chaos. Bikers were scrambling to leave, their heavy machines spinning their wheels in the dirt.

Like scattering rats, he thought. The heat hit him as he reached the gate. White-hot flames leaped into the air, the smoke a dark, choking black. Doug held his shirt over his mouth, remembering Art had bottles of chemicals in the cabin.

Summoning his courage, Doug ran towards the fire, knowing he was crossing into Hell.

Days later, what was left of the cabin was still smouldering. The police had come and gone. They'd wandered into the old net shed, which miraculously suffered only minor damage, searched the site and declared Art Whilley dead.

The bikers never returned. Wayne was gone. Dennis Havers acted as if he'd never known Art Whilley. It was as if he'd never existed.

One morning, Doug walked up to Art's place. He'd never called it Hell's Half Acre. When he got there, he saw a woman standing by the ashes, her head bowed, as if in prayer. It was Clara Bell. Doug raised his hand to wave, and she looked up. She gave him a stiff nod and walked away.

Doug hauled away the burnt-out Mustang. It was the last time he ever went there. He'd thought it was all over. But now, he had a sinking feeling he couldn't shake off.

Doug finished his cigarette and turned to go back into his workshop. Hearing vehicles approaching, he waited to see who it was. An RCMP cruiser and a dark sedan passed his house and headed towards the Daggs'.

This was it, then. Doug looked upwards and sent a silent prayer and apology to his mother.

CHAPTER THIRTY

Lee slumped in the uncomfortable metal chair in the interview room. He had no idea how long he'd been there. An unsightly film was forming on the surface of the mug of tea in front of him.

An officer, one of those who'd driven him to the detachment, had placed the mug on the table.

"Someone will be with you soon, sir," he'd said, and with a gesture of sympathy, had gently squeezed Lee's shoulder before leaving him alone.

That was a while ago. Maybe an hour? Five? Lee didn't know.

Time wasn't important right now, except he knew Katie would be worried. Thank God she had Terri. Terri had been like a mother . . .

The thought caught on his emotions like barbed wire.

Mother. Motherless. Katie was motherless. Officially.

Lee almost laughed at the absurdity of it all. All these years he'd wished Nadine would either mother her daughter or just move along and let them be . . . *Well, that's what they say, isn't it? Be careful what you wish for?*

Is this my fault? he'd wondered, sitting in his living room earlier that day. He had his arm around his daughter. He was confused. He was trying to understand what the two RCMP officers had just told him.

He must have said it aloud because he saw the officers exchange glances.

"How did she . . . ?" He couldn't say the word out loud. It was inconceivable Nadine was dead.

Look around, he wanted to shout at the officers. *See this couch? Nadine bought it. And these cushions? We argued about these fucking cushions. Now you're telling me she's not coming back?*

The officers explained a little. It still didn't make sense. She was belly dancing. For fuck's sake. At the Fat Chicken. All the people there knew her. They knew she was a flirt. They knew everything about her. She'd grown up in this town.

"She's an administration officer at the city," Lee had said. "She works for the mayor." He didn't know why that seemed important to him, but he wanted these officers to know Nadine was a serious person. She wasn't just some flaky middle-aged woman who liked to dance in fancy dress. She was . . . more.

"Yes, sir," they'd said respectfully. And then, "Is there someone who could look after your daughter?"

Lee had become aware of Katie clinging to him, her body heaving with sobs.

"Go to Terri's," he'd told his daughter. "Go there and I'll be back soon, I promise."

"Come with us now, sir."

He'd obediently walked out to the waiting car and got in the back.

He didn't know why, but he thought they'd take him to see Nadine. But instead, they arrived at the detachment. And now, he was waiting.

Lee was aware of activity and noise outside the room. *They must be busy*, he thought distractedly. And then remembered why.

Lee laid his head on his arms and started to cry.

* * *

Katie watched in disbelief as the RCMP cruiser took her father away. Her legs wouldn't hold her up. She sank to her knees on the porch.

Her mother was dead? And they thought her father killed her?

A voice came from a long way away, and she noticed a police officer speaking to her.

"Katie? Is there someone who can stay with you? I'm afraid we must search the house now."

Katie looked up and managed to whisper, "Terri."

"It's OK, officer," she heard a familiar voice boom, "I'll take Katie to my wife."

Katie held her hand out, but Doug South ignored it and put his arms around her, as if she were a small child.

The officer was talking again, something about keys, and Katie realized they would pull the house apart. She cried again.

"Shh, it's OK, Katie. They have a job to do. They'll find out your dad has nothing to do with any of this. He'll be home before you know it."

Katie nodded. She felt in her pocket for the door keys and a piece of paper fluttered to the ground. Doug bent down to pick it up.

He turned the card over and over in his hand and then hugged Katie tighter.

As he helped Katie home to Terri, who was waiting for her with outstretched arms, Katie didn't understand why Doug kept whispering to her, "I'm so sorry, Katie."

CHAPTER THIRTY-ONE

Jade was having the strangest dream. She was laughing with Summer about an old black-and-white movie. They used to watch them all the time. When she was little, Jade's favourite was Charlie Chaplin. He made her laugh until she couldn't stop. Summer used to do an imitation of the way he walked and doffed his hat whenever Jade felt sad after a hard day at school. Summer also used to pretend to swoon, like Chaplin's leading ladies, her hand held dramatically to her forehead as she dropped onto the couch. Jade would rush over, joining in the pretence, and pat Summer's cheeks or wave imaginary smelling salts under her nose, until Summer grabbed her daughter and tickled her, both of them collapsing with laughter.

That's what I need, smelling salts, Jade thought, not understanding why she couldn't pull herself out of this deep sleep. Why was it so dark? Was it the middle of the night?

Her eyes opened, and she realized she was sitting up, and for a minute she had a rush of panic. Did she fall asleep at her desk? What was that smell?

Everything smelled musty and damp, like dirt. Jade wanted to cough and tried to bring her hand to her mouth. But she couldn't. When she moved her hand, something dug into her flesh, and she cried out. Was she still dreaming?

Gradually her eyes got accustomed to the dark, and her groggy mind began to clear.

She remembered the phone call, just before she was about to leave the office. It was from Mr Knight. She remembered his calm, measured voice, asking if she could spare a minute and meet him at the fish plant?

She hadn't wanted to go to the Fat Chicken. She'd been so worried since Ricky Havers was found. She just wanted to go home, but she knew they expected her at the belly dancing display. Nadine had reminded her about six times. But a quick visit to the fish plant seemed a welcome distraction, just for half an hour, and besides, it was work, wasn't it?

She'd left the office without telling anyone. Nobody would miss her for a while, she was sure. She'd walk down to the fish plant and when the meeting was over she would take a stroll along the boardwalk and think about what she was going to say to Inspector Vega. She couldn't put this off any longer. The guilt was tearing her apart.

When she got to the fish plant, it was deserted. Only the gulls called to her and pecked and fussed in the evening air. The ocean lapped lazily around the pier, and Jade thought how beautiful this place could be, what potential this waterfront lot had, once the derelict fish plant was finally torn down.

Jade tried opening the door to the plant, but it was locked. Of course it was, she remembered, it was dangerous. They didn't want kids running all over it and getting hurt.

She wandered round to the other side of the building, wondering if Mr Knight was waiting for her there.

Nobody.

Maybe she'd got the day wrong? Maybe he meant tomorrow evening, and she'd misheard, maybe deliberately, because she didn't want to go to the Fat Chicken?

She sighed. Couldn't put it off any longer. Mr Knight would call again.

She heard something, she couldn't think what it was now. Maybe a gull shrieking? And then the crunch of footsteps running, someone saying something to her, but she couldn't hear. It all went dark.

Then confusion. It felt like ten people were pushing and pulling her and whispering in her ear. It got darker and colder and then someone — a man — put their lips to her ear and said two words.

And then nothing. And now? Where was she? Why had this happened?

Jade began to cry. And then she tried to scream. But her voice seemed muffled, as if she were shouting into a pillow.

What was it that man had said to her?

"Daniel's girl."

Who was Daniel? She wasn't Daniel's girl! They had the wrong person.

Or had they? What if this was payback for Ricky?

Jade hung her head, and as she cried, she felt an overwhelming urge to sleep.

CHAPTER THIRTY-TWO

Vega stood at the front of the room.

"OK, people, I need your attention. It's been a long day and it's not over yet. We're going to put together what we know so far, the limited amount of forensic data we have and information we've gathered from interviews and statements so far."

He paused and looked around the room. His team had been working since the early hours of the morning. On a normal day, most of their shifts would be over. But this was not a normal day, and eyes looked expectantly back at him.

He continued.

"We'll eat on the go — pizza and coffee are on the way, courtesy of Hephzibah's."

There was a murmur of appreciation in the room. Nobody had managed to eat so far that day, and given the scenes they had all witnessed, Vega knew that most of the officers wouldn't have much of an appetite. But he needed everyone to bring their best to this case. And officers who were too tired and hadn't eaten were not on the top of their game.

Vega continued. "Right, we have two crime scenes. Two more crime scenes. Both are homicides, and we're treating them as one investigation at the moment, with potential links to the Ricky Havers case."

Vega pointed to the board. Stuck to it were the unpleasant but necessary pictures of the dead victims taken at the respective crime scenes.

"First, Nadine Dagg — throat slit, found at the back of the Fat Chicken pub. Time of death was after midnight, we believe, but probably before three in the morning. Not confirmed yet, but we'll have that soon. Over here are Dennis and Sandra Havers. Found this morning by their housekeeper, Joanna Campbell. Dennis shot in the head at his desk, and Sandra shot in her bed. Both shot with Dennis's gun, it appears."

An officer interrupted, "Is it a possible murder-suicide, sir? Or a suicide pact? Given the recent discovery of their son?"

"No. It's a reasonable theory, except forensics believe Dennis was shot first, and although there may have been an attempt to make it look like a suicide, because Dennis was shot in the side of the head, the angle is all wrong. But the safe was left open, and Dennis left a note. So it's possible he'd intended to kill himself but was helped along. Dennis also reeked of booze, and there was an empty bottle of Jack Daniel's at the scene. The coroner says it's unlikely he could have held his hand steady enough to fire a shot."

"What did the note say, sir?"

Vega preferred the questions to come at the end, but he grabbed his notebook.

"The note specifically is not addressed to anyone. But it was in the same envelope with the housekeeper's name on and it was full of cash. Joanna Campbell, the housekeeper and unfortunate soul who found the victims this morning, said Dennis always left her cash on his desk. The note says just one thing: '*I am responsible for the death of Daniel Ellis. I am truly sorry. I have always loved Sandra. I am so sorry. Dennis.*'"

"Nothing about Ricky? And who is Daniel Ellis?" another officer asked.

"All questions we need answering, and quickly," Vega said briskly. "At the moment, we have one person connected to all three deaths: Lee Dagg. Lee is Nadine's husband. We know from more than one statement that Nadine and Dennis Havers were having an affair and weren't too discreet about it. The affair had been going on for years. Several people confirm that Lee was pretty fed up with his marriage and Nadine was, let's say, a 'high-maintenance' wife who liked to spend beyond their means. Ricky Havers' remains were found on the Daggs' land — in the middle of the woods, where people would be unlikely to walk."

"Wasn't it Katie Dagg who found Ricky?"

"Good point, Officer. Katie Dagg arranged a field trip of sorts for the historical society, and by Lee's own admission, he had no idea the event was taking place. Our working theory, based on the evidence we have at the moment, is Lee Dagg, a humiliated husband, seeks revenge on his wife and her lover by first snatching the lover's son and killing him and then, when the affair doesn't end, killing his wife and her lover. There doesn't seem to be a reason for killing Sandra unless she was just collateral damage."

The room was silent. Everyone seemed to be taking it in.

Then an officer said, "Lee Dagg wasn't at the Fat Chicken. He could have dropped Nadine off, and then gone to the Havers', killed them both and then come back to pick up Nadine, right?"

Vega nodded.

"Dagg was informed of Nadine's death as her next of kin earlier today. So far, he's been unable to tell us where he was all night. Katie says she heard him come home in the early hours, and she assumed it was Lee and Nadine, after the belly dancing night. She says she was at the neighbour's house all evening, and her dad wasn't home when she got back. She thought he was at the Fat Chicken. Everyone at the pub confirms he was not there."

Vega looked around the room.

"There are holes in this theory. I want you all to gather evidence, please. Keep an open mind. Do not discard evidence or statements that don't fit with this," he added, and he banged the whiteboard. "Too many investigations have gone sideways because we only looked at evidence that worked with our theory. But we do need to know where Lee Dagg was all night."

"We also need to know who Daniel Ellis was," Sergeant Fowler said. "He was important enough for Dennis Havers to be thinking of him just before he died, so he's important to us. Was this killing revenge for Daniel Ellis's death?"

Vega let Fowler take over and assign tasks to the team. She was efficient and knew what needed to be done.

"OK, folks—" he looked at his phone — "it's six. Grab something to eat, get on with your assignments and we'll meet at eleven. Let's make progress, please."

PC Matt Beaufort knocked on the door.

"Inspector? I think you need to hear this. Summer Thompson is in an interview room. She says her daughter Jade is missing."

"The mayor's missing?" Vega was astonished. Then he remembered Andi had told him Jade hadn't made it to the Fat Chicken.

"OK," he told PC Beaufort, "I'm coming."

He threw a glance at his whiteboard as he left the room. He knew he'd told his team to follow the evidence and not the theory, but was it possible Jade's disappearance was connected? And did that mean they had no leads at all?

CHAPTER THIRTY-THREE

Summer Thompson stood up as Inspector Vega entered the interview room. She looked anxious, and he saw she was rubbing her hands nervously. He saw Matt Beaufort had supplied Summer with a cup of tea which she hadn't touched. Matt had also started to take some notes.

Vega gestured for Summer to sit down at the table and also indicated for Matt to take one of the empty chairs. Vega sat down in the other.

"OK, Summer," he said, "Matt here is going to take notes as we chat and then we'll get all available officers out looking for Jade. Let's start with when you last saw her."

Summer took a deep breath.

"I saw her yesterday when she left for work. I didn't actually see her. She likes to be quiet in the mornings, get her head together for the day ahead, so I give her some privacy. But I got up and watched her car drive away."

Vega raised his hand. "You know it was Jade behind the wheel?"

Summer nodded. "Yes, Inspector. And I know she was in the office yesterday because I've already checked."

"Good. OK, carry on."

Vega knew they would verify everything, but he wanted Summer to tell him everything she knew first.

"I wasn't expecting Jade back for dinner, as I knew she was going to that awful belly dancing thing at the Fat Chicken. So I watched some TV, but I thought she'd be back by midnight. I fell asleep on the sofa, and when I woke up, she still wasn't home, and it was about one o'clock in the morning."

"Did you try to call or text?"

Summer shook her head miserably.

"I wish I had, but I thought she might have stayed with Hephzibah or something . . ." She trailed off and looked at Vega. "The thing is, Inspector, she's a grown woman, not a teenager. I didn't want to be fussing, and we agreed when we moved in together, we would give each other space, so I didn't want to seem . . . hysterical . . ." She put her head in her hands.

Vega reached out and patted her hand. "I would have done the same. This morning? Nothing from her?"

Summer raised her head. "No. I expected her back for a change of clothes before work, but she's been busy and stressed, so I left it again, and then when I went to get a coffee, I heard about poor Nadine, and I just thought she must be talking to you. I saw her car in the city parking lot. I went home and expected to see her. I knew she would be distraught about Nadine. It's so terrible. And then, when I didn't hear anything, I went down to her office and the lady on reception said Jade hadn't been in all day. I came straight here, thinking she might be in an interview or something . . . but she's not and now I'm really worried, Inspector. This isn't right. She would never just go off, not with everything going on . . . Something terrible has happened, hasn't it?" The last words were a whisper.

Vega decided to be straight with Summer.

"It doesn't seem right, I agree. Let's not panic, but Matt here is going to ask you a few more questions about Jade, so we can circulate a description. Her car is still in the parking lot?"

Summer nodded.

"Right, so she'll be on foot . . ."

Summer finished for him, "Or in someone else's car."

"That is possible," Vega conceded.

There was a knot in his stomach. He didn't want to frighten Summer, but with four murder victims, he feared for the young mayor. And he was convinced, even without solid evidence, that all four victims were connected somehow, and Jade must be part of this puzzle. So he leaned forward and said, "Summer, you have to answer me honestly. I can't do my job if you don't, and time is not on my side. So, I'm going to ask you once: is there a connection between Jade and Ricky Havers?"

Summer's reaction was confirmation. She physically flinched, as though Vega had slapped her.

Damn that woman, Vega thought. Andi was right.

"Summer, let me have it now."

"A long time ago Ricky Havers assaulted . . . no, raped my daughter." The words came spilling out as Summer clasped and unclasped her hands. "It ruined my daughter's life, Inspector. She never told a soul, not me, not anyone, until she got some counselling last year. She always hated visiting me here at Coffin Cove, but last year she told me why. She was very angry, Inspector." Summer looked at Inspector Vega, almost pleading. This was it, he thought. What was it Dennis had said on the phone? *My son wasn't an angel. He did things to people.*

She continued, "She was angry because Ricky had that damn Smoke Room store, right in my backyard. Whatever shady deal Dennis was cooking up, that store was causing daily problems. We — that is, the trailer park residents — we petitioned, but Dennis was mayor, and whatever he wanted, he got." Summer sounded bitter. "Jade was so angry. One night it all got too much. She took my gun."

Vega couldn't help but raise his eyebrows.

"A gun? What did she do, Summer?"

"She never meant to hurt him. She just wanted him to admit what he had done. Acknowledge it. She confronted him. But I got there, Inspector, and although she fired, the shot went wide — she wasn't used to guns."

But knew enough to load one, Vega thought. He was transfixed, but he was aware PC Beaufort was scribbling this down.

"Was he hurt, Summer?"

She shook her head.

"He fell. They were both on the roof of the Smoke Room and Ricky lost his footing and fell. But I'm sure the worst that happened to him was a sprained ankle. Jade and I ran home. She was so . . . I don't know. The next morning, we both expected the RCMP to come knocking. But they didn't, and I drove past the Smoke Room to see if he was hurt badly, but he wasn't there. We assumed he decided not to report Jade because he didn't want anyone to know what he did to her. I'm certain Jade wasn't the only one."

"But then Jade decided to run for mayor?" Vega said, almost to himself. "And Ricky went missing."

The fall explained the broken ankle and clavicle, he thought. And there was no way Ricky could move far with those injuries. Somebody must have taken him.

"Jade wanted to tell the RCMP. But it would have hurt her candidacy, so I persuaded her not to," Summer said. "It was my fault, Inspector. I should have known something was wrong when she was a teenager. I failed her. She wanted to be mayor because she hates injustice of any kind. And Dennis and his cronies have been running this town into the ground for years."

Vega sat back in his chair.

"Summer," he said, watching her closely, "are you aware both Dennis Havers and his wife Sandra are dead? Shot sometime in the early hours of this morning?"

He watched as her eyes went wide and both hands flew to cover her mouth.

"Summer—" he leaned forward — "I have to ask you this. Do you still have that gun?"

CHAPTER THIRTY-FOUR

Matt Beaufort made a surreptitious call to his wife. It was nine o'clock, and the detachment was still buzzing. It felt chaotic to Matt, as phones were ringing and Vega's officers were rushing in and writing notes on the whiteboard or shouting to each other from behind their computer screens.

Inspector Vega stood in the middle of the room, calmly taking calls and assigning new tasks. Occasionally, he'd clap his hands as if he were the coach of some sporting team, encouraging them towards a win.

Matt told Lily he'd be late again. He didn't have a specific task, but every so often, someone would stick their head out of the office and ask him to copy something or look something up.

All day he'd been making cups of tea for interviewees and sometimes taking notes for Vega's detectives.

So far, the media hadn't descended on Coffin Cove. But Vega had warned Matt it could happen soon.

"Hello?"

Matt looked up. He recognized Walter, the owner of the Fat Chicken.

"Yes, sir, can I help you?"

"Could I see Inspector Vega, please? I have some information for him. I'm not sure it will help, at least . . . I think . . ."

Matt smiled at the man. "Inspector Vega is busy. Maybe you can tell me?"

Walter nodded, "You're right, of course. He must be run off his feet."

Matt came out from behind the small counter and pointed to a couple of chairs in the foyer. "Sit down, sir. I'll make some notes."

Walter sat down. "You know, it sounds crazy, but I've talked to my wife, and then we called Jim Peters and we all think it's peculiar."

Matt was getting impatient. "Sir, the inspector can decide if it's crazy or not."

"I've seen a man in town the last few days. He looked familiar, but I couldn't place him. He's been staying at the Wilson Motel, and he told Peggy he was some kind of real estate developer. He was in the pub for the belly dancing thing too. And then, when I was in Andi's apartment, I saw a photo on the wall. And I knew who the man reminded me of. Except the more I think about it, I think it's really him. But . . ."

"But what, sir?"

Walter looked sheepish. "This is the crazy part. The man I think it is . . . he died years ago."

* * *

Vega was frustrated. He stared at his cell phone, which was on loudspeaker, and wanted to hurl it across the room.

"You need more manpower, I know, Inspector. Unfortunately, there's been a gang shooting here on the mainland, and a homicide in Prince George, so at the moment, you're on your own until I can get more of our guys over there. However, you'll have more locals at your disposal in the next hour or so. You can use them for door-to-door and interviewing."

"Yes, ma'am." There was no use whining to the superintendent, it wasn't her fault.

"It's a bad business, Andrew." Her voice softened. "I disliked Dennis Havers, but nobody deserves that. Are you sure it wasn't suicide? A pact, maybe, between him and his wife?"

"No, ma'am. He looked like he was planning suicide. He left a note with a weird confession of sorts, but somebody finished the job for him. The gun was left at the scene. Wiped clean, of course, but I've got a team going over the house now."

There was a brief silence.

"A confession, you say?"

"Yes. He said he was responsible for the death of a—" Vega looked down at his notes — "Daniel Ellis. We've looked him up, but it seems like he died years ago in a fishing accident. Dennis was not on the boat, so we don't know what he meant. But we're looking into it."

"And the woman?"

"Identified as Nadine Dagg," Vega answered.

"Cause of death?"

"Her throat was slit," Vega said. "I'll know more when the reports come in."

Sinclair was silent again at the other end of the phone. Vega knew she wanted to ask more, but she never asked her officers to speculate. She'd wait for the report.

Vega continued, "And now Jade Thompson, the mayor, has gone missing."

"Christ."

"Ma'am, I have Summer Thompson here at the detachment. I've applied for a warrant to search her home. It seems she owns a gun. And there was an incident last year between Ricky and Jade Thompson. It seems Jade fired at Ricky, but Summer swears he wasn't hurt. He went missing after that. I'm checking the dates."

"And now Ricky's body just showed up, and Dennis and Sandra are dead," Sinclair said. "You're thinking this missing persons report is designed to throw us off?"

"I have to think Summer Thompson, and possibly Jade, are suspects, ma'am, at least until we can rule them out."

"And the other victim?"

"Not so sure about Nadine Dagg. It was a very clean slice, and I doubt either Jade or Summer would have the strength to do that. But forensics will tell us more. Hopefully, there's some DNA evidence."

"So you're still looking at the husband for that?"

"In the absence of any other leads, ma'am, yes."

Before Sinclair ended the call, Vega remembered something.

"Ma'am, there's something else I could use your help with."

"If I can, Inspector, what do you need?"

"Remember you told me about an old investigation Emma was involved in — a drug cartel on the island? It involved a biker gang?"

"Yes, that's right. Didn't go anywhere."

"Does Emma have the old files, ma'am?"

There was a pause. "I can get them for you if you think they'd help. What are you thinking, Inspector?"

Vega hesitated before he answered, "Just a thought, ma'am, that's all."

There was a pause. "There were a lot of bad things going on in Coffin Cove back then, Inspector. Havers was involved, and I think you'll remember Summer Thompson was right there in the middle of it. Except back then, she was a victim."

"Victims sometimes seek revenge, ma'am," Vega said simply.

"You're right, Inspector. Sometimes they do."

They ended the call, and Vega stared down at his phone. He couldn't tell his superintendent he was following Andi Silver's "gut feeling", could he? And yet, nothing was making any sense at all.

"Damn it, I need ten times the manpower," he said out loud.

And if Summer was telling the truth about Jade's disappearance, then he was running out of time.

There was a knock at the door and Charlie Rollins was standing there, looking miserable.

"Do you have a minute, sir?"

"Not really, Sergeant, but come on in." Vega was irritated. Hadn't this idiot done enough damage?

Charlie walked into the room, and without waiting, slumped down in a chair and held his head in his hands.

Vega stared at him. *What now, for Christ's sake?* He took a breath and tried to keep the annoyance out of his voice.

"What's this all about, Charlie? Come on, man, I've got multiple murders on my hands. Let's have it."

Charlie Rollins straightened up.

"Yes, sir. Sorry." His voice trembled a bit. Vega looked at him. Oh God, had he been crying?

"Sir, Dennis Havers and me, well, we were good friends. We went way back."

Vega nodded and cursed himself for being so insensitive. Of course Charlie would have known the Haverses well.

"Charlie, I'm so sorry. Forgive me. I completely forgot how close everyone is in this town. The last few days must have been very hard for you."

Charlie waved his hand. "Thank you, sir, but it's not that. It's just . . . well, I used to help Dennis once in a while. Nothing illegal or anything . . . but . . . well . . ." The man was stammering.

Vega closed his eyes.

"Charlie. Please tell me everything. Now."

"Dennis didn't mean to get Ricky killed. He just . . . he was frustrated with his kid. Ricky never worked a day in his life and Dennis knew he would cut corners with this weed store. It was all about the money for Ricky. And Sandra gave Ricky everything he wanted. Dennis just wanted to scare him. . . you know, try to teach him about real life, so . . ."

"So he told you not to pay any attention if Ricky was reported missing?" Vega finished for him. "Good God, man, what was supposed to happen? Did Dennis get someone to abduct him?"

Charlie shook his head slowly. "I don't know, sir. He told me that Ricky would be gone for a while, and when he got back, he and Sandra would toe the line."

"What did he mean by 'toe the line'?" Vega exclaimed. "You do remember that kidnapping is a crime, right? Even if it's someone you know? What happened to you, Charlie? Been so long in the back of beyond you forgot everything about being a police officer? Jesus."

"I'm sorry," Charlie mumbled.

"So you think Dennis had his kid killed?" Vega demanded.

"No, no, sir. After a couple of weeks, Dennis was worried. He said the people he'd hired to . . . teach Ricky a lesson, they hadn't got him. They couldn't find him. So then Dennis started thinking someone else must have grabbed him. And that's when you came over, and I got some searches underway . . ."

"But by that time, it was too late," Vega finished for him.

Charlie nodded.

"Why didn't you come forward before?" Vega asked, trying not to leap up and throttle the man sitting opposite him.

"I was going to . . . When we found Ricky, I tried to call Dennis. I thought he should tell you everything. But Dennis wasn't answering. And now he's dead." Charlie hung his head.

"OK. Have you told anyone else?" Vega asked.

Charlie shook his head. "But then the article came out. And now the whole community blames me for Ricky's death. I can't . . . live with myself." His voice cracked again.

Vega suddenly felt sorry for Charlie.

"Listen, man, no one's blaming you for Ricky. We have a killer in Coffin Cove. I need you. You know this community.

You made a mistake and so did I. But now, I need you to focus and help me, can you do that?

"Yes, sir, I'll try." Charlie still had his head down but didn't sound so desperate.

Vega patted him on the shoulder. "Good man. We'll talk again later."

"Thank you, sir." Charlie left the room, standing a little straighter.

Vega felt like his head would explode. He and the team were being buffeted in all directions. Were they being manipulated? As soon as they started chasing down one investigation, another bomb went off. These killings were connected. And whoever was behind this spree must be laughing at them all racing around chasing their tails.

First, Vega had Dennis under the spotlight for Ricky's death, and considering Charlie's confession, he might have been on the right track. But now Dennis was dead, and so was Sandra. Maybe Dennis's hired thugs made a mistake. And then took Dennis out, in case he came clean. But how was Nadine connected to this? She and Dennis were having an affair, but why kill Nadine? And how on earth did Jade Thompson fit in to all this, except to unseat Dennis as mayor? And who the hell was Daniel Ellis?

Vega was suddenly tired. Tired of this investigation and tired of Coffin Cove and its damn secrets. That was the problem with this town, everyone was still living in the past. Everyone was looking back, not forward.

Vega sat up. Maybe that was it. These cases must be linked by something or someone from the past. What was it Andi said about this town? *Everyone knows everyone else's business.* Well, someone knew the connection between the Havers, Daggs and Thompsons. He just had to find that person. Or maybe it wasn't a person. Maybe it was a place.

He leaped up and opened the door. "Charlie?"

The sergeant came running. "Yes, sir?"

"What's the history of the chapel? Why is it there?" Vega felt, for some reason, this was the key to everything.

Charlie looked blank. "I don't know, sir. I don't think the Daggs built it, I think it was the previous family, the Whilleys. But they've all been dead for years."

"Right." Vega felt deflated. He had one more question for Charlie. "Do you know who Daniel Ellis is?"

Charlie shook his head. "No, sir. Never heard of him."

PC Matt Beaufort appeared behind Charlie Rollins.

"Inspector? Have you got a minute?"

Vega spread his hands in resignation. "Sure, why not? What is it?"

"Walter from the pub is in the interview room. I think you should hear what he has to say."

"OK, Constable, I'll be right along."

Vega clapped Charlie on the shoulder. "Go home, man."

But Charlie didn't move. "You know who could tell you more about that chapel, sir?" he said. "Clara Bell. She knows just about everyone's history in town. And she'll know that Daniel Ellis if he's from Coffin Cove."

CHAPTER THIRTY-FIVE

Andi couldn't imagine eating. There was an acidic burn of stomach bile at the back of her throat and her head was pounding. She felt chilled and shivered uncontrollably. She wanted to lie down and rest but was terrified that Nadine's glassy dead eyes would haunt her thoughts and dreams. So she struggled to stay awake, propped up at the galley table, absently petting Bruno's head and grateful for the warmth of the dog's body as he snuggled up to her.

Walter had arrived with Bruno when Andi got back to her apartment, after giving her statement. Walter took one look at her and told her to pack a bag. Minutes later, Harry arrived.

"You can stay on the boat for a few days," he said gruffly, while Andi threw a few things in a bag and packed her laptop. "You can have my stateroom. And Bruno's coming with us. He likes it on the boat."

Andi hadn't argued. The last place she wanted to be was this apartment. She didn't think she could ever stay here again. She thought for a moment and picked up Terri's photo and slipped it into her bag. She called Jim and told him where she was going. He agreed it was the best idea all round.

Harry followed her down the steps, and then, with a hand on her shoulder, gently steered her away from the trash cans where Andi had found Nadine that morning. Andi couldn't look. There was nothing there. The forensic team had finished a few hours before, and Andi guessed they were at the Haverses' house. The news of Dennis and Sandra's killings was like a gut punch. Andi had been too shocked to speak. Suddenly, her quest for a story seemed childish, even obscene. Three senseless deaths in one horrific night, on top of the murder of Ricky Havers.

Andi couldn't think of any connections. She felt tired of it all. She felt like she'd unearthed something larger and more sinister than she'd ever imagined possible and somehow unleashed this evil. She didn't know what the "something" was. Logically, she knew none of this was her fault. But as she buried her face in Bruno's fur, she just wanted it all to go away.

Harry stood with his back to her, slicing and throwing garlic, onion and vegetables into a large frying pan on the galley stovetop.

He poured her a glass of wine without asking and put it in front of her.

"What are you cooking?" Andi asked, as the aroma of spices filled the cabin. Andi searched her mind for the last time she had smelled food like this and could not remember.

"Halibut cheeks," Harry said.

"What?" Andi looked at him, confused.

"You asked what I'm cooking," he said. "It's OK. You're still in shock."

"I didn't know halibut even had cheeks." Andi managed a smile.

"Best bit of the fish," Harry said as he put a plate of food in front of Andi. "Eat. You'll feel better."

They both ate their meal in silence, as it grew dark outside.

From the cabin window, Andi watched as the moonlight threw a shaft of shimmering light over the ocean, and the gentle rhythmic ripple of waves comforted her a little.

"It has a calming effect," she said to Harry. "Being on the water, I mean. Is that why you live out here?"

"Hephzibah rents my house," Harry answered. "As much as I love my sister, there's no way I want to live with her. She has too much stuff."

Andi laughed.

"The boat suits me," Harry continued. "I have everything I need." He looked at her curiously. "What about you? That little apartment. It's OK, but I thought it was temporary . . ."

Andi looked down at her plate and fiddled with her cutlery. She hadn't been hungry, but somehow the plate was empty.

"It was. I didn't know what I was going to do. I promised Jim I'd stay for another year, but now . . . I don't know, I just keep thinking I've fucked up somehow."

She felt the tears come and wiped her hand over her face.

"How have you fucked up?" Harry demanded.

Andi looked up. He was serious.

"Well, in my continuing obsession for a good story, I published details of the investigation I wasn't supposed to, I practically accused Charlie Rollins of killing Ricky Havers, I didn't find out anything for Sandra Havers and now she's dead, and so is Dennis and poor Nadine."

"Are you finished with your pity party?"

Andi jerked her head up. Harry laughed.

"Good. Now, I'm going to pour you another glass of wine while you get all those photos and documents out and fire up your laptop."

Andi looked at him in surprise.

Harry laughed. "What's the matter? C'mon, girl, you won't be happy until you've figured this thing out. Stop feeling sorry for yourself and get back to work."

He filled her glass. "The way I see it is this: someone waited until Ricky's body was discovered before he — or she — went on a killing spree, right? So whoever it is must either be fucking crazy or full of rage for something. Something that links the Havers and Nadine Dagg. And I don't think it's Lee Dagg. I went to school with Lee. And sure, he might regret marrying Nadine, but he wouldn't do anything to hurt Katie. He might punch out Dennis in the pub after too many beers, but Lee Dagg wouldn't snatch Ricky Havers and then kill Dennis and Sandra, and the mother of his daughter, no way." He was emphatic.

Andi nodded.

"I still think Jade and Summer Thompson are connected to Dennis Havers in some way."

"Unlikely that either of them killed Nadine," Harry said. "Nadine wasn't tiny, and she wasn't a fragile little flower. She'd have put up a fight."

Andi nodded. "That's what I thought."

"So, get out your stuff and let's see what you've got. Maybe I know something that'll help. And you know there's somebody in this town who knows what's going on. Vega can collect all the fingerprints he wants. My bet is there's something in the past that set off these killings. All we have to do is work out what it was."

"I think we can help with that." Jim Peters stood in the galley doorway. Andi could see the figure of someone behind him. "Any more of that halibut left?" he asked.

"Sure. Who have you got with you?" Harry asked.

A woman stepped into the galley, holding rolls of paper. She had a shock of white hair and wore a long black skirt with a jacket made of some kind of animal hide.

"Hello, Clara," Harry said. "Take a seat. Plenty of fish to go round."

CHAPTER THIRTY-SIX

Vega listened to Walter.

In his mind's eye he could see the brand-new Mercedes E-Class sedan parked outside the motel room next to his. He'd even nodded at the owner, although Vega couldn't remember anything about him, except he was dressed expensively. What had Peggy Wilson said his name was?

"Knight," Vega said. "He called himself Mr Knight. Who do you think he is?"

Walter looked relieved.

"Art Whilley. He lived where Lee and Nadine — well, not Nadine now, I guess — he lived on that plot of land, but he lived in his parents' cabin. He was supposed to have died in a fire years ago."

"OK, Walter, I don't know if this is significant or not, but I need to get a look at that photo and find out where Andi got it. Is she home?"

"No," Walter said. "She's staying with Harry on the *Pipe Dream*. Poor girl. She didn't feel safe in the apartment."

For some reason, Andrew Vega's heart dropped when he heard that. Pushing the feeling to one side for a minute, and hoping it hadn't shown on his face, he pulled out his cell phone and spoke to Andi.

"You have it with you? Great. No, I'll come to you. I'll be about half an hour, I've got a quick briefing first. Just hang on there."

He shook Walter's hand.

"Thanks for coming in."

As he watched Walter leave the detachment, he turned to Matt.

"Call Peggy Wilson. No, go to the motel and see if Mr Knight has checked out, or if his car is still there. Get any information you can from Peggy Wilson — but swear her to silence. Threaten to arrest her if you have to. I can't have gossip spreading and screwing up this investigation, got it? And Matt, do you know Clara Bell?"

Matt nodded. "I know who she is, sir. She was with Katie Dagg when they found Ricky. You want to speak to her?"

"Yes. Ask her to come in — I know it's getting late, but tell her it's important, OK?"

Matt nodded and hurried out.

Vega went into the office and called for attention.

Keeping it as concise as he could, he briefed his detectives on Walter's information.

"I need everything we can find out about this 'Art Whilley'. Can we connect Whilley or Knight, or whoever it is, to Jade Thompson? Anyone got anything?"

One young officer put his hand up.

"This might be something, sir. We went through the mayor's office to see if there was any clue to her whereabouts — you know, a diary, a scheduled meeting or something, but there was nothing concrete. But we did find an envelope with what looks like a building or development proposal for the old fish plant. One of her staff heard Mayor Thompson and Nadine talking about it the other day. The company name on the papers is Knights Development Ltd."

"OK. Good. So it's possible Jade met up with Knight when she left the office? The fish plant is within walking distance."

Vega looked round at the nodding heads. "But let's not get carried away here. This 'Knight', or whoever he is, might just have the misfortune to look like a dead guy. He could genuinely be a real estate developer. And there's nothing to connect him with any of the Haverses or Nadine."

There was something else bothering Vega. He'd heard the name "Knight" before. He said this out loud, and Diane Fowler said, "That dirty little scumbag squatting in the bookstore, you remember? At the strip mall, near the Smoke Room. He claimed to be Ricky Havers' right-hand man. He was going on about being rescued by a knight in shining armour. He thought it was hilarious. I just thought he was stoned."

Vega nodded. "Where is he now?"

"Passed him on to Nanaimo, sir. Thought he could help with their new drug problem. We found some pills in his stuff, matched the description they've been circulating."

"Good, Sergeant, get on to them and see if they've got anything helpful."

"On it, sir."

Vega was pleased at the information flowing in the room, but they still weren't any nearer to finding Jade Thompson. Uniformed officers had interviewed nearly everyone in City Hall. Two people had seen Jade leave on foot and walk in a direction that could have taken her to the fish plant. And then, nothing. And despite Diane Fowler's keen memory, Vega knew he'd heard the word "Knight" somewhere else.

He checked the time. Andi was waiting for him, and he needed that photo. At the same moment, PC Matt Beaufort put his head round the door and a detective finished a call.

"Sir!" they both said in unison.

"You first." Vega pointed to Matt.

"Peggy Wilson says Mr Knight checked out this morning. She didn't see him go, she just found the key in the box, which is normal if someone's checking out early. He paid by credit card and she says she knows nothing more about him, apart from what we already know: he was a real estate developer. We have the registration of his car, and I've started the paperwork to get the credit card details."

"Outstanding work," Vega said, and Matt beamed at him.

"You next, Detective," Vega called out.

"The search on Summer Thompson's place, sir. It turned up a gun — doesn't look like it's been fired recently, but we sent it in to ballistics anyway. Nothing else out of the ordinary — Jade's clothes in the closet, doesn't look like she left in a hurry. We also checked with Hephzibah Brown. She did see Summer this morning, checking if Jade had stayed with her. Says Summer was really worried."

"OK. She's not off the hook yet, but it looks like Mr Knight is our best bet for Jade. Let me think a minute."

The room went quiet. Then Vega said slowly, "There's only one road out of Coffin Cove. Is there any chance at all that this godforsaken town has a camera anywhere on that road?"

He saw heads shake. He knew it was a long shot.

Then Diane Fowler blurted, "The Smoke Room, sir! It has a security camera set up over the door that faces the parking lot. If it's still operational, it might have a view of the road — enough to see vehicles pass, maybe?"

"Right. Who would monitor that camera?"

Diane said, "I'll find out. Maybe Dennis Havers kept the payments up, even after Ricky disappeared. Otherwise the company would have retrieved their equipment, I'm sure."

"Follow up, please, Diane. Get the registration of Knight's car from Matt. And get the registrations of all the vehicles leaving Coffin Cove today. Let's check them all."

Feeling like they were making some progress, Vega left the detachment and drove the short distance to the government dock. He didn't have time to enjoy the evening air. He had a bad feeling Jade didn't have time on her side either.

CHAPTER THIRTY-SEVEN

Andrew Vega arrived at the government dock. The sun had lowered behind the cliffs hours ago and the wind was blowing in from the ocean. Clouds scuttled across the sky, obscuring the moonlight. Vega could see the glow of light from the *Pipe Dream*. A shadow fell across the deck, and he could hear Harry's voice.

"Over here, Inspector."

Vega didn't know why it bothered him that Andi was staying with Harry.

Was he jealous? Vega had this overwhelming feeling it should be him who was "rescuing" Andi, not Harry. Not that she would welcome being rescued.

He didn't have time for this. He pushed those thoughts away and shook Harry's hand as he stepped onto the *Pipe Dream*.

"Sorry to disturb your evening, Harry. But this is important."

Harry waved away Vega's apologies and showed him into the galley.

Vega wasn't familiar with boats of any kind. The galley was cosy, but there was plenty of room for a kitchen area and dining table. He could smell the aroma of something delicious and was aware he hadn't eaten in hours.

Andi was sitting at the table with her laptop in front of her. Vega saw with relief her colour was back and she looked alert, although worried. Beside her was Jim Peters and an older woman he didn't recognize.

"Inspector, this is Clara Bell," Jim explained.

Vega nodded at the woman, who looked at him with a grim expression. "Pleased to meet you, Clara. My officers are trying to reach you, so I'm glad you're here."

Vega took a seat and Jim started to talk. "Inspector, we have some information we think is relevant to your investigations. In fact, we think it's possible a man we all thought was dead has returned to Coffin Cove and for various reasons has . . ." Jim's voice faltered. "He's killed our neighbours. It wasn't until today after Nadine and the Haverses, well . . . now this makes sense. I'm only sorry we didn't make the connections before these killings. But I don't think he's finished yet."

Vega nodded and interrupted Jim. This was making some kind of sense. But he didn't have much time and needed to formulate a plan.

"Jade Thompson is missing," Vega said without any preamble. "You were right, Andi, there was a connection between Ricky and Jade, but it's not what you thought, and it has nothing to do with Ricky's death. I'm certain of that."

Their faces, especially Andi's, registered shock.

"Shit!" said Harry.

"I thought something was wrong when she didn't show last night. I was going to call her, but then . . ." Andi tailed off. Vega guessed she was thinking about Nadine.

Jim asked Vega, "Did you talk to Walter yet?"

Vega nodded. "I did."

Andi asked, "What's going on?"

"Walter saw a photograph in your apartment earlier. When he came in with tea for you, remember?" Vega explained.

Andi nodded.

"He thinks the man in the photo is either the same man who may be involved in Jade's disappearance or someone who looks a lot like him."

Andi pulled out a file from her laptop case and opened it. "This is the picture." She handed it to Vega.

Andi pointed to the men in the photograph. "That man is Wayne Dagg, Lee's older brother, and that's Art Whilley. That's Daniel Ellis, and that's Doug South—"

"Wait," Vega said, his mind racing. "Did you say Daniel Ellis?"

"Yes," Andi said, surprised at the urgency in his voice. "I thought you were interested in this one?" She pointed to Art Whilley.

"I am. It's just the name has come up."

"You think he's the killer?" Andi asked. There was a hint of the old Andi in her voice, and Vega smiled.

"I can't say yet," Vega said. It came out sounding pompous, and Vega was annoyed with himself. He needed Andi's help, and he didn't want to argue.

"It's not Daniel, that's for certain," Harry said.

"What?" Vega and Andi said together.

"Daniel Ellis cannot be the killer," Harry said. "He was lost at sea. Fishing accident. Well, more stupidity than accident, but the same result. I saw him leave the dock with my own eyes, and he never came back."

Vega shook his head. "When Walter came in, he was talking about Art Whilley. He believed Art died in the fire, but Walter swears Art Whilley is wandering round Coffin Cove pretending to be a real estate developer. Now the mayor's missing, and she's been in contact with this mysterious man in the last few days. I need to find him, if only to eliminate him from our enquiries. I have my officers looking into the death records," he said grimly, "but so far they can't find anything."

Vega rubbed his hands over his face. He felt exhausted.

"I have four people murdered and one person missing. I need to know as much as possible about this Art Whilley, and fast. Jade could be in real danger. So please, no speculation. Just facts."

Harry grunted. "There've been so many stories about Whilley and Hell's Half Acre over the years, it's hard to separate fact from fiction. Where did you get the photos anyway?" he asked Andi.

"Doug and Terri South," she replied.

"Figures," Harry said. "Doug was sort of involved with all that biker gang stuff. So was Dennis, if you can believe it."

Vega nodded. "Our mystery man, who may or may not be Art Whilley, he's calling himself Mr Knight."

Harry's eyes widened. "Holy shit. And you think he snatched Jade Thompson?"

Vega said, "I don't know. It's a lead we're following, and at the moment, it's our only lead. Jade was supposed to have a meeting with Knight or Whilley the evening she disappeared. She was last seen walking towards the fish plant. But I have no connection and no motive. So I need to know what you have. Everything."

Jim jumped in. "Inspector, if you'll let me, I'll tell you what we've found out."

"Go ahead, Jim, but get to the point, please."

"Art Whilley was an abused boy who grew up to be a disturbed young man. Despite a few friends — Clara here, Ann and Doug South — he was a loner. He was also very smart. He liked to mess around with chemicals, and he read a lot. He concocted some kind of drug, a bit like LSD. Somehow, Wayne Dagg, Daniel Ellis and Dennis Havers found out."

Jim paused. "I think it's important for you to understand these three men were Art's tormentors when he was a boy. They used to 'hunt' him, like some kind of animal. Art found some solace with Clara, who taught him how to hunt properly and taught him the old ways of surviving. She did it to help his confidence, but inadvertently showed him how to shoot and use a knife and string up animals — all skills useful for a killer."

In his mind, Vega saw the brutal images of Nadine, with her throat neatly slit, and the bodies of Sandra and Dennis Havers. Ricky too, he thought. He was trussed like an animal. They'd thought it was a gangland killing, but Vega realized they were wrong.

Jim continued. "Wayne, Dennis and Daniel came up with this scheme. They would sell the drugs and split the profits with Art."

"Was this Doug South involved?" Vega asked.

"I don't think so. I believe Doug is hiding something, but not that."

"Go on," Vega said, beginning to feel like a lot of things were slotting into place.

"They were successful with the drug business. Wayne had connections with a biker gang, so distribution was easy. Art spent his money on a Mustang, and even had a girlfriend for a while — Nadine Dagg, who broke up with Lee to go out with Art."

"Is Lee the jealous type?" Vega asked, aware that Lee Dagg was still at the detachment waiting to be interviewed.

Harry shook his head. "No. Lee was hurt, and pissed, but who wouldn't be? Stood up by your girlfriend and then she turns up with the town weirdo in front of all your friends?" He shook his head. "But that was Nadine. Back then and now. Well . . ." He tailed off, remembering.

Jim said, "Wayne discouraged the relationship. It sounds as if he tried to control everything in Art's life. Eventually, the scheme fell apart. Daniel died at sea, and we suspect, although we have no proof, that Daniel was also transporting drugs by boat. It's possible he took a risk when the weather wasn't good."

"Or maybe he was encouraged," Vega said, remembering Dennis's note.

"Maybe. Doug said Daniel was the weak link in the organization. He was reluctant to be involved, and when he met Summer Thompson, she wanted him out. And Art hated her for that, we think because Daniel was kind to him."

"So that's the connection between Art Whilley and Jade? Her mother?" Vega asked.

Jim nodded. "We can't find any trace of Wayne's whereabouts. Wayne disappeared, but not before he somehow became the owner of Art's property, Hell's Half Acre. Wayne may have conned Art. Art was smart, but not very worldly, and maybe looked to Wayne as his business mentor. If he thought Wayne betrayed him, it's another reason for Art to hold a grudge against the Dagg family."

Jim became very serious. "If we're right, Inspector, Art Whilley is destroying all the people who tried to destroy him. The Haverses, Nadine, and now you say Jade Thompson is missing. We believe Lee and Katie Dagg are in his sights too. They're living at Hell's Half Acre. It was taken from Art and now he wants it back."

Vega let this sink in. Then he asked a question.

"What did the bikers call themselves?"

"The Bold Knights or the Knights something," Harry said. "They ran the biggest drug distribution network on the island for a while. You lot tried to nail them, but they were always one step ahead. They were supposed to be using a network of tunnels, the old mining tunnels. They were used by smugglers in the old rum-running days."

Sinclair's report. That's where Vega had heard the reference to "Knight" before. Everything Harry and Jim were telling him now clicked into place.

Just then, Vega's phone rang. He glanced at it, and then said, "I need to take this," and he stepped out the galley onto the deck.

When he came back a few minutes later, he said, "Doug and Terri South are at the detachment with Katie Dagg. Summer Thompson is still there too. So I have to get back and verify some things you've told me. At the moment we think Whilley or Knight hasn't left Coffin Cove. But it's an extensive area, so I need to call in some help."

Clara Bell hadn't said a word. She'd eaten her meal, listening to the conversation, her bright eyes moving from one person to another.

As Vega went to step out on the deck, she said to the departing figure, "I know where Arthur is."

* * *

Vega wasted no more time. But he needed one more piece of information before he called Superintendent Sinclair.

Summer Thompson was sitting in an interview room. Her head was bowed and her hands clasped in her lap. For a moment, Vega wondered if she was praying. Then she looked up.

"Any news?" she asked anxiously.

Vega shook his head. "No, I'm sorry. But I have to ask you a question and I need you to be straight with me."

He pulled up a chair and sat directly opposite her. He looked into Summer's eyes. She was terrified, he could see.

He asked, and when she'd answered, he patted her hand.

"Thank you," he said. "This will stay between us."

CHAPTER THIRTY-EIGHT

After Vega had spoken to Summer, he and Sergeant Fowler sat in another interview room with Katie Dagg and Terri and Doug South. Trembling, Katie Dagg pushed a wrinkled business card towards him.

In a low voice, she said, "Inspector Vega, for the last few days I have been living in a nightmare. It's surreal. I found Ricky Havers' dead body, or at least, Clara Bell and I found him. Then my mother was murdered. Then Ricky's father and mother were murdered, and you think my dad had something to do with it. My dad . . ." Her voice got stronger. "My dad wouldn't hurt anyone. My parents had problems. They've always had problems. But Dad's never been violent. It isn't in him."

"Katie," Vega started, but she cut him off.

"I've been trying to figure out why this is all happening to us. And I don't know why. We don't deserve it. But it started when this man—" she indicated the card — "this man here suggested I find the chapel and research that stupid story. I know this sounds crazy, Inspector, but I think he sent me there on purpose. I think he knew I'd find Ricky. And . . ."

Vega held his hand up and looked at the card. *Knights Development Ltd.*

"Katie," he said, "we know about this man."

Terri put her hand over Katie's and Doug started speaking.

"Inspector, you may know about this man, but you don't know everything. The thing is . . . I think he is not Mr Knight or whatever name he's calling himself. I think it's Arthur Whilley."

Vega nodded. "Go on."

Doug took a deep breath. "Inspector, a long time ago, Art Whilley wanted to escape from Coffin Cove. For lots of reasons, he felt trapped and desperate. People here, apart from my mother and Clara Bell and me — well, most people treated him pretty badly. Including his own family. It got wild back then, and Art was into some bad stuff. He wanted out, and he staged a house fire." Doug's voice faltered. "Art was good with chemicals and knew how to make a fire burn really hot, so nothing would be left. There'd be no way to tell if he'd burned up in there or not. But he wasn't in that fire. Nobody noticed. Everyone was stoned or drunk, and all I had to do was scream that Art was in the house, when the fire had caught on enough for nobody to chance running in."

Doug looked at Inspector Vega and shook his head slowly. "I thought I was helping. My mother, before she died, she asked me to look out for Art. And . . . and I tried . . . but I had no idea this would happen." He hung his head.

Vega felt bad for the man, but time was seeping away. "Doug, do you know how he left?"

Doug nodded. "He used the old mining tunnels. Smugglers used them. He left a boat at the end of one of them — comes out at Sharps Point. I helped him. If he'd left in his car, Dennis and Wayne would have known. But as it happens, Wayne went AWOL a couple of days before."

Did he? Vega thought. *I wonder.*

Vega stopped the interview. He turned to Katie. "Katie, I can't let you or your father leave yet. It's not safe." And then to Doug, "I'll need you for a while longer. The person you know as Art Whilley, and we know as Mr Knight, we believe he's abducted Jade Thompson."

Doug's eyes widened. "The mayor? We hadn't heard that."

Vega said, "She disappeared yesterday. We think she went to meet Knight . . . er, Whilley, and he snatched her. We think he's holding her underground, possibly in the same tunnel he used to escape last time. We also believe he came back to Coffin Cove and murdered Nadine Dagg and the Haverses. We've heard the story you told Jim Peters, and the information from Clara Bell. We're either about to embark on a search and rescue mission, or, if we're too late, a recovery mission. Either way, we need to act fast. And I need your help."

Vega left Doug and Terri with Sergeant Fowler.

"Come with me," he said to Katie, and led her to the interview room where her father was still waiting. Lee was slumped over the desk when Vega opened the door.

"Lee, you're free to go," he said as Katie rushed over to her father and flung her arms around his shoulders. "I know this is a terrible time for you. But if you would be willing to stay and answer a few questions, you may help prevent someone else suffering the same pain you're going through. Would that be OK?"

Lee Dagg looked up.

"Whatever you need, Inspector," he said in a gruff voice.

Vega nodded.

"Thanks. I'll be back in a short while."

Vega went outside. The detachment was buzzing, and he needed some peace to make his next phone call.

"Superintendent? I need more resources."

Vega tried his best. But Superintendent Sinclair wasn't convinced.

"You want me to mobilize an Emergency Response Team based on this story?" she asked incredulously. "Andrew, you have no direct evidence for any of this. It hasn't been for-ty-eight hours since Jade went missing, and you want armed officers running around looking for a man who two journal-ists think has risen from the dead?"

Vega was silent. He knew how it sounded.

Sinclair sighed on the other end of the phone.

"Hold off until you have more to go on. Wait for more forensics and see what you can do in the next twenty-four hours. Then we'll assess."

Vega ended the call and felt like flinging his phone across the parking lot. He knew Sinclair's hands were tied. She had limited resources, and Nanaimo was in the middle of a drug war.

But what was he to do?

He couldn't wait twenty-four hours. He'd have to use what he had, even if it was entirely against protocol. Sinclair had left him no choice. He rubbed his hand over his face, suddenly aware how tired he was. Before he could head back inside, he heard the door open behind him.

* * *

Andi heard the frustration in Vega's voice as he finished his phone call. The blue glow of his cell phone screen illuminated his face. He looked at the end of his tether, Andi thought. It probably wasn't the best time for this conversation, but before she could turn and go back inside, Vega turned to face her.

"Andi."

"Andrew, sorry, I didn't mean—"

"It's OK," he interrupted her. "Are you alright?"

There was genuine concern in his tone.

"I'm fine. Look, Andrew, about that article—"

Vega waved his hand. "I don't care about that now, Andi."

"I know. But still, I wanted to . . ."

"Explain? Apologize?"

Andi felt irritation rise, until she saw Vega smiling at her.

"Well, both, I guess." She tried to smile back, but instead felt like crying.

Vega must have noticed, because he stood close to her and touched her shoulder.

"It's been a very bad day," he said so softly that Andi strained to hear him, "and the only thing I care about is that you are safe."

He pulled her close to him for a moment and hugged her, and Andi found herself hugging him back.

She felt him gently kiss the top of her head before he released her.

"I need to get to work. Will you help me?"

* * *

Vega called his team together. Clara, Harry, Andi and Jim gathered at the back of the conference room.

Andi saw Charlie Rollins and Matt Beaufort standing at the side of the room.

Andrew Vega stood at the front and briefly shared Jim's information. Andi saw his team nodding. *They trust him*, she thought.

Sergeant Fowler stepped up to the front.

"We believe Knight is still in Coffin Cove. There have been no sightings, but he hasn't left town as far as we can tell. We have a roadblock checking all the vehicles leaving town. We believe Jade Thompson is in imminent danger, so we have to act fast with the very limited resources we have. So Inspector Vega and I have put together a plan. It's . . ." she hesitated. "It's unorthodox but we didn't respond to a missing person report before and now that person is dead. So we're not taking any chances." She threw a meaningful glance at Andi.

Andrew Vega stood up again.

"I take full responsibility. But we act now. Sergeant, explain the plan and get everyone organized for first light tomorrow. Clara and Harry, I need you to come with me."

Harry and Clara followed Vega to the interview room.

"I need to look at your maps. We don't have much manpower, so we need to narrow down the places Whilley might be holding the mayor."

Clara spread her maps across the table.

"He'll have her down a mineshaft. He knows 'em all."

"Which one?" Vega asked Clara. It was a tall ask, he knew. He didn't want to put Clara under pressure. "It will be my final decision," he told her, "I just need to rule out those shafts which are too dangerous or difficult to access."

Clara didn't hesitate. "These," she said, pointing to three shafts. "These have black damp."

Vega looked at her questioningly. "What's that?'

"Gas. Bad gas. It'll kill you, but you'll not know it until it's too late," Clara explained.

"These are too far, and there's no way out," she said, pointing to others on the outskirts of Coffin Cove. "If he wants to take the girl."

If she's still alive, thought Vega.

"This one, this one and this one," Clara said.

Harry peered over her shoulder. "That one is an old smugglers' route. The exit is here, near those rocks. He might go that way."

Vega thought for a moment. "Doug South said he left via Sharps Point before. Where's that?"

Clara and Harry showed him.

"OK," Vega said, "here's what we'll do."

* * *

Vega stood on the steps in front of City Hall. Jim had done a good job, he thought. The response from the community had been better than he'd hoped.

A sea of expectant faces looked at him as he called for attention.

"Thank you for coming. Mayor Jade Thompson is missing. We believe she's been abducted by the same man who killed Nadine Dagg and Dennis and Sandra Havers, and we believe he's still in the Coffin Cove area."

He waited until the murmur of shock subsided. It was only a few hours ago, Vega realized. It felt like another lifetime to him, but some people here might not have heard about the murders. Was this a good idea? Too late now, he thought. Jade needed him, needed everyone.

"We've narrowed down four areas where we think he's most likely to be holding Jade. I do not have the resources I need to search them all without alerting the killer and allowing him to move Jade and escape. So I need your help."

Vega looked at the crowd, at the faces of men and women who had answered Jim Peters' call for help.

"We have to find Jade Thompson. We'll divide up into four search parties. My officers will be with each party, and we'll search one area each. We'll conduct a grid search — we'll explain how that works — and hopefully, hopefully, we will locate Jade. If any of you see this man—" Vega held up a picture — "do not approach him. Let my officers do their job. Please do not discharge your firearms." He looked sternly at the men in the crowd carrying shotguns. "I need this man in custody. Let him face the consequences of his actions. And please, do not place yourself in any danger."

Vega let Sergeant Fowler arrange the search parties. He walked over to Andi.

"Are you feeling OK?" he asked.

Andi nodded.

"Good," he said. "Join that party over there." He pointed to a group of people gathered around an officer. It wasn't until she joined the group that Andi saw the officer was Charlie Rollins.

CHAPTER THIRTY-NINE

Clara Bell pulled the lines free and threw them on the deck. Then, nimble as a goat, she hopped on board. The low chug of the diesel engine was barely audible above the cry of the gulls, as the *Pipe Dream* idled away from the dock.

Harry sat in the wheelhouse steering the boat. When they reached the edge of the no-wake zone, Harry pushed the throttle forward and the *Pipe Dream* picked up speed, slicing through the silver-grey waves. He looked down and saw Clara standing on the deck, her face tilted up slightly into the morning breeze. She was wearing her customary long dark skirt, and her white hair was lifting and billowing behind her. She reminded Harry of a Viking warrior, invoking his own Norwegian heritage.

Harry was fond of Clara. There was more than one mixed-up boy who had sought refuge at Clara's trailer. Before Greta, Harry's mother, had left Ed, Harry had escaped from the drunken violence of his home and found a protector in Clara. She'd never stood in judgment of either.

"It's a sickness, boy," she'd told Harry once, when he'd stormed to her in anger, cursing his father and his drinking.

Now, Clara looked out for Ed. She dropped in to see him, leaving food in the fridge and occasionally sitting with him on the porch.

Harry could understand how young Art Whilley had befriended this solitary woman. What he couldn't understand is how that boy had become a murderer, and, in cold blood, cut short another human's life. Not once, but four times over. Clara had taught Harry compassion. Unwittingly, she'd taught Art Whilley how to kill.

The first glow of sun was appearing on the horizon. By now, the search parties would be well underway. Harry frowned to himself. He wished Andi had stayed at the detachment, where she'd be safe. He didn't understand why Vega sent her out with Charlie Rollins, of all people.

Harry shared Andi's opinion of Charlie, but she didn't understand that he hadn't been angry with her over the article, just frustrated. It wasn't the way to change things in Coffin Cove. The people who lived here didn't want to be told they were wrong, or backward, or living in the past. They knew they couldn't be cut off from the rest of the world forever. But Andi Silvers and Jade Thompson would not change things overnight. And it would take more than Andi's articles or Jade's plans for funky murals and new bistros for Coffin Cove's violent past to fade into the mists of time.

Harry was aware of another uncomfortable feeling. He was worried about Andi. He cared for her more than he wanted to admit. He'd felt tension between Vega and Andi and wondered what that meant. But if that man cared for her, why would he send her into the bush while there was a killer running loose? Then again, he thought, it would do no good trying to tell that woman what she should do. Maybe Andi was more suited to Coffin Cove than he thought.

Harry pulled his wandering thoughts back to the task at hand. He glanced down and caught Clara's eye. He beckoned her to come up to the wheelhouse. He climbed up the steps and PC Matt Beaufort followed her. He was not a sailor, Harry could see. Telltale beads of sweat were forming on his top lip. Harry reached into a small compartment near the wheel and tossed Matt a small container.

"Take two of those," he said. "I get seasick too some-times." He didn't, but why make the boy feel worse?

He watched Matt gulp down two pills quickly.

"Thanks, Harry."

"Not too far now," Harry said to Clara. "That's Sharps Point over there." He pointed to the dark shape of a rock formation coming up in front of them.

"Round the other side," Clara said. "If the tunnel's still open . . ." She left the sentence unfinished. If Art were to use this old smugglers' route as an escape, they'd see some kind of boat moored. Otherwise, the trip was a waste of time, and they'd have to hope one of Vega's teams had better luck.

Just then, Matt Beaufort's radio crackled into life. Harry couldn't hear much over the drone of the engine, so just watched as Matt held the radio to his ear.

* * *

Jade tried to open her eyes. She was disorientated. She thought she heard voices, but perhaps they were only echoes or dreams. She thought she heard Summer calling her.

"Mom," she murmured and tried to move, but stomach pain followed by intense nausea stopped her.

In her confusion, she felt a hand on her shoulder.

"Time to go," a voice said.

"Where?" she asked. "Where am I going?"

"To meet your father," the voice said, and someone pulled Jade to her feet.

* * *

Charlie Rollins was panting. Andi could see he was strug-gling. They were beating a path through heavy undergrowth. Clara had directed them to an abandoned mineshaft a kilo-metre west of Hell's Half Acre. Years ago, a vast concrete tipple had unloaded coal into rail cars for transport to the dock in Coffin Cove. Now, the stone skeleton was crumbled and overgrown, but the shaft and the tunnel still remained.

"Arthur knows these tunnels," Clara had said. "This one is easy to get to, if you know where to look."

There were several openings where it would be possible for Art to have got into the underground tunnels with Jade, she'd explained. But the tipple opening would be the easiest.

"The tunnel takes a fork a short way from the tipple. Arthur knows which way to go to get to Sharp's Point. The other way leads east of Hell's Half Acre."

Vega had made the decision. One party led by Charlie Rollins would search around the tipple, and another, led by Vega, would search the tunnel from the east end.

"I hope we're right about Art using the tunnels," Vega had said grimly. To be sure Whilley wasn't just lying low, waiting for them all to be tramping around in the undergrowth, Sergeant Fowler had set up a road block to catch him if he left by vehicle, and a group of determined-looking fishermen were patrolling the government dock.

"It's the best we can do," Vega had muttered. Andi had wanted to give him a reassuring hug, but instead she strode over to Charlie Rollins and held out her hand.

Charlie had looked at her for a moment, and then, to her relief, had shaken Andi's hand.

They'd been hiking for a while.

It was a challenging walk for a fit person. Andi was feeling the strain in her leg. But for Charlie, overweight and desk-bound for years, it looked like torture. Sweat was glistening on his brow, and Andi could see damp patches forming around the collar of his shirt.

Andi offered him water. Charlie grunted and refused. He stopped to take off his Kevlar vest.

"Is that wise?" Andi was nervous. Charlie was the only one authorized to engage with Whilley if necessary. Vega had been adamant about that. It didn't seem a good idea for the only police officer in this group to be exposed if they ran into the madman on the loose in the woods.

"I know what I'm doin'," Charlie snapped at her. He was clearly still holding on to the remnants of a grudge. There was nothing she could do, except hope for the best. They didn't have time for a debate. Andi shut her mouth.

The small group pushed on, crunching through the bushes, as the sun peered through the trees.

When they'd started, it had been dawn. Now, two hours later, Andi was feeling the warmth.

She stopped to peel off a layer of clothing.

Charlie called out "Stop!" and held out his hand. He was a short distance ahead, and the group of searchers gathered around him. Andi tied her sweater around her waist.

"It's here," Charlie called out. "I can see the tipple. The shaft must be around here somewhere."

The group dispersed and Andi jogged over to help. Charlie pointed to his left.

"Try that way."

Andi kept her eyes to the ground, careful to step only on solid ground. She heard Charlie calling out to the group to be careful. The last thing they needed, she thought, was for someone to fall down the shaft.

After a few minutes of fruitless searching, she looked up to see where the others were.

The dappled light made it hard to see. Andi shielded her eyes. She saw a figure in front of her. *Charlie?*

"Have you found it?" she called and stepped forward into a shadow. The figure said nothing. *Charlie?* Her eyes adjusted as she saw in horror a man holding a gun and pointing it straight at her.

Andi was frozen. Everything around her melted away. The last time she had been near a gun, she was running to save someone else. It was impulsive. She hadn't stopped to think. But now, this gun was aimed at her. It felt like slow motion as the man readied his weapon and aimed. Andi saw a glimpse of his face as he moved slightly, and she saw he was smiling. Art Whilley. It must be. Andi took a breath and willed herself to move, but it was too late. She heard a loud crack and then everything fell silent.

Andi was still standing.

The man took off running.

"He's going towards the tipple!"

Andi heard the other hikers crashing through the brush. She wanted to call to them, to remind them that it was only Charlie who could apprehend Whilley, but her voice seemed stuck in her throat. Was she really OK?

She looked down at her arms and legs, expecting to see blood. But it was true, she hadn't been hit. She heard a groan from behind her. She willed herself to turn, terrified that somehow Art Whilley had doubled back and would attack from behind. But the only person she saw was Charlie Rollins.

He was lying on the ground, face up. Blood seeped from his chest.

Andi dropped to the ground and grabbed his radio. "Help us! Help us!" she screamed. "Charlie's been shot!"

CHAPTER FORTY

"This is as near as we get," Harry said, pulling the throttle back. "It's too shallow and rocky to go any further." He killed the engine and looked at Matt. "What did they say? On the radio?"

Matt had lost all his colour.

"They've sighted Whilley. They think he's in the tunnel, probably headed our way. Vega's called the coast guard to help."

"And?" Harry could see by Matt's face there was something more.

"Someone's been shot. I lost the signal and couldn't hear who it was."

Harry nodded. He couldn't trust himself to speak. He felt panic rising. *Please, God, don't let it be Andi. Not again.*

Clara had Harry's binoculars and was looking at the beach.

"There," she said, pointing and passing the binoculars to Matt. "I see a boat."

Matt nodded. "A speedboat of some kind." He fumbled for the radio. "I'll call for backup."

Harry looked at him. "Son, it'll take a while for even the coast guard to get here. I know Vega alerted them, but

Whilley could come out of that tunnel any second and get away in that boat. He could be at the border in minutes. Call Vega, but in the meantime, we need to disable that boat."

Harry left the wheelhouse and went to the bow of the boat to drop the anchor. Matt and Clara waited for Harry on the deck while he went into his galley and came out with a shotgun.

"What are you doing?" Matt asked in alarm.

"I don't think I can get a shot into that boat. At least, not to do enough damage to stop him trying to use it. I might just put Jade in danger of drowning."

"So what are you thinking?"

"We can get onto the beach and make sure Whilley can't even start the boat. We'll use my skiff." Harry pointed at a small dinghy chained to the stern of the *Pipe Dream*. "We'll get over there, pull some wires on that speedboat and get back here. Then at least Whilley's stuck here, or he'll have to go back the way he came. Hopefully, Vega has manpower at the other end."

Matt nodded. "OK, makes sense."

Harry was relieved Matt agreed. He sensed the young constable was a bit out of his depth. But he seemed to be calm, and Harry respected him for that. Now he had to focus on the task ahead, and put his worry for Andi out of his mind.

Harry wound the cables and lowered the skiff into the water. He climbed over the side, holding his shotgun.

Matt grabbed his arm. "You can't take that," he said. "I have a gun. I'm the only one who should use it."

Harry frowned, but remembered Vega's instructions. He'd been clear on this point. Only officers may carry guns and engage with Whilley. Harry handed his gun to Clara.

"You stay, Clara. Radio if you see Whilley. Let Vega know if he runs back in the tunnel."

Harry started the outboard and steered the little skiff until they reached the rocky beach. Matt hopped out and dragged the boat into the shallows.

Feeling his heart pounding, Harry ran over to the speedboat and started pulling at wires under the dashboard. If Whilley made it to the end of the tunnel, he wouldn't be going any further.

* * *

Matt could see what Harry was doing. He wished he'd been able to take charge as effortlessly as Harry. He was still feeling sick after the boat ride and nervous about what would happen next. He felt as if thirty years of police experience had been crammed into the last few days.

"Get the fuck away from my boat."

Matt turned to see Art Whilley standing partially behind a rock, with his arm around Jade Thompson, who seemed semi-conscious. She was leaning heavily on his arm. In his other hand, he had a gun. It was pointed at Harry.

Matt could see a large hunting knife hanging from Whilley's belt.

"Let the girl go, Art," Matt said, hoping his voice wasn't shaking. "Then you can go. We only want Jade safe and sound."

Whilley carried on speaking. It was as if Matt didn't exist.

"You're Harry Brown," he said.

Harry nodded. "I am. Haven't seen you for a while, Art. Last I heard, you burned in a fire. But you're looking well enough now."

Harry's tone was casual, as if he were bantering with a buddy in the pub. Whilley's attention was fully on Harry, and Matt knew this was the moment to take Whilley down.

As Harry talked, Matt eased his Smith & Wesson from his holster. He tried to keep calm and remember his training.

"When you pull your gun, all bets are off," he remembered his instructor saying. "It's not a negotiation after that. You shoot to kill, not to wound."

"Art Whilley, put your gun down," Matt shouted as loud as possible, hoping to catch Whilley off guard.

Instead, he swung round and pulled Jade Thompson closer.

"You won't shoot. You won't risk killing the mayor here."

Harry said, "Come on now, Art. It's all over. We all know what's going on. What's the use of taking Jade? What do you think you're going to do with her?"

Art Whilley looked back at Harry and then at Matt. Then he started laughing.

"You're just a kid. Still wet behind the ears. I bet you've never shot that gun in your life, have you?"

Matt ignored what Whilley was saying. He could see the older man's arm holding Jade was trembling. *He must be in his sixties*, he thought. *He's just trekked through a long tunnel dragging Jade. He can't hold on for much longer. He'll have to make a break or drop her.*

Whilley waved his gun at Harry.

"Get out."

Harry did as he was told but tried again. "Art, Clara's on my boat. She tried to help you, remember? And what about Ann South? She cared about you. Don't let them down, man."

Art seemed to hesitate. "They all betrayed me. They took everything. I tried to make them like me . . . but I was no better than an animal. Prey. And now I'm doing the hunting. Just like Clara showed me."

"Whilley, I won't ask you again, drop the gun and move away from Miss Thompson," Matt said, as calmly as he was able.

"No, I've got a better idea."

In one movement, Art dropped Jade and aimed the gun directly at Matt.

This was it. He must not fail.

Matt pulled the trigger. But he'd forgotten. "Twelve pounds of pressure on that trigger," the inspector said. "You can't hesitate."

A gun fired. Matt looked down. It wasn't his. He was still standing. Harry was still standing. Time seemed suspended as Matt tried to figure out what had just happened.

Art Whilley looked confused. Jade Thompson was sprawled on the ground. Art Whilley crumpled slowly, blood gushing from a hole in the side of his head.

Matt and Harry rushed forward.

"Clara," Harry said. "Got him behind the ear. Took him down like a deer."

Matt looked back at the *Pipe Dream* and saw the woman standing there, still aiming the shotgun, her white hair blowing in the sea breeze.

"Matt!" Harry brought Matt's attention back to the present. "Jade's unconscious. What's wrong with her? Did he poison her?"

Matt felt Jade's pulse. "She's still alive. Her lips are blue and her breathing's shallow. I think it's carbon monoxide poisoning."

"Right, gases from the tunnel," Harry said. "What do we do?"

"Nothing," Matt said. "Nothing we can do, except hope she can hold on until help comes."

Just then they heard a rhythmic *thump, thump, thump*.

Matt looked up.

"Thank God. Or Clara. It's the coast guard helicopter."

EPILOGUE

Jim climbed down the ladder.

"All hooked up," he said to Clara and stood back to admire the new solar panels installed on her trailer. He'd been checking in on Clara every few days, until she'd told him to stop.

"I'm fine. Don't be bothering me," she'd told him.

But Jim turned up anyway, fixing a few things in her trailer.

"How do they work again?" Clara asked a little suspiciously, gazing up at the sleek panels which looked out of place in her rustic homestead.

Jim laughed. "It's OK, Clara, it's easy. You don't need to do anything."

He explained how they worked and showed her how to switch to the generator as backup.

"So less diesel, then?" Clara asked.

"Way less," Jim said, and her face broke into a wide smile.

* * *

An excavator blocked the sun.

Mayor Jade Thompson-Ellis cut a ribbon and waved to the operator.

A large metal claw descended slowly, crashing through the roof of the old fish plant. It grabbed a load of rotten rafters and debris, like a giant mechanical bird collecting twigs, and swung back and deposited them in a massive dumpster.

There was a ripple of applause from the watching crowd. Summer Thompson was at the front, beaming with pride.

Andi was surprised to find herself so elated to see the crumbling fish plant being demolished. *It's just a building*, she thought. But it symbolized so much more — as if it was bringing closure to a horrible murder and an end of sorts to the trauma of the last few months.

Andi thought Jade had bounced back quickly. After being treated for carbon monoxide poisoning, she'd taken a few weeks off and had some counselling. Jade had handed Andi a business card when Andi interviewed her. It was for a counselling service in Nanaimo.

"She helped me, and she's still helping me," Jade said. "Why suffer when you don't need to? Doesn't make any logical sense."

The card was still in Andi's purse. She'd taken it out and put it back several times. But she was sure she would make and keep an appointment. It was time those nightmares stopped for good.

Andi saw Charlie Rollins in the crowd. It was the first week of his retirement. This morning, the *Coffin Cove Gazette* carried a photograph of him smiling and accepting an award for bravery, accompanying Andi's story about Charlie saving her from a crazed killer.

Matt Beaufort stood beside him. He was staying on for the time being, he'd told Andi. He wanted more experience before he transferred to a city. Besides, the detachment was getting an overhaul and some new equipment. Plus, the mayor had found enough money in the budget for an extra full-time officer. It was the service Coffin Cove deserved, she'd said.

Doug and Terri South were not there.

Andi knew they had a special appointment. Today, Art Whilley would be laid to rest in the Coffin Cove cemetery.

It was a controversial decision, Doug said he knew, but the secret ceremony was to remember the boy, not the killer. It would have pleased Ann, Doug's mother. Andi had decided not to report this in the *Gazette*.

Katie Dagg stood beside Lee. The museum was open, and the first exhibit was called "Pioneer Women" and featured Clara Bell, who had offered to tell stories to the tourists. For a fee, she had told Katie sternly.

Jim tapped Andi on the shoulder.

"I hear Lee and Katie are moving," he said. "Hell's Half Acre will be vacant. Unless Wayne comes back."

Andi nodded but said nothing. The last time she'd talked to Andrew Vega, he'd told her about a second set of human remains they'd recovered from the chapel, just where they had found Ricky Havers. Forensics were still working on it, he said, but he was certain they belonged to Wayne Dagg.

Andi and Andrew Vega had met for a coffee before he caught the floatplane back to the mainland. Andi had felt awkward at first, remembering the intimate moment they had shared. Maybe Vega felt the same, because at first, he'd talked a lot.

Vega had been suspended. Superintendent Sinclair had no other option, he explained to Andi. He'd simply not followed standard procedure.

"But you saved Jade Thompson," Andi said. "If you hadn't authorized the search parties, she'd be dead now. And maybe more people. Doesn't that count for anything?"

"It does," Vega said, smiling, "but an officer was shot, and a civilian killed a suspect. There are rules, Andi, in my job. I broke them, and now I have to pay the price."

But he went on to tell her the better news. Nanaimo RCMP had credited his team for helping crack the drug ring. Kevin Wildman had provided enough information to lead the drug squad to the Knights' headquarters. In a small warehouse, they had found a stash of drugs matching the "dukes" on the street. Interestingly, they also found a freezer and traces of embalming fluid. Vega was sure they would link the warehouse with Art Whilley.

"Can I print that?"

"Sure. It's a scoop, right?" Vega had teased her. But then he'd looked serious. "You were right about a lot of things, Andi. You have good instincts."

Andi had wanted to ask what it was she'd been right about, but the distant throb of an engine got nearer, ending their conversation.

As the floatplane taxied to the dock, Andi had impulsively blurted out, "What now? For you and me, I mean."

Andrew Vega had stood still and then reached out an arm to pull her into a hug.

"I hope there can be a 'you and me', Andi. But . . ."

"But I'm a journalist and you're a police officer?"

Vega had nodded.

"It would always be complicated."

Jim poked her in the ribs, interrupting her thoughts. "Are you ready? Harry's cooking."

"I know," Andi said and smiled. "Hey, Jim, did you know halibut have cheeks?"

Jim rolled his eyes. "Everyone knows that," he said, and they walked down the boardwalk to the *Pipe Dream*, where Harry was waiting.

THE END

Thank you for reading this book.

If you enjoyed it please leave feedback on Amazon or Goodreads, and if there is anything we missed or you have a question about, then please get in touch. We appreciate you choosing our book.

Founded in 2014 in Shoreditch, London, we at Joffe Books pride ourselves on our history of innovative publishing. We were thrilled to be shortlisted for Independent Publisher of the Year at the British Book Awards.

www.joffebooks.com

We're very grateful to eagle-eyed readers who take the time to contact us. Please send any errors you find to corrections@joffebooks.com. We'll get them fixed ASAP.

Made in the USA
Columbia, SC
23 June 2021

40893833R00164